ZOMBIEKILL

RUSS WATTS

SEVERED PRESS
HOBART TASMANIA

ZOMBIEKILL

This book is for those who prefer to show compassion instead of hate and mercy instead of aggression.
Although perhaps it is for those who do a little of both.

"Happy are those who dare courageously to defend what they love."

Ovid.

PROLOGUE

Charlie smiled as her mother performed a clumsy pirouette. Some days were better than others, and today was a *good* day. Her mother was happy, showing off in her revealing red dress which had sequins around the hem and a little red bow at the back. The dress was ankle length and very glamorous, and Charlie knew it was an old favorite of her mother's, one of those items that never got used, but was too good to give away. Smiling was too much of a rarity these days, especially now the rain had stopped. It was another sunny day, which normally would be reason enough to be happy. Yet they longed for rain. The winter hadn't been a problem, but now they were getting longer days and less rain, and that meant less to drink. They all knew what it meant, yet nobody wanted to confront the matter, preferring to wait and hope. Getting through the winter was hard, but the coming summer would be far worse. The rain would stop, and the water would dry up. Charlie knew they were facing some serious problems for which there was no easy answer. There were plenty of fresh lakes and rivers nearby, but actually getting to them was nigh on impossible. Venturing outside was not an option. The corpses were still fresh and strong; maybe not as quick as they used to be, but they were still dangerous. Any attempt to move through the streets of Peterborough would've meant death for anyone insane enough to try it. Charlie tried not to think about the future too much. It was too hard to picture it; to think that one day this might all be over. All they could do was live in the moment, make it from one day to the next, and wait for the rescue.

There was little else to do right now, so her mother had decided they would host a fashion parade, trying on all their old clothes that hadn't seen daylight for years. Charlie loved these days when her father was busy strengthening the fence outside leaving them alone. As much as she loved her father, there was a special bond she had with her mother. It had been there for as long as she could remember. Her father was under a lot of pressure, she knew that, and he found it hard to relax. That meant her mother felt his burdens, too, and having the opportunity to just relax and laugh with each other didn't come along too often.

"It's great, Mom, really good. You should show Dad."

"Oh, I don't know," replied Jemma as she curtsied in front of her daughter. "I feel a bit silly. It's a little revealing for someone my age." Jemma tugged at the waist. "And it barely fits anymore. This is such an old dress. I haven't worn it for years. Maybe one day I'll get the chance. I just need to lose twenty pounds."

"Oh, whatever," said Charlie as she jumped up off her bed to stand beside her mother. "If anything you could gain twenty pounds." They stood side by side in the full length mirror looking at each other. Since they had been forced to lock the front door and barricade the windows, and with no prospect of going out again, their diet had meant they had all lost some weight. They had to keep to strict rations, and there was no snacking between meals anymore. Charlie knew she was lucky though. Her father, Kyler, had seen it coming and stocked the house to last them several months. He had got as much as he could from the store before it closed its doors for the last time. It was a strange situation, but it wasn't forever. Charlie knew it would get sorted out eventually. One day the army would roll through town and announce it was all over. They were just sorting out the large cities first, and they had a lot to sort out, so she knew she just had to be patient. One day the dead would be gone, and Peterborough would be a nice, quiet little town again. One day she would be able to go back outside without fear of being attacked. With *them* out there, going out onto the streets meant certain death. One day, things would get back to normal. One day.

Charlie suddenly became aware of how boring she looked compared to her mother. Every day she dressed in the same old thing: jeans, a loose baggy top, and a UCLA sweater on cold days. She never bothered with make-up and tied her blonde hair up in a bun. If she kept her blue eyes hidden, she could almost pass as a boy. It was something they joked about occasionally, about how her father had been so desperate to have a son that he had gotten both a son and a daughter in Charlie. When she was younger he would take her out on his boat and show her how to fish, how to *really* fish. The days of going out on the lakes were gone, but she remembered them fondly. Right now she wanted to be a girl, to be Charlotte, not Charlie, and decided she would try on a dress too. She couldn't even remember the last time she had put a dress on. That was a lie. She could remember exactly when.

Jackson had taken her to Portland to some Italian restaurant. She had worn a slinky black dress that night and even let her hair down. They had been going out for six months, and she was sure that he was going to ask her to move in. Jackson had broken up with her over dessert, and that was the last time she had bothered to put on a dress.

Charlie felt a little insecure beside her mother who had long blonde hair and a shapely figure that was very attractive for a forty-nine-year-old woman. Charlie hoped she had the same figure when she was older. It was just effortless for her. Her mother was a real woman, not a girl pretending to be one.

"Why don't you try it on?" Jemma turned her back toward her daughter. "Go on. Unzip me, and try it on. I'd love to see you in it."

Charlie reached for the zip but hesitated. "Wait. Why don't you show Dad first? Go on, I'm sure he'd love to see you in it. You look hot, Mom."

Jemma turned around and smiled. "Thank you for saying so, but I don't think your Father wants to see me like this. He'll just say I'm wasting time."

"What a load of crap. Wasting time? What else are we going to do? Go for a hike? Go fishing or get in the car and pop over to Manchester for some retail therapy?"

Charlie laughed but then saw the sadness spreading over her mother and wished she hadn't suggested anything. Talk of going outside was akin to blasphemy. It was impossible, and they all knew it. When you couldn't have something, it was easier to ignore it than talk about it.

"One day, Charlie, I'll take you. I'll take you wherever you want to go." Jemma turned around and offered her back again to her daughter. "Now get me out of this dress. I'd rather see you in it than look at myself any longer. You're beautiful, Charlotte, and don't ever let anyone tell you otherwise."

When her parents spoke there was often something in their tone, a sadness that seemed to invade their every waking moment. It would lift now and again, but it was back now. It was the thought of leaving, or of *not* leaving that had brought it back now. What if Peterborough never changed? What if the military couldn't clear the corpses away? What if the streets stayed full of them, and there was no way out of this, ever?

"One day, Mom, you can take me to Boston," said Charlie as she brought her hands up to the zipper. "We'll go and stay in a five star hotel, Dad can go to the Patriots, and we'll shop like we've never shopped before. Just you see."

"One day," mumbled Jemma.

Charlie had to believe this wasn't it. It had only been a few months. Surely they were getting on top of things by now? The TV had said the military were going to concentrate on the major cities first and would work their way to the outer suburbs eventually. They were to wait for rescue, but so far there had been precious little sign of any. The corpses walking through the streets of Peterborough had appeared months ago, just when they had appeared around the rest of the country, and they had not gone anywhere. Their ranks had only been swelled, and now there were thousands of them. Once the TV and radio had died, the power had gone with it a few days later. People had panicked then. Their neighbors and friends had all gone outside to make a run for it, to find help, to find shelter; Charlie was thankful her father had convinced them to stay put. She had seen so many of their neighbors killed, the corpses taking them down in the roads and streets and gardens, that she often wondered if they were the only people left alive in the whole town.

There was a knock on the bedroom door and then it swung open. Kyler came into the room, his work boots banging loudly on the wooden floorboards. He was like a whirlwind, bringing with him a blast of fresh air. He wore a thick green jacket covered in oil patches and tears, and his hair was unbrushed as if he had only just got up out of bed. He was carrying a large spanner in one hand and a greasy cloth in the other.

"Jemma, have you seen my…" He trailed off when he saw his wife in the resplendent red dress. His mouth dropped open and his eyes widened. "I…well, I…you…"

Charlie broke out laughing as Jemma walked over to her husband. "Have I seen your what?"

"Have you seen the…"

"I think what you're trying to say, Dad, is that Mom looks good, right?"

Kyler looked at Charlie and then back to his wife. He looked her up and down and nodded. "Yeah, totally. I mean I'm just not used to seeing you like…like this. You look…different."

"Different?" Jemma winked at Charlie and then flicked her long blonde hair over her shoulders. In a low husky voice, she said, "Different or sexy?"

Kyler let out a low laugh. "Mrs. Robinson, are you trying to seduce me?" He leaned in for a kiss and giggling Jemma shrieked, pushing him away.

"Kyler, no, you'll ruin the dress. You're going to get your dirty hands all over me."

"That's the idea," replied Kyler playfully as he stole a quick kiss on his wife's cheek and threatened her with his thick grubby hands.

Charlie sank onto her bed. Her father looked like he wanted to rip that dress off her mother, which was a little more than Charlie could stand. "All right you two, get a room."

"Oh I'm sorry, Charlie," said Kyler sarcastically. He smirked as he looked upon his daughter. "Are we disturbing you? Don't you have some homework to do? Some errands to run?"

"No. I'm happy here in *my* room, thank you." Charlie loved seeing her parents happy together. Sometimes she felt guilty for being at home; for getting in the way. Sometimes she wished she had gone to college as she had planned instead of staying behind and working in the local grocery store. Then again, she had to admit that she was content in Peterborough, and if she had gone she would've missed out on seeing her parents so much.

"Say, Charlie, why don't you pop downstairs and help me in the garage. I'll be down in ten minutes," said Kyler as he continued admiring his wife.

"Ten minutes?" Jemma frowned and put her hands on her hips.

"Sorry, you're right, of course," said Kyler. He turned to Charlie. "Make it five."

As her parents burst out laughing, Charlie put her hands over her ears. "Ugh, gross. Get out, Dad, get out, get out, get out. You're disgusting, both of you!"

"See you later," said Kyler as he left the room chuckling. "Take care of each other."

"Right, Charlie, you have to help me out of this thing," announced her mother as she sauntered back over to the bed. "Seriously, it's only staying up because I'm breathing in. I need more oxygen, so get it off me."

Charlie stood up grinning. "Okay, turn around." Charlie ran her fingers over the silver chain that ran around her mother's neck. A small silver heart shaped pendant dangled from it, a present from Charlie two Christmases ago. Charlie slid her hands around her mother's shoulders and rested her head on her neck.

"I love you, Mom."

"What's wrong?" asked Jemma.

"Nothing. I'm fine," said Charlie, lying. How could she tell her mother she was jealous of her? Seeing her parents together had made her think of Jackson. He was long gone, and though she had loved him, those feelings had gone quickly after he had broken up with her. The truth was that she felt lonely. She got way more attention now the world was full of zombies than she ever had before. The problem was the only men out there weren't interested in taking her out to dinner. They wanted her *for* dinner.

Jemma put a hand on her daughter's. "It's going to be all right you know. They'll find us one day." Her voice was soft and all the playfulness was gone. When she spoke, she was serious but kind. "You'll be fine, Charlotte. You're twenty-one, and you've got your whole life ahead of you. Just remember that. Not every day is going to be shitty, and not every day is going to be a rainbow full of dancing unicorns. But I can tell you that every single day that you're on this planet I will love you and look out for you. Your

Father too. We'll always be here for you. So quit your worrying, and get this damn dress off me before I pass out."

Charlie sucked in a deep breath and raised her head. She began to tug at the zipper on the dress. "Okay, Mom, no need to get all sentimental on me. I was just thinking—"

"Wait," said Jemma suddenly. "What's that?"

"What?" Charlie peered over her mother's shoulder at the window. The thin curtains were drawn leaving a gap in the center only an inch wide. She preferred not to look outside too often. Not much changed, and there were so many zombies out there that she didn't need any reminders.

"There. Someone's running. I just saw them skirt around that van." Jemma went to the window and drew back one of the curtains.

Charlie nervously approached the window. Their house overlooked a narrow road that bordered the edge of town. There was a field beyond the road fringed with tall grass and even taller weeds. A lone oak tree protruded from the tall grass like a lighthouse, its branches spreading out far and wide like beams of light. Charlie looked up and down the road, scanning for the van in amongst the horde of corpses. She had spent too many hours looking at the road from her window, and knew where the van was. It was an old courier van parked outside Mr. Riley's house. The delivery guy had made his last delivery there and had never been seen again. Neither had Mr. Riley.

"You see anything?" asked Jemma.

Charlie saw a lot of things. She saw Mr. Riley's front door swinging on its hinges as the dead walked in and out of his house freely. She saw the hundreds of zombies littering the road, staggering around looking for the living. She saw a dead girl in a pink vest gnawing on a clean white bone. She saw a tall man with a bald head stumble in the middle of the road as his intestines slopped out of him, wrapping around his thin legs. She saw a small boy clutching a toy fire engine in his hands, half of his skull missing, and a gaping hole in his chest where his heart should be. She saw a lot of things, but she didn't see anyone running.

"No, Mom. Maybe you imagined it. Maybe it was one of the corpses."

"I don't think it was." Jemma scratched at a small spot forming on her neck. "We haven't seen one of them running for a while now."

"Mom, forget it. There's nobody out there." Charlie pulled away from the window, not wanting to look any more. It was too much. There were so many people, so many dead neighbors and friends always there, always just *there*. She hated it. Her bedroom was the one place she had to herself. She had her books and music and photographs and memories, and now they had ruined it. Below her window the dead clattered clumsily into cars, into the walls, into each other; the noise was a constant reminder of the death that awaited them all. It was as if they were poking fun at her. Think you're getting rescued? Ha, the only place you're going is straight to Hell.

Charlie sat back down on her bed as Jemma continued to watch out of the square window. "Come on, Mom, forget it. We might not have seen them running for a long time, but in case you forgot, that was also the last time we saw anyone else alive out there."

"Don't forget Arthur Atwood. He's still up there," said Jemma quietly, without taking her eyes away from the window.

Charlie hated it when her Mom talked about Arthur Atwood. He was once the richest man in the area who built himself a mansion up on the hill. He made a fortune in Portland selling real estate before moving out to Peterborough, claiming he wanted to 'get away from it all.' He became a self-styled philanthropist and did a lot of good for the town, which was why they turned a blind eye to the ugly mansion he had built on the hill outside town. It was something of an eyesore that the locals tolerated. At night Charlie could see it, just, from her bedroom. Even now the lights came on suggesting he was still there. As far as Charlie cared, he could stay there. It would be impossible ever reaching the house, and was he really any better off than them? All the millions of dollars he had, and he was still stuck in his house just like them with nothing but a few thousand zombies for company.

"So what? You think it's Arthur out there? Maybe we should invite him in for a coffee?"

"Charlie Gretzinger, stop being stupid. I'm telling you there was someone out... There! A woman!"

Charlie bolted up and looked out of the window. She gasped when she saw that her mother was right. A figure darted from behind the courier van to the large witch hazel shrub by Mr. Riley's house. It was a woman, though she was so filthy that she almost looked like one of them. Her clothes were rags, and the color of her hair was indistinguishable from the rest of the grime that covered her from head to toe.

"Jesus, Mom, who is it?" Charlie peered anxiously through the window. The woman was thin, probably starving. She had to be desperate to have gone out onto the streets. "What do they want?"

Jemma unlatched the window and pushed it open. Instantly, the sounds of the dead grew louder, and Charlie felt sick. They mumbled and groaned, and the sound of their feet scraping along the road made her skin crawl. There was nothing evil about them; they didn't show menace or emotions or kill through anything other than what seemed to be basic, natural impulses. They were disgusting, and Charlie turned up her nose as the corpses' smell began to permeate her bedroom.

"Mom, what are you doing? Shut it," whispered Charlie. She tried to bring the window closed, but Jemma pushed her back and glared at her.

"No. We have to help her. We can't leave that poor woman out there."

"We don't even know who she is. For all we know she could be—"

"Could be what?" Jemma bit her lip and looked at Charlie. "Look, I know you're scared, but she needs our help. We can't just turn her away. If we leave her out there like that she'll die. We have a nice house and plenty of room, and I'm not going to turn away and forget I saw her."

Charlie watched as her mother swung the window wide open and leaned over the ledge. Jemma let out a low whistle. Calling out would only alert the dead and cut off any hope of safe passage to the house. She needed to try to get the strange woman's attention carefully. Jemma whistled again and began beckoning over to the house with both hands.

"Is she coming?" Charlie kept her voice to a whisper, afraid that anything louder could suddenly bring a hundred dead people up into her room. They couldn't climb the fence around the house, but with the window open, she didn't feel very secure.

Through the open window, Charlie heard the woman scream. "Help, me!"

"Fuck." Jemma turned away from the window and ran across to the door, the red dress flowing gracefully around her.

"Mom, what's happening?" asked Charlie nervously. She didn't want to look. She couldn't stand to see it happen again. In the early days she had seen too many people die horribly. She didn't need to watch it happen again.

"She's making a run for it. She's coming here. I've got to get down to the front gate and let her in before they catch her. Get your father."

The woman outside screamed again, her voice echoing around Charlie's bedroom and coating the walls and floor with a desperate plea for her life. Charlie felt sick again and shook her head.

"No, Mom, we can't. Dad said it was too dangerous. We should—"

"Charlie, just get your father—now! I am *not* leaving her out there to die." Jemma raced out of the room, leaving Charlie foundering. The noise from outside the house was increasing, and her mother's footsteps were thundering through the house as she ran downstairs. Who was this woman? Who was crazy enough to go outside? It was selfish, that was what it was. They were going to draw all the zombies to the house, and then they would be stuck forever. Charlie knew she had to get her father. He would know what to do.

"Dad? Dad!" Charlie sprang into action and raced out of her room, down into the lounge. Shafts of bright sunlight shone through the blinds illuminating the room, but he wasn't there. "Dad?"

Charlie called out frantically, but she couldn't hear any movement from within the house. He had been looking for something. Was he in the garage?

"Dad, where are you?"

As Charlie ran out of the back door into the driveway, Kyler came running from the garage. He wielded a large crowbar above his head, and his eyes were wide open. They were no longer full of lust but worry and fear.

"What's going on? I heard a scream. Where's your Mother?"

Charlie sucked in a deep breath. "It's a woman. Out there. She's the one who screamed. She was by Mr. Riley's house, and... I don't know who she is. I told her to forget it, but Mom wanted to help. I didn't know where you were. I thought..."

Kyler grabbed Charlie's shoulders, and his eyes bore into hers. "Where's Jemma? Where's your Mother?"

Charlie glanced back at the long driveway that led to the front gate. High brick walls sheltered the driveway from the neighbors, and the front gate was made of thick iron railings. "She wanted to let her in, before the others—"

Kyler shoved his daughter out of the way and sprinted down the long driveway toward the road. "Jemma. Wait, Jemma. Don't open the gate."

The sun warmed Charlie as she stood there watching her father run after her mother. He ran like a maniac, as if he were possessed. He was waving the crowbar above his head like a soldier going into battle. Surely her mother would wait? She knew how risky it was to open the gate. They hadn't opened it in months. There was just no need. They ran the risk of letting the corpses in if they did, so it stayed shut. Kyler had drilled it into Charlie to never go out there, not that she needed any convincing.

"Jemma!"

Charlie heard her father call out and then began the long walk down their drive to the road. Charlie felt a sinking feeling in her stomach as she walked through the yard to the side of the house. This woman was going to ruin it all. Today was supposed to be a good day. Instead she had fucked it up. Her father was angry, understandably, and her mother was risking the security of their house by letting her in. The woman had ruined everything.

As Charlie turned the corner, she broke into a jog. Her father was almost at the end of the drive, and beyond him Charlie could make out her mother. There were figures shambling around in the road, and Charlie saw the woman running for their house. Several corpses were following her, and Charlie felt the knot in her stomach tighten. The front gate was open.

"Mom?"

Charlie shivered in the sunlight as she broke into a sprint. She ran as hard as she could, trying to catch up with her father ahead of her. Something wasn't right. Why wasn't her mother answering? Why had she rushed ahead like that? The woman was almost at the gate now. To Charlie she seemed to be running slowly, as if she had no energy left. How long had she been out there? Charlie knew her mother was right. They couldn't ignore her. They couldn't turn the other cheek and pretend they hadn't seen her. As Charlie ran and neared the end of the drive, she saw her father raise the crowbar and bring it down sharply on the head of a corpse that had gotten near the front gate. Christ, what had her mother done?

The gate was open.

Charlie's whole body shook as she ran. Sweat stung her eyes as she neared the gate, and she saw her father drive the crowbar through the forehead of a corpse trying to push its way through. Behind him, the screaming woman fell to the ground. Three zombies immediately pounced on her, with more following. Charlie watched as the woman was submerged beneath a tide of moving dead corpses, all biting and scratching and pulling at the woman's skin. The screaming stopped quickly.

That's when Charlie noticed her mother. She was laying on the ground just outside the gate, her blood pooling on the road around her red dress. There was a huge gash in her neck and blood around her head too. Jemma's mouth was open, but no sound came out. A zombie had hold of her legs and was biting her thighs, ripping out huge chunks of flesh.

"Mom!" Charlie raced to the open gate, but Kyler blocked her path. He slammed the crowbar into another zombie and shoved Charlie back. She fell over and watched as her father extended a hand through the gate.

"Jemma. Take my hand. Come on. I can't... I can't..."

Charlie watched as her mother reached out a hand, but she was too far away. She had gone outside the gate, onto the open road. She was only six, maybe eight feet away, but she may as well be a hundred. Another zombie found Jemma and jumped on her, plunging its gaping jaws into her abdomen. Charlie saw her mother screw up her eyes, and her face contorted and twisted in pain as a huge piece of flesh was ripped away from her stomach. The silver pendant around her neck reflected the sunlight and briefly dazzled Charlie. She blinked away the tears, and when she looked back at her mother, the life in her eyes had gone. Her body had stopped moving, and her arms had gone limp. Another zombie had discovered her and was gnawing on her left leg, pulling away the smooth skin with its teeth as if shredding a chicken.

Charlie rolled onto her stomach and threw up. Her vomit was sour, and she started to panic. They were all going to get in. They were all going to die. Her mother was going to die. Her mother was dead. She was dead, dead, dead. It wasn't the sight of the blood that brought more bile and vomit up Charlie's throat, it was the bloodcurdling scream that her father uttered. She knew then that it was over.

With a huge shove, Kyler pushed the gate shut and locked it. He dropped the crowbar on the drive and then crawled over to his daughter. He pulled Charlie to him, and Charlie waited for him to pull her closer so they could share their grief, so that they could comfort one another. Instead she felt the sharp sting of his slap and she recoiled, clutching a hand to her cheek.

"What...?" Charlie looked at her father, not recognizing the man who sat before her. Sweat ringed his face and dripped from his nose. As he swept his brown hair from his eyes she saw a fierce anger in them that she had not seen before. She felt terrified of him in that instant and knew things would never be the same again as he grabbed her shoulders. "What have you done, Charlie? You know what they can do. What the fuck have you done?"

The tears flowed freely down her cheeks, and Charlie wished her mother was back inside the house. She wished she had found her father sooner and that she was anywhere else but here. There was nowhere to run. Her father slapped her again, and he dug his fingers into Charlie's soft skin as he shook her shoulder like a rag doll.

Kyler screamed in her face, spit spraying his daughter's face. "What were you two doing? How could you let this happen, Charlie? What the *fuck* were you doing?"

Kyler pushed Charlie away, and she fell back, cracking the back of her head on the hard driveway. He stood over her like a giant, pointing a thick finger at her, anger burning his cheeks.

"I told you to look out for each other, didn't I? *Didn't I?* Have I taught you nothing?"

Kyler stormed away to the house, and Charlie curled up into a ball, tears pouring from her eyes for her dead mother and the life that awaited her now.

CHAPTER 1

"Look, Schafer, I appreciate what you're saying, but this is my house. If I hadn't taken you in, where would you be right now? I'm not trying to score points. I'm just saying that you need to listen to me. I've got it right so far, and I'm right on this one. Leave it be. We're good here, and there's no need to go upsetting the apple cart."

Schafer looked at his wife Magda for a clue as to whether he should push it or not. She could read these situations better than him and pick up on things that he missed. Schafer could analyze a chessboard and work out potential moves well in advance of them being played out. He loved the game and its ruthlessness and the paradox between its structure and freedom. He would play games with his friends whenever time allowed and often saw similarities in reality to the game. This was another occasion when Jeremy was playing to win. He had all the pieces lined up and knew Schafer couldn't afford to risk pushing forward. They were locked in a battle of wills, and as much as Schafer was enjoying it, he had to bring himself back from the edge sometimes. Magda always knew when he should cool it or go for broke and push his Queen forward. He looked at her now for reassurance: should he push on and go in for the kill or keep his advantage for another time and stay back?

The look on Magda's face was telling him not to go there. If he tried to argue further it could make things worse. There was enough tension in the house already without him adding to it.

"Okay, okay," said Schafer scratching his unkempt gray beard, "let's do it your way. You're right. Of course, we are your guests. I'd just like for you to think about the future and how long it's realistic for us to stay here. That's all I was trying to suggest. But it's okay. No problem, Jeremy, no problem at all."

Schafer offered his hand, and Jeremy shook it. The two men had an uneasy friendship; one based more out of necessity than real respect. They got on with each other because they simply had to. There was no other choice given the circumstances. Both knew it, and both tried to maintain a cool distance from the other. There was no hatred between them but always that distance. It was safer that way. They had learned not to get too close to people. It was easier than when they left.

Schafer walked across the cold linoleum to Magda. "Okay. Let's go chat with Rilla. She'll want to know."

Magda was an ample woman, large framed with a pudgy face and thick arms. She had begun to lose a little weight given the restriction on how much food there was available now, and her clothes were starting to look a little loose around her waist. They weren't hanging off her yet, but Schafer knew his wife was going to need a whole new wardrobe if they were still here next winter.

"Ja, okay. Natürlich."

Schafer winced when she spoke. Her English was not as good as his, and he knew how much it pissed off Jeremy when they spoke in their own tongue. He turned around to face Jeremy.

"I'm sorry, my wife…"

"It's fine. You go talk to Rilla. I should be helping Lyn out in the garden anyway."

Schafer could tell that Jeremy was trying to hide his annoyance. Had they not already been arguing then, Magda's German may have led to another 'discussion' about the respect for other people's wishes, but as it was Jeremy let it slide, and disappeared quickly out of the sitting room. He said nothing when he left and made little noise when he walked. He was a tall, slim man matching his tall, slim wife, and Schafer still didn't feel at ease in his presence. They were just too different in their backgrounds, their attitudes, and culture. The only thing they had in common was the need to protect their families. Both of them had done well up to today, and together they could say they were survivors.

Schafer pressed his flannel shirt down, trying to get the creases out of the collar. He still tried to keep a good appearance despite the conditions. Washing was a rarity and, of course, they had no clothes of their own. Having to borrow clothes made Schafer feel uncomfortable, and wearing Jeremy's shirts meant Schafer always felt a little uneasy around him. Even the way they dressed was different. Schafer chose red checks and stripes, whilst Jeremy was dressed as usual in dark clothes. Today he wore a black shirt tucked into dark jeans, and keeping tabs on him was like watching a shadow dance in the dark.

Schafer pulled on his beard thoughtfully. "Magda, please, remember we talked about this. Jeremy doesn't like us speaking Deutsch."

"Aber, ich-"

"Nein. *No*." Schafer took his wife's hand, noticing her fingers were thinner and that her wedding ring fitted a little loosely now. The pale band of skin underneath it was beginning to show, but getting a wedding ring resized would prove extremely difficult. "It's not easy for you. I know this is awkward, but with me and Rilla helping, you can do it."

"Okay, okay. Yes, I will try. I find also it is…schmerzlich. I mean it is not easy for me. I don't like this American."

Schafer squeezed his wife's hand. Her eyes met his, and he wished he had been able to convince Jeremy that staying was not a viable long-term solution. Jeremy's house was large enough for them all to sleep comfortably in their own rooms, and safety wasn't an issue. The house was well built, the windows and doors were always locked, and the retaining wall around the back garden meant they had a barrier between them and the corpses which was practically insurmountable. Jeremy had turned the whole garden into a vegetable patch before Schafer had even arrived with his family, and it looked like they were settled in for the long haul. Schafer was worried though, worried a lot.

"You don't have to like him. But we do have to get along. Come, let's see Rilla. If we're going to live with him and his family any longer, then we need to understand them, to work with them, and make this happen. We need to do it for Rilla." Schafer led his wife through the house, past the closed windows and blinds, and up to the guest room that had become their daughter's room. Pushing open the door, Schafer found his daughter lying on the bed reading a book. He looked around the room, impressed at how tidy it was. Everything was neatly folded or correctly stored, the books lying neatly on the dresser. For a seventeen-year-old girl, she was impeccable.

"Rilla, are you okay?"

As Schafer entered the room, Magda went straight to their daughter and sat down beside her on the bed. The duvet cover crumpled immediately, and there was a popping sound as one of the springs in the mattress went.

"Ja, obwohl ich bin gelangweilt. Mein buch ist nich sehr gut. Es ist eine dumme Zombie-Roman. Was haben Sie sprechen mit Jeremy uber?"

"English please, Rilla. We need to help your Mother. You know how Jeremy doesn't like it when-"

"Okay, fine. *In English*." Rilla rolled her eyes and put her book on her pillow. "Jeremy doesn't like anything."

Schafer smiled. His daughter's brown eyes sparkled when she got angry. She reminded him a great deal of his own mother. It wasn't just the physical similarities, but the personality that was starting to shine through now that she was getting older; turning from a child into her own woman. Rilla was strong but smart with it. She knew when to pick a fight and when to stay quiet. That was something she had learned from her own mother.

"Maybe not. But he saved our lives, and we are in his home, so we have to respect that. I cannot make him do anything."

Rilla hugged her mother and then shrugged. "So what? We live here forever? Wait until we run out of food?"

"Jeremy thinks he can grow enough food for all of us. He said Lyn has got a lot of vegetables growing, and until they are ready we have enough tins of food and supplies to last."

"You think he's telling the truth?" Rilla looked at her mother. "Do *you* think so?"

Magda nodded. Her face was sad. "Ja. He tells truth."

"He's not trying to trick us, Rilla. You have to understand that he's been through as much as we have. What he's made here with Lyn and Victoria is a good thing, and I can understand he would not want that compromised." Schafer went over to the window and parted the curtains. He wanted to see them. He needed to see them, to be reminded that they weren't gone, that the dead were still all around them. He needed to remind himself why he had agreed to stay here. "All he wants to do is protect his family. You can understand that, can't you? I'm not saying I agree with him, but I can see his point of view. It's far safer to stay behind these walls than to go out there."

Schafer peered through the pale yellow curtains at the streets below. There were at least two dozen of them that he could see. A few of the corpses were motionless, sitting or lying on the ground, but he knew that was just laziness. As soon as something or someone got their attention, they would jump up. The others bumbled around, crashing into vehicles and walls as if they were drunk. It was just an illusion. These people were neither drunk, nor as harmless as they appeared. Yet nor were they alive anymore. Their teeth could rip a man apart in seconds. A single bite from their diseased dead bodies would mean death to the recipient. Schafer had seen too many people fooled into thinking they could get past them—just run past the zombies with ease. It was an easy mistake to make; one that had been made too many times early on. It wasn't taken seriously enough, and when it was, it was too late. A lot of people had died, and Schafer recognized they were more than indebted to Jeremy for making sure he and his family was alive too.

They had arrived from Germany for their annual vacation several months ago now. Schafer knew it was the last time they would all get away as a family. Rilla was already complaining about being away from her friends for so long, and she was likely to go off to university in a year. Schafer knew there was one friend in particular, a boy called Franz, whom Rilla was going to miss the most. His daughter was growing up, and there was nothing he could do about that. The flight to Washington had been uneventful, and the few days they had spent there acclimatizing to the time zone and looking around the museums had been happy. Magda especially loved museums and cities, and it was she who had pushed for them to go to Washington, a city they had never visited before. Unfortunately, they were never likely to visit it again. A million corpses now filled the streets of the capital city, and the museums were populated by the dead. If there were any survivors left, they would not stand a chance. Schafer knew they had been lucky. If they had not left when they had, there was a very good chance they would be dead now too.

Schafer remembered catching the flight to Portland and hearing the first stories then. He had a text from a colleague back in Nürnberg about some trouble in Berlin: rioting, fighting, and people being attacked in the street. It sounded strange. There was no political motivation for it; no terrorist outrage. It felt surreal standing in the quiet airport reading about the problems back home. Being on vacation, Schafer usually avoided the news and liked to forget the world's problems, but they were catching up. Whilst waiting to board the flight, he overheard two men talking about some sort of incident in Boston, a gang war that had somehow got out of hand. A lot of people had died. There were reports that one of the gangs had attacked a hotel, but he missed the details. It sounded too far-fetched to be true, and he ignored the rest of the conversation, preferring to think about the huge trout he was going to catch the next day up at Peterborough.

After picking up the rental car at Portland airport, they made their way down through Manchester and reached Peterborough just as night was creeping up on them. The motel was basic but perfectly comfortable, and that first night had gone well. Magda and Rilla enjoyed some pasta in the local Italian, and having received no more texts from his colleague, Schafer went to bed forgetting about the whole thing.

The next morning his phone had been alive with messages, all warning him to get back home before it was too late. Trouble was spreading and people were panicking. Whatever had caused the riots to break out in Berlin had spread fast. It wasn't just in Germany now, but a problem that was growing exponentially. First France, then Spain all reported the same things. People were attacking each other. Checking the news whilst Magda and Rilla went to find coffee, Schafer sat on the end of his bed in the small motel room watching as the news feed told him of problem areas and no-go zones on the Eastern seaboard. All flights to Europe were cancelled. The threat level to the United States had been raised, and a curfew was being imposed in all the major cities and larger urban areas. He heard reports of viruses and infections, of corpses reanimating, and stores being looted for food and bottled water.

When Magda and Rilla returned with coffee and pastries for breakfast, they could not believe what he had to tell them. All three of them sat in their little motel room watching the TV news as horror story after horror story unfolded. They didn't leave the room at all that day, and only when it grew dark did Schafer venture outside. He found the closest store, bought all the food he could, and returned to the motel knowing the vacation was over. All night the sirens wailed, and the noises and screams they heard were terrifying. Peterborough was supposed to be a quiet town, the perfect place to 'get away from it all' for a week of relaxation. Instead, they spent the night locked in their room wondering if they were going to make it through the night.

"It's just the same as before. We might have escaped that motel room, but all we've done is trade one prison for another." Rilla lay back on the bed and folded her hands under her head. "We should've stayed in Germany. We should've—"

"Okay, Rilla, I wish we were home, too, but we're not are we? So let's just deal with what we've got. You want to go back to that motel?" Schafer closed the curtains. It was only two or three miles away, but getting from there to this house had been a nightmare. "You really think we'd be better off if we had stayed there? I remember how hungry you were after the third day. I remember how frightened you and Magda were when those men knocked on the door. I remember having to…" Schafer looked at his wife, her round eyes sad and tired. "Look, we are better off here. And if Jeremy says we stay, then we stay."

"Wir sind so weit von zu Hause," muttered Magda.

Rilla glared at her mother. "Yeah, Mom, I know how far away we are from home. Like that's helping."

"Rilla, Jeremy thinks we can wait it out," said Schafer. "He is adamant that we have enough food. I know this isn't what we wanted, but we can't exactly get back to the car, drive the three hours back to Portland, and jump on a plane back to Nürnberg. We stay here, and that's the end of it."

"It's not just the food, Dad." Rilla looked at him. "It's what's out there. Those people, those corpses—they're not going anywhere. They *know* we're here. Don't tell me you can't hear them at night, because I know you can. The way their fingernails scratch at the brickwork, the moaning sound they make, and the grinding of their teeth. One day they'll figure out how to pull down that fence, or get over it, or get under it, or something, and then we're fucked."

"Language, Rilla," said Magda quietly.

"Es tut mir Leid." Rilla sat up and rested her head on her mother's back. "Sorry, Mom."

"I know, I tried to explain to Jeremy, but he thinks it will hold." Schafer peered at the fence panels through a crack in the curtains. They might hold, but he wasn't prepared to gamble the lives of his wife and only child on 'might.' The fence was the only thing that was separating the house from being invaded by a hundred dead people. Rilla was right. If the dead found a way in, they were screwed. There was no back way out. Jeremy had ensured the house was protected on all sides, and the fence doubled as the main entrance to the property. The door in it had been nailed shut ensuring the only way in was gone. Rilla was right about another thing too. Schafer did hear them at night scratching and clawing at the wood as they tried to get in. He had become accustomed to the noises, but that didn't mean he had gotten used to it.

"Okay, so what do you think, Magda? You want to go or stay?"

Magda brushed a hand through her daughter's hair and looked forlornly at her husband. "I think I want to stay. If you and Rilla stay, then I stay."

Both Schafer and Rilla knew that their mother would go wherever they went. It wasn't that she had no opinion, but she was too far out of her comfort zone. Her grasp of English was tenuous, and ever since the zombies had appeared outside their motel room, she had become more and more withdrawn.

"Dad, let's go. You know what I'm talking about." Rilla sat bolt upright, her deep brown eyes lighting up when she spoke. "That house on the hill is our best bet of seeing this through. I know that getting to Portland or Washington—or even back home to Germany—is out of the question. For a long time, it would seem. So for the next few weeks or months, or however long it takes for this situation to be resolved, we need to be somewhere safe. This isn't the place. Jeremy and Lynn took us in. But like the motel, it's just another stop on the road."

Schafer looked at Rilla with a heavy heart. She spoke the truth. "Mr. Attwood's place?"

"Sure. The mansion. Why not? Jeremy said it was like a fortress. You heard what he said. Attwood was a rich old man who built himself more of a castle than a home. High perimeter fencing, security cameras, even a moat fed by the nearby river. You know he's there; the lights still come on at night. We've all seen it, so I don't know why Jeremy can't see it too."

"Rilla, I'm not sure..." Schafer knew the house his daughter spoke of. He had seen it, too, and discussed it with Jeremy. There was nothing else like it around for miles. Jeremy had told them how Attwood had built it a few years back. He was a millionaire and had spared no expense, buying up all the land around it too. Getting there wouldn't be easy, but if they could get inside, then there was no doubt they would be safe. Schafer wanted to go, but it wasn't the right time.

"Dad, it's the best place for us. You know it, and I know it. If you can't convince Jeremy, then I can." Rilla got off the bed and walked toward the closed door. "Let me talk to him. I'll make that idiot listen to me."

Schafer turned away from the window, the sun warming his back as he approached the door. Rilla hadn't opened it yet, and he needed to make sure their conversation stayed private. "Just remember who took us in, Rilla. When the motel was overrun, when there was nowhere else to go, Jeremy and Lyn opened their doors to us. You know what would've happened if they hadn't, and you also know that they didn't have to do that. They put themselves and Vicky in danger when they did that."

"I know, but—"

"*We* are the reason those corpses are mounting up outside that fence; outside this house." Schafer remembered the day they had turned up on Jeremy's doorstep no more than minutes from death. Escaping the motel had taken all their energy, and they had not known where to turn. There was no help, no police, nowhere to run except away from the zombies, away from the motel; they had run through the streets of Peterborough aimlessly, at one point circling back on themselves in error. They didn't know the area, and it was only a fluke they found Jeremy's house. Schafer saw movement in a window and had dragged Magda and Rilla with him, hoping it meant someone was alive inside. As it turned out, he was right. Jeremy had let them in with caution and locked the fence behind them. The zombies chasing had been barricaded outside and had not gone anywhere since. It had been a beautiful sunny day, just like today, and the memory of it was still fresh in Schafer's mind. He thought he was going to lose his family that day. He thought he was going to watch Magda and Rilla torn apart at the hands of the corpses that now populated the world, and yet Jeremy had shown kindness and let them in. He owed Jeremy, they all did, and that was why they had to respect his wishes now. Stay in the house; stay where they knew they had food and water. There was a certain logic to it, Schafer had to admit. What Jeremy couldn't see was that one day it would all come tumbling down. Schafer just hoped they weren't there when it did. In the meantime, they had to play the waiting game and show to Jeremy that they weren't about to jeopardize what he had created: a safe haven, an island surrounded by a storm of death that refused to dissipate.

"We cannot throw away all the trust we've built up over the last few months," said Schafer firmly. "Let's not burn our bridges yet, Rilla. We can wait a bit longer. I'm worried about the future too. I'm worried about tomorrow and the next day and the next. But this is the way it is now, Rilla."

The bed creaked as Magda got up, and she joined her husband's side. "Please, Rilla. We must stick together. Ich vermis Nürnberg. I want to go home. For now, we must do what Jeremy says. So please, listen to your Father. Werden Sie es für mich tun?"

Schafer kissed his wife on the cheek. Having her on his side meant a lot. If she had sided with Rilla, then he would've had a great deal of difficulty in stopping her from talking to Jeremy. It wouldn't have achieved anything except create more tension between the two families. They might be living under the same roof, but they were a world apart when it came to decisions on how to live.

Rilla's shoulder's dropped, and her eyes hit the floor. Schafer knew she would calm down and realize they were doing the right thing. He wanted to offer her something; a sign that she wasn't completely in the wrong, a glimmer of hope that they weren't trapped in a stranger's house forever. "Rilla, maybe when the food and water start to run out, maybe then I can talk to Jeremy and Lyn again. I'll make him see. Maybe—"

Rilla snapped her head up and looked at her parents. Her hand hovered over the door handle, and she wanted to rush out and scream at Jeremy. She wanted to run away, all the way home to Nürnberg, but she knew she wasn't going anywhere. Every day they spent here, every night she slept in a strange house in a stranger's bed, she felt not just afraid but frustrated. "Maybe when the food and water have run out we'll be too weak to go anywhere. Maybe we'll just have to start eating each other. Maybe the fence will give way tonight, and none of us have a tomorrow to worry about."

"Rilla…"

A knock on the door interrupted them. Three soft taps told Rilla exactly who it was, and she opened the door, pleased that Vicky had given her a reason to leave. Jeremy and Lyn's daughter had celebrated her tenth birthday last week, and they had strung up balloons and banners inside the house. Lyn and Magda had even managed to make a cake with what few ingredients they could muster, and they had played games until it got dark. It was after they had all eaten that Vicky had asked why none of her friends had been able to come to her party. She knew it was something to do with the dead people outside, but couldn't understand why they hadn't at least telephoned to say happy birthday to her.

Vicky was the one thing that gave Rilla hope. Vicky was such a cute girl. Her curly brown hair still ringed her freckled face, and her naturally outgoing attitude meant she enjoyed spending time with her. Rilla was an only child, and Vicky had become like a younger sister to her. She displayed none of the mistrust that her parents did and simply enjoyed every day. She had her moments, of course. There were the days when she couldn't understand why she wasn't allowed to go to school or why she couldn't go swimming down in the lake as she had done last summer, but on the whole, she was a good natured child, and a ray of hope in an otherwise bleak situation.

"Hi Vicky, what's going on?" Rilla knew there was no point in arguing with her parents anymore. Schafer had made his mind up which meant that Magda had made hers up too. Rilla would rather spend the rest of the day with Vicky than discussing something that wasn't going to happen.

"What are you all doing in here?" asked Vicky, innocently.

Schafer smiled. "Nothing, my dear, just having a little talk. Are you all right? Where are your parents?"

"They're in the garden." Vicky sighed. "Booooring. They're planting seeds. Mom said it was something called zookeenee. I don't know what it is, but it sounds horrible."

Rilla bent down to Vicky. "You want to play hide and seek?"

Vicky's face brightened up, and she clapped her hands together. "Yes, yes, yes, yes. I'll hide first. You have to find me."

"Okay," said Rilla as Vicky darted off downstairs, "but remember you have to stay in the house."

"Yeah." Vicky's voice was lost as she ran down the stairs.

"Rilla, watch out for her, don't let her go—"

"I know, Dad. I'll be careful. We'll talk later." Rilla smiled at Magda. "Right now I've got a ten-year-old girl to find."

"Ich liebe dich," said Magda quietly as her daughter left the bedroom.

"It'll be fine, Magda," said Schafer, as he put an arm around his wife. He heard the zombies banging on the fence below, recalling how close they had been to getting in the day they had arrived here. He felt nervous, as if he could feel them getting closer, scratching one more layer of paint off the fence with every day. One day the wood would get too thin, it would crack and shatter, and ten thousand corpses would pour into Jeremy's house. He pulled Magda to him and hugged her, burying his face in her hair. When he spoke he tried to keep his tone light, hiding the fear he truly felt. "Gott meine Familie zu schützen. It will all work out, you'll see. Rilla will come around. It'll be fine."

CHAPTER 2

Charlie picked up the linen basket full of wet clothes and trudged outside with it. . The washing machine had long since stopped working, so everything was done by hand now. When enough rainwater had collected, she would soak their clothes in the bathtub and hang them out to dry, letting the sun do its job. They didn't bother with washing often; it was far too arduous, and quite frankly it seemed all rather pointless. They never saw anyone, never went anywhere, so why should she worry about how she looked? Sighing, Charlie went out to the small garden they had. When she reached the clothesline, she began to peg the clothes up one by one. She started to hum a tune, an old song by an old band that she used to like. She hadn't actually listened to music for months now, not since they had run out of batteries. She still remembered, though; still had the music in her head, and sometimes she thought she could hear it floating across the wind, as if her favorite bands were all lined up outside, playing in Peterborough just for her. The music would get so loud she had to force herself to stop listening. It was all in her head, of course, and when the music stopped she wondered why her brain did that; why sometimes she would wake in the middle of the night with a rock song blasting out so loudly that she had to muffle it with a pillow over her head. Eventually her brain would turn the music down, but it took a concentrated effort to make it do so. It was as if she was stood in front of the radio, her fingers barely touching the dial, unable to change the setting. Today, however, as she picked out one of Kyler's freshly washed shirts from the basket she wanted the music. She needed to block out the sounds, the noise that *they* made. It was like a foreign language, all the moaning and groaning that passed their cracked, dry, dead lips; she hated it and turned the volume up. A song came into her head, one about a girl falling in love with a boy who already had a girlfriend, and she started humming along, breaking out into a smile when she remembered the singer and how much she fancied him.

'*I want to kiss your mouth, hold your hand, and all I feel is the distant wind as you turn your back on me.*'

That was over a year ago now. The singer was probably dead, and as much as Charlie wanted to grieve, to feel sorry for him and his family and his fans, the truth was she didn't really care. He was like a cartoon character. Had he ever been real? He was only ever in a magazine or on the TV, just like the rest of them. It was as if her old life had been just an illusion.

Charlie heard the zombies rattling the fence and groaning, and she turned the volume up louder. "Jesus, can't you just be quiet for one fucking minute?"

When she'd finished putting the last shirt up on the line, she turned the basket over and left it on the grass, and then made her way over to the long driveway. It had been three weeks since she had last stepped foot on the drive. It had been three long weeks since she had lost her mother, and neither she nor her father had gone back to the fence, to that spot where she had died.

They were loud today, the deadly sounds of the walking corpses filling her head until she couldn't hear the singer's voice anymore. Who gave them the right to take over? Who had decided to let them in and turn the country over to them? It wasn't fair. Charlie was annoyed and angry. She had woken up with a headache, and the sky was a dreary gray. Kyler had made her do the washing and then proceeded to open a bottle of wine whilst giving her a list of chores. It had become something of a routine in the last couple of weeks. Ever since it had happened, since the screaming woman had destroyed their world, Charlie had been forced to watch her father drink all day and night. He refused to talk about what happened that day, and from his attitude, Charlie could only assume he still blamed her. He had shut her out, speaking to her only to trade insults or order her to do some menial task around the house. Since that day, she had become a tenant in her own home, no more than a live-in cleaner on hand to serve her master.

"For fuck's sake, quit it." Charlie turned the music off. It was impossible to hear it over the racket they were making. "What do you want?"

Charlie strode purposefully onto the drive, turned the corner of the house, and stared at the fence. It was *them*: the invaders, the foreigners who had just taken over the country with no regard for any of its people. It was *them* who had ruined everything. Charlie looked at the motley group of bodies, at the disparate people torn from their own lives forced into destroying others. Some days they seemed quiet, withdrawn, yet other days they were noisy. Today they were noisy. A crowd of around thirty were gathered futilely around the gate as they tried to get past the lock to her and Kyler. Charlie walked slowly down the driveway, trying to keep one ear out for her father. If he caught her he would only say she was shirking her duties to pleasure her own morbid curiosity. She was curious, true, but only as to why they kept coming. There was no logic to it. They couldn't get in, it was impossible, and yet they kept trying.

Charlie wondered if they were being led by something or someone. Perhaps an invisible force that somehow drove them here to the house where they lived. It had stopped feeling like Charlie's home and was just a place she lived now. More than that, it was a place to exist. Living would imply a sense of being, of working toward something, a future, a life; her father had ensured that any hope had been extinguished alongside the death of her mother. As Charlie ventured further forward down the driveway, she spotted the crowbar lying on the road where her father had left it. Not far away, there was a dark stain on the concrete, just a small circle of dried blood that hadn't been completely erased by the wind and sporadic rain yet. It was the last evidence of her mother's death.

Charlie looked at the zombies straining to reach her, their arms all pushed through the small gaps in the fence. Their hands were clutching at the air, grasping at nothing, reminding her of babies, feeble hands curling up and unfurling as they desperately tried to find something to grab hold of. But there was nothing. Charlie knew well enough to stay well away from the fence. The men and women there could kill her with a single scratch. Once the dead got hold of you, there was only one end. In the early days, they said it was a biological parasite that was transferred in the blood of its victims, much like the Zika virus that had left so many deformed and dead in South America. Then the guesses stopped, and the focus turned on how to survive, how to avoid the dead. Finally, everything stopped. It didn't take long for *them* to take over and ruin everything.

"I hate you," muttered Charlie. Her eyes scanned the corpses standing at her fence. There were men and women, partially dressed, some still wearing blood-stained clothes, some with arms and hands missing, some with chunks ripped from their necks or torsos, and some rotted away so they appeared more like ghoulish cartoon versions of their true selves. There were children too. Those were the ones she hated the most. They hadn't been able to defend themselves. They had suffered the most, and now they were stood outside Charlie Gretzinger's home, their small hands trying to grab a piece of her to shove into their rotten mouths. As they lined up to eat her, their faces pressed up against the fence, they reminded her of refugees from another country, as if they were just people looking for somewhere to turn, their hands outstretched for mercy and a hand-out, their open mouths waiting for food. She hated them for what they had done to her family, to her town, and what they had done to the world. She thought about picking up the crowbar and ramming it into their heads, thrusting it through all of their brittle skulls until a mountain of bloody zombies lay at her feet. She should, she knew, but she couldn't. What purpose would it serve? It wouldn't bring her mother back, and even if she killed these, then more would come. They always did.

The dead were dressed in rags, faded clothes that over the months had lost all their color, and yet in the throng she caught a glimpse of bright red. It was just a flash of color, but it was definitely there, hiding behind a fat woman with half her face missing. Charlie's heart pounded. Could there be anyone alive out there? Charlie took a step forward, trying to find the burst of color again, and then she found it, this time appearing briefly behind a man with nothing below the elbows except for a straggly piece of meat and tissue that looked like spaghetti.

"Hello?" When Charlie spoke, her voice sounded faint and pathetic. She wanted to shout, but she was scared. Even the single word she spoke had aroused the dead, and they pulled and pushed against the fence with more force. They wanted her, but they weren't going to get her.

"Is anyone—?"

Charlie turned the music up to full volume quickly, filling her head with snippets of her favorite songs, of thrashing guitars and piano chords, desperately trying to take her mind off what she could see. The glimpse of red from earlier was now in full view. It was part of a dress, part of a bright red dress that had been torn and ripped, but the owner was still wearing. The person wearing the dress was now at the driveway entrance, their hands pushing through the small gaps, and their bare feet kicking at it as they tried to get to Charlie. The zombie's teeth clacked together loudly, and Charlie tried to focus on the music. It was impossible.

"Mom?" Charlie hated them all. *They* had done this, changed her, killed her, and taken her away from her family for what?

Jemma no longer resembled the beautiful woman who had married Kyler, but was a skeletal figure missing huge chunks of flesh. There was a gaping hole in her stomach, moist red tissue surrounded by patches of dark brown and purple skin where she had started to rot. One breast hung low over her abdomen, whilst the other was missing, eaten away exposing her ribcage. A silver pendant still hung around her crooked neck, and her face was riddled with bite marks. One eye had been sucked from its socket and eaten whilst the other swung loosely upon her cheek, hanging on by a thread. Patches of hair had been pulled from her head, swathes of skin ripped off, leaving her head a patchwork quilt of bruises and bloody flesh. Odd white pieces of her skull poked through the remaining thin hair. As Jemma pushed her arms through the fence, her body stuck on the other side, one of her hands opened out revealing there were only two fingers left, the others now just short bony stumps.

Charlie gasped, turned away, and began walking quickly back to the house. How could this be happening? Had her mother returned because she was drawn there by the crowd or corpses, or had she led them there? Her mother was dead, dead and gone. Charlie couldn't reconcile what she had seen with her loving mother. They weren't the same person. Her mother had died, and whatever was stood at the fence now was just a Doppelganger, a freak, a parody of the real woman. Her body might be moving, her legs walking, but that thing was not her mother.

Returning to the clothesline, Charlie sank onto the grass, and grabbed hold of the empty basket. It was real, something she could feel in her hands. That thing back at the gate that looked like her mother wasn't real. It was one of them now, not a real person. Charlie was trembling, her breath coming in quick gasps, and she knew she had to contain her anguish. She didn't want her father to see her like this. He would want to know what she had been doing, and she couldn't face having to tell him what she had seen. Charlie stayed on the grass, focusing on the music in her head, letting it soothe her until she managed to calm down. Every time the vision of her dead mother popped back in her head, she forced herself to concentrate on the necklace that was still around her mother's neck. If Charlie forced her eyes to look at the necklace, she found she could ignore the terrible wounds on her mother's body and ignore the terrible pain she knew that her mother must have been in when she died.

Eventually the music faded away, the guitars stopped playing, and the call of the zombies became background noise. She didn't know how long she had been sat out on the garden like that, but it didn't really matter. As she looked at the house that she still called home, she realized that her father hadn't come out to look for her. Had he even noticed she hadn't returned? Did he care? Charlie felt like staying out there a while longer. What was the point in going inside when all that faced her was more work? And for what? Kyler clearly didn't give a shit about her anymore, and the truth was, she beginning to resent him. She loved her father, but he had changed. Since that day, he had become withdrawn, drank a lot more, and treated Charlie like she was worthless. She didn't want to hate her father, but he was making it easier with each day that passed.

A muffled bang broke her thoughts. Looking up at the house, it took her a moment to work out what it was. The house looked quiet, empty even, yet she knew her father was in there somewhere, working on getting drunk enough to make it through another day. On the ground by the back door there was a bird. It had jet black feathers, and as Charlie stood up to look at it, she realized it was a crow. It was hopping around on the floor, turning around in circles, unable to get off the ground. Charlie looked at the large window that now had a thin crack in it and understood that the bird must have flown into it.

"You poor thing." Charlie wondered if she should approach it or leave it be. If she spooked it, then it might do itself more harm. But if she didn't attend to it, would it be able to fly again? There was a good chance it had broken a wing, and she knew it might need caring for. Wasn't that the right thing to do? There was probably an old shoebox in the garage she could use. She could find worms for it in the garden, provide it with a little water, and coax it back to life. Here was a chance to do the right thing. Her mind made up, Charlie slowly began to approach the bird. It had stopped flapping around and was sat on the ground with its feathers puffed out as it watched her.

"Don't worry, Mr. Crow, I'm going to help you," she said with a lilt in her voice. She didn't want to scare it and walked very slowly. The bird seemed to be breathing fast, its chest heaving rapidly. It was more than likely petrified. Charlie knew she must look like a giant to it, and picking the poor bird up might not be as easy as she thought. "It's okay, it's all right," she cooed. "I'll take care of you."

The bird suddenly flapped its wing, and Charlie expected to see it soar up into the air. She had probably misdiagnosed it. Maybe its wing wasn't broken, and the crow was just momentarily stunned. The bird cartwheeled and then landed back on the ground. It had at least one broken wing and wasn't flying anywhere.

"Settle down now, Mr. Crow. It's okay." Charlie was only six feet away from it now and was preparing to grab it. She didn't want to hurt it, but she knew she couldn't just leave it.

"Charlie?" Kyler stepped out of the door into the sunlight and raised a hand above his eyes. The stubble around his chin was several days old now and threatening to turn into a full blown beard. The light hurt his eyes, unaccustomed as they were to seeing the sun for themselves without the soothing haze of alcohol to protect them. "What's going on out here? You should've been back an hour ago. I heard a bang. Have you been in the garage? You know I don't like you messing around with my stuff."

Charlie ignored the gruffness and accusing tone to his voice. "There's a bird, Dad. See? It flew into the window and hurt itself. I was just going to—"

"A bird?" Kyler saw it sitting on the ground and took a step toward it. "You're out here playing with a bird? We've far more important things to be doing. You should be fixing that hole in my shirt I've been telling you about. Then there's the inventory to do. We need to figure out exactly how much food we have left. Come on, Charlie, you're supposed to be an adult now. Quit playing, and get on with your work. Jesus, I'm sick of having to tell you what to do. How about you start taking some damn responsibility for this house? You think *I'm* going to do everything?"

Charlie wanted to scream at him, to tell him to wind his head in, but more than anything she just wanted to help the bird. Whatever work had to be done inside would keep. They weren't going anywhere. "Dad, I'll be there in a minute; I'm just going to help this—"

"Like hell you are." Kyler walked to his daughter, causing the bird to stir. It flapped its wings uselessly as Kyler grabbed his daughter's arm firmly. He pulled her toward the house.

"Ow, Dad, that hurts. Stop it." Charlie couldn't win in a physical fight with her father, but that didn't stop her from trying to pull back and stay to help the bird.

"I'll stop it when you start acting like a damn adult. You think this is all fun and games? You're supposed to be twenty-one, not a little girl anymore."

Charlie managed to wrench her arm free of her father's grasp. "Let go of me!" she screamed. She could feel the tears threatening to erupt, but didn't want to give him the satisfaction of knowing he had made her cry. Not again. "Just let me help this bird. Piss off, Dad. Just go back inside and leave me alone."

Kyler grabbed her arm again. "You wouldn't have spoken to me like that if your mother was here." He drew his face up to hers. Anger burned in his eyes. "Come here. You want to help? You want to do something useful?" Kyler dragged Charlie toward the bird.

"Dad, please, just stop it." Charlie felt her cheeks flush and knew tears were the next step. Why was he acting like this?

"Broken wing, huh?" Kyler put his other arm on Charlie's neck and forced her to look down at the bird. They were only a couple of feet away now, and the bird was breathing heavily. A fleck of blood was encrusted on its yellow beak, and its eyelids were drooping as if it were sleepy. "This bird will make a good dinner. You want to help, then put it out of its misery. Snap its fucking neck and be done with it."

Charlie was shocked. "No. I can help it, Dad. I can make it better. Please?" She felt like a little girl when he scolded her. She couldn't stand up to him, and when she did she felt like everything she said only angered him more. Her father's grip on her neck was strong, and there was no way she could throw him off. He was in control now and she had to make him understand. She had to make him see there was more to all of this than just death. "No, I'm doing it. Mr. Crow can still make it if we help him."

"Mr. Crow is just food. He's part of the food chain. Don't you get how this works, Charlie? The crow eats worms, we eat the crow, the zombies eat us, and then when their bodies finally rot and turn to mulch in the ground, the worms come up and eat them. It's the circle of life."

Kyler laughed. He forced Charlie's head down lower. The bird sat on the ground motionless, exhausted, and Charlie felt the first tears fall from her eyes. He had lost it. Her father had totally lost it, and over what, an injured bird? Charlie thought she should tell him about his wife, her dead body at the fence, and then she'd see how he'd cope. She wanted to tell him, she wanted him to hurt, to suffer as she was. She wanted to make her father cry as he did her. But she said nothing and listened to her father's cruel laugh.

"It's not going to recover," said Kyler. "There's only one way to end this. So do it, Charlie. You think you're a woman now; you think you can handle everything without me, *so do it*." Kyler suddenly released his grip on her and Charlie stumbled forward. She jumped over the bird, worrying she was going to tread on it, and then stood up.

"I'm not going to hurt it, Dad," Charlie said through her tears. She was shaking, yet she couldn't bring herself to do it. She had to make him see that he was wrong. "I think we can save it. I think—"

Kyler shook his head. "You've got to grow up one day. You have to fight or you die, Charlie. Your boy bands are gone. They're not making another Star Wars. There are no more trips to the golden arches or the mall, so grow a pair."

"No!"

Charlie screamed as Kyler reached down, scooped up the crow in his hands, and snapped its neck. The sickening crack sent shivers up and down Charlie's spine. Kyler held the lifeless bird in his hands and walked toward his daughter.

"Here." He thrust the bird to her and instinctively Charlie held out her hands. Kyler dropped it into her hands.

"You can serve it tonight with that tin of potatoes we've been saving. I need a good feed for a change. I've had enough of this shit. It's time for you to start taking on some more responsibility, Charlie. Hurry up and get inside." Kyler walked back to the house and turned in the doorway. He looked at his daughter holding the dead bird, her face a mixture of shock and fear. "If I don't see that bird on our plate tonight, maybe I'll snap your fucking neck too," he said calmly, and then disappeared back inside.

Charlie stared at the bird in her hands. Its head lolled loosely around in her palms, and yet it was still warm. Its feathers were soft and its body fat. She knew she had to do it. Would her father hurt her or hit her or kill her if she didn't? She doubted it, but he would make her life Hell.

"I'm sorry, Mr. Crow. I thought...I just wanted to help."

A song started playing, a distant voice that soon turned into a full choir. It was the song she had used earlier to drown out the noise of the zombies. Now it was drowning out her thoughts.

'*I want to kiss your mouth, hold your hand, and all I feel is the distant wind as you turn your back on me.*'

The thought that kept coming to the front of her mind was how she wished she could swap places with her mother. Charlie didn't want to wish herself dead and she didn't want to remember her mother like that, or remember how much her father had willfully hurt her. So she played the song at full volume and slowly walked back toward the house, toward her home, and letting the tears fall, she began to think how she was going to cook Mr. Crow for dinner.

CHAPTER 3

"You sure about this?" asked Rilla. "I mean, maybe we should wait. He listens to Lyn. I'll talk to her."

Schafer shook his head. "It's too late for talking. He won't listen anymore. The more you try to explain things to him, the more he digs in his heels. It's like he's making a point now. No, this is our best shot, Rilla. I'll be careful. I'll be fine. Just look after your mother. Magda's not doing so well. She's worried. She... just look after her for me."

"Okay, but..."

Schafer kissed his daughter's forehead, his gray beard tickling her skin. He was worried about venturing out into Peterborough, but he saw no other choice. They would run out of food in two more days if they didn't find more, and they had enough water for three or four days maximum. Jeremy was insistent that it was too dangerous to go out, and that they wouldn't find anything if they did. He thought they should wait for the crops they had planted a few weeks ago; wait for the bountiful harvest that his garden was supposed to bring. Schafer knew that waiting was not an option anymore. They had tried it Jeremy's way, and it wasn't working anymore. Magda had lost even more weight and was becoming lethargic with every passing day. They had all lost weight, and if he didn't do something about it today, then tomorrow might not come. Schafer knew his headache was a result of becoming dehydrated, and it was another reason why he had to leave the house. He had tried talking to Jeremy about it, but he was continually shut down. Over the last week they had argued more and more, until it just wasn't worth the effort anymore. If Jeremy wanted to stay and starve to death, then Schafer knew he couldn't convince him otherwise. That didn't mean he had to let his family suffer too.

"I'll be okay, Rilla."

Schafer had found one of Victoria's empty backpacks and pulled the straps around his shoulder to make sure it was secure. He was going to use it to hopefully bring back some food. Schafer patted his pocket, checking the kitchen knife was safely stowed away, and gripped the old baseball bat in his hands. Rilla had found it in the back of the garage collecting dust, probably one of Jeremy's old toys from his own boyhood, and she had stolen it away for her father, insisting that he take it.

"Just keep quiet, don't draw attention to yourself, and get back here if you run into any trouble. Don't take any chances, okay?"

"Promise." Schafer winked. "Now go. Just make sure you're here when I get back."

From the confines of the laundry room they ceased their whispering, and Rilla stepped out to head for the kitchen. She had to cause a distraction to make sure that Jeremy and Lyn were looking at her and not at her father who was about to sneak out the back. Jeremy would never allow Schafer to go out, so they had planned how to do it carefully. Rilla would make a lot of noise in the kitchen from where the back yard was hidden from view. Schafer meanwhile would run out back and use the garbage bins to scale the retaining wall into the neighbor's property. If Jeremy or Lyn asked where Schafer was during the day, then Rilla would simply say he wasn't feeling well and was still in bed.

Schafer waited patiently in the laundry room, for Rilla to start shouting and drawing everyone to the kitchen. He looked around the room as he waited, marveling at how white and clean everything was. With everything that had happened, it was surprising how Jeremy and Lyn liked to keep up appearances. Lyn regularly swept and cleaned the house, even dusting the TV when it hadn't worked for months and wasn't likely to ever again.

A short scream sounded from within the house, and Schafer knew that was his cue. It was Rilla screaming, and he could already hear the others running to the kitchen. He crept silently out of the room, down the corridor to the back door, and outside where the sun was waiting for him. He heard Rilla scream again and shout something about rats, and then he was gone, running over the brown garden and the dead vegetable patch to the wall. It looked higher than he remembered, but he couldn't afford to back out now. He dragged two of the garbage bins over and pushed them right up against the wall. Clambering on top of them, he put his arms on top of the wall and began to pull himself up. When he reached the summit, he looked back briefly, noticing the crowded zombies around the front of the house. When they did go, they would all have to go over the wall too.

Before he jumped down, Schafer scanned the neighbor's yard, ensuring it was clear. The drop, about ten feet, wasn't as high on this side as the land rose up, and he knew he could safely let himself down without breaking anything. The whole area had been concreted over and seemingly used to store old car parts. Bits of engine lay all over the place, and dead leaves had collected in the corners of the yard. The small house beyond looked deserted. Two small windows upstairs were open, and the dark rooms within appeared to be empty. There was one large window downstairs, also open, and Schafer dropped to the ground. As he landed he dropped the bat, and it rolled into a rusty old carburetor, sending out a clanging sound that echoed around the yard. Schafer bristled, but nothing came running from the house. He scooped up the bat and paused. If the noise had disturbed a zombie inside the house, then it would be out any moment. At least if he were here he could scale the wall and be back over at Jeremy's safely and quickly.

Nothing came. Cautiously, Schafer approached the house. It was similar in style to Jeremy's, though it didn't appear to be in such good repair. The paint around the windows was cracking and peeling, and the yard was dirty. There was a small path leading around the side of the house where Schafer noticed a discarded child's bike, its wheels flat and a cobweb stretching from the faded pink seat to the handlebars. A spider scuttled away under the rim of the seat as Schafer came nearer. The bike was on the ground, probably abandoned when the occupants of the house had left town. He had learnt that as many people had run as had stayed, and he hoped this was one family who had left town. Though he was prepared to do what it took to help protect his family, he didn't really want to have to face one of the zombies. Putting down an animal was one thing, putting down another human was something else. Escaping the motel, he had managed to push them away, avoid them, and dodge their clutches. He wasn't actually sure what he would do if he came face to face with a zombie directly and was hoping he wouldn't have to decide anytime soon.

Schafer put his hand on the back door and pushed. It opened easily, revealing a dark interior. Stepping over the threshold, the warmth of the sun on his back evaporated quickly, and the still coldness of the house wrapped around him. The air was cool, and Schafer had to force himself to breathe naturally. He felt like he was breaking in, even though the door was open, and he held the bat firmly in front of himself. It didn't come naturally to him to break and enter, and he was no hero.

"Food. Find the kitchen." Schafer needed to speak to break up the silence. Rilla had wanted to come with him, but there was no way he would let her. It was far too dangerous, and he would move quicker on his own. He didn't want to spend half of his time looking out for her when he had to concentrate on watching himself.

Schafer didn't have to look far. He walked through the ground floor of the house slowly, looking solely for where the kitchen was. Soon he found it, a small, dirty room buzzing with flies. The sink was piled high with dishes and the counter was filthy, riddled with leftover food and stains that didn't need close inspection. Schafer wasn't looking for fresh food and left the rotting meat to the flies. He needed tins and packets of preserved food, maybe bottles of drink too. He opened all the cupboards, coming across cutlery, dishcloths, plates and utensils, none of which were of any use. He finally opened a cupboard that contained two small tins at the back. The rest of the cupboard had been cleaned out, but he grabbed the last two remaining cans and examined the label.

"Macaroni cheese." He didn't know what it was and the picture on the front of a yellow mush looked foul, but he took it anyway. If that was all he found all day, he was going to go home disappointed.

The rest of the kitchen turned up nothing useful, and he carefully went to the front door. There was a broken pane of glass at the top of the door, and he stood up on tip-toe to see through it. As he looked out onto the front of the house, he tugged at his beard. The corpses were everywhere, not just at Jeremy's house, but all over the street. Rotting bodies walked slowly up and down the street as if waiting for an order; men and women bumping into one another without even noticing. Some held onto bloody bones like teddy bears or as if they were security blankets, their fingers wrapped tightly around the white femurs and humeri. Others looked around trying to find something of their own, their blank gazes only coming to life when they spotted raw meat. Schafer knew if he stayed at the door too long they would find him. It would only take one, and then it would bring more. He retreated into the confines of the dark house. The road was too full of them, so clearly he was going to have to stick to using the back yards to get around for now. He just hoped they didn't all have such high walls as Jeremy's.

Schafer went back to the yard and examined the wall leading to the next house. It wasn't too high, and he knew he could get over it with a little help. Spotting a spare tire, he dragged it over to the wall, the effort of it making him sweat. All he had eaten in the last twenty-four hours was half of a dark chocolate bar and a cold tin of tomato soup. They were down to one cup of water a day each, and it wasn't enough to keep them going. He ignored the pain in his head, and using the tire to lever himself up, he climbed the wall to the next house.

The neighbor here obviously took more pride in their house, and the garden, though overgrown now, clearly had been loved at one point. There was an abundance of flowers and roses that had intertwined around each other, unattended too for months, and vines had grown all along the length of the dividing wall. Dropping into the garden, he landed softly on a mound of earth, his feet sinking into the dry dirt. The house proved less successful than the last, though, as all the doors and windows were locked. Schafer reckoned he safely had three or four hours before he would have to turn back, and it would be easier moving from house to house as the fences got lower and easier to climb.

Using a discarded trampoline, Schafer clambered into the next property and found one more dead end: another locked house, and no way in. He could have smashed a window, but was reluctant to draw any attention to himself with the inevitable noise that it would make. Plus, if he accidentally cut himself, he didn't want to bleed to death before he could make it back to Jeremy's. As he made his way over another fence, he realized he had reached the end of the small terrace. The last property had no fence bordering it and the garden gave way to a small path, and then the open road. He spotted a couple of zombies meandering amongst the discarded vehicles on the road, and he quickly ran to the back porch. There was a glass atrium over a wooden deck where the occupants of the house had probably spent many hours enjoying the sunshine. Schafer didn't want to stay outside for long and expose himself to the corpses close by, so he entered the house quickly, finding the back door wide open.

The heat in the atrium was intense and he moved fast, jogging into a downstairs sitting room furnished with photos on every wall. A black and white picture hung above the couch of a couple on their wedding day reclining in an orchard surrounded by flowers. The man wore a smart suit and tie; the woman a white dress. Both had gleaming white teeth and large smiles. They were beaming with happiness, and suddenly Schafer felt overwhelmed by sadness. Where were these people? Had they left and made it somewhere safe, or were they rotting in a field, their decomposing bodies exposed to the elements, their wedding bands destined to be buried forever in the earth? Schafer looked closer at the other photographs around the room, all immaculately mounted in plain silvery chrome frames: in one the woman held a tiny baby, in another the baby had grown into a small boy and was playing with a plate of spaghetti and had it draped over his head as he laughed. Schafer saw drawings made in crayon, stick figures holding hands as a purple sun shone down on an over-sized house with blue grass and a giant fish inexplicably floating in the sky above them all. They were the sort of drawings that Rilla used to do before she grew up and got into boys and partying. As Schafer made his way around the room, he tried to shun the feeling of sadness, to summon up his energy and concentrate on finding what he had come here for.

Next to a bureau full of papers was another open door, and he made his way to it. Sat atop the pine bureau was a square fish tank, the liquid in it a murky dull gray. The parapet of a plastic castle poked above the thick soup-like shallow water, and the tiny skeletons of two fish lay on the crusty surface, reduced to nothing but bones amid dirty sludge. Feeling queasy as he moved through the house, Schafer wanted to hurry. The hallway stretching from the sitting room was dark with no windows to allow in any light, and he almost dropped the bat as his sweaty hands fumbled past a coat stand and onto another door.

He felt uneasy looking around the family home of dead people and was relieved when he finally found a large kitchen through the next doorway. The curtains were drawn, and the kitchen was clean and tidy, aside from a large brown stain on the floor in the center of the room. Moving swiftly, he started to ransack the cupboards, instantly finding a packet of chips and two unopened bottles of Sprite. He dusted them down and shoved them into the backpack, grateful it hadn't been a wasted trip. If nothing else, he would be able to go back with a few supplies to tide them over. It also meant he could concentrate on the next part of the plan; the true reason he had left Jeremy's house.

Aside from gathering food, he needed to do some more investigation of Peterborough. With the food and water rations all but gone, it was important to replenish them, and in the short-term they needed anything he could lay his hands on. But whatever he found was only going to be a stop-gap. With six mouths to feed, they simply could not all go on living together at Jeremy's place. There would never be enough to go around. Schafer needed to check out the house on the hill. It was their best chance of making it. Germany was a dream, but the house was attainable. It was barely visible from Jeremy's, and Schafer had to get closer. He needed to check it out, to see if it really was an option. He wanted to know if it was as secure as they thought, if the walls were still intact, or if it had been overrun with zombies. Rilla was convinced it was safe; sure that if they could all make it there then they could ride out this whole zombie thing. Schafer wasn't so sure. Jeremy and Lyn had filled Rilla's head with tales of Attwood and his house. Intending to warn her off the place with stories of how obscenely rich he was, and how the mansion wasn't suited to the area, they had inadvertently put the idea in his daughter's head that it was in fact the safest place in the whole area. It was run more like a compound or a military base than a rich man's sanctuary. Maybe they were one and the same thing. Schafer just knew he couldn't risk taking his wife and daughter out onto the dangerous streets of Peterborough based on rumors. He had to know what they would be getting themselves into if they left.

Creeping forward to leave the house of death, Schafer turned back to the hallway. As he made his way back past the coat stand, he heard a noise coming from above his right shoulder. A carpeted staircase had hidden the slow footsteps of the women until she was almost upon him. Hopeful he had found a survivor, Schafer turned to discover the woman with her hands reaching for him, her fingers already brushing his shoulders. A nervous excitement made his skin tingle, and he felt suddenly energized, ebullient for the first time in months.

The eviscerated woman had been dead for months, and her skin was tight and yellow. The left side of her face had been eaten away exposing her broken jaw, and where her nose should be there was a well of maggots. A knife was stuck between the woman's shoulder blade, only the hilt still showing. The white cotton top she wore was caked in dried blood, yet the lower half of her emaciated body was naked. The long brown hair that hung drably from the woman's skull like a worn mop reminded Schafer of the photographs. He had seen this woman before at a time when she had been happy, when she had been surrounded by her family, and facing a glorious future instead of an ignominious death.

All of Schafer's excitement dissipated in a moment, his spirit broken like an egg shell. Suddenly he felt very alone and very afraid. "Who are-?" Schafer recognized the woman, but he didn't recognize the deathly veil that hung over her. The life that was in her eyes was all gone now, and as she lunged for him a cluster of blow flies crawled from a fissure on her skull.

Schafer stumbled back, the woman lurching down the last step and grabbing at him. Her face pressed up against his and he felt the woman's bony hands dig into his shoulders as she tried to hold him. Her mouth opened, and her rotten teeth tried to clamp down on his neck. Schafer felt the woman's ice-cold skin brush against his beard, and he screamed, terrified she was going to take a chunk out of him. He had the bat in his hands, but there was no way he could bring it up to strike her.

Schafer used his body weight and one free arm to push the woman back, but she was surprisingly strong, and managed to keep hold of him. His back was to the front door, and as he tried to repel the zombie, he heard a banging noise at the door. It wasn't the sound of anyone knocking to come in—it was the same thumping noise he associated with the night. When the zombies outside Jeremy's house tried to break through the fence, they made the same sounds. Like children banging on toys with no purpose or aim, just to create as much mayhem and destruction as they could, so too the zombies acted like children, hoping they could just bash their way to what they wanted.

Schafer refused to submit. He had a lot to achieve, a lot to live for, and making sure Rilla and Magda were going to be okay was top of the list. He grunted with the effort and managed to push the dead woman away from him. Her feet tripped on the lower step, and she fell onto her back on the stairs. Schafer pulled at the knife in her shoulder, intending to run it through her brain and put her down, but the knife was stuck in bone and refused to budge. As he let go of the knife, the woman pushed herself up, and began to come for him again as he stepped back.

Schafer gripped the baseball bat with both hands and lifted it to head height. The woman had been so happy. Were her husband and child upstairs? Had they died together? Had she turned first and eaten her child? All he knew was that *they* had gotten to her. It might have been a bite, a small wound that had insidiously changed her slowly, or it may have been a full on attack. The streets weren't safe with them outside, and the woman had paid for her country's lack of protection. Her whole family had probably paid the price, and now Schafer was left to clear up the mess.

He spat angrily and cracked the baseball bat against the dead woman's skull. The bone splintered, and the woman staggered to the side, her arms unable to protect her as she tried to remain standing. Schafer aimed the bat at her again. He swung with all the force he could muster and smashed the woman's skull again, this time bringing her to her knees. The woman looked up at him with something approaching reproach and pity in her eyes. He knew he was imagining it. These people, these abominable creatures, didn't think or feel or desire anything but death. Schafer put it out of his mind. Remember the woman from the photograph, he told himself, remember the beautiful mother she once was instead of the pathetic zombie now trying to cling to life.

Schafer cracked the bat a third time against the woman's skull, and it smashed open like a coconut, exposing the liquid innards that sprayed against the wall and staircase. The woman went down, and Schafer bent over her as he brought the bat down again and again, pulverizing her head until it was obliterated beyond recognition, and she stopped moving.

"Es tut Mir leid," he whispered. "I'm sorry for your family."

He had let his guard down and almost been caught out. It was something he rarely did in chess, and he had forgotten the strategies and advantages that playing with caution could bring. He was so busy focusing on his goal, on taking the King, that he had taken his eye off the board. There were a lot of pawns still on the board who would happily take a bite of him and bring him down. Then it would be game over.

Schafer cursed and vowed to take more care in future. The house had appeared vacant, but death was still a real and present danger. The thumping noises from the other side of the front door increased, and Schafer knew he was going to have to run. He didn't have the strength to fight more of them, and if he stayed in that house he would end up trapped, overwhelmed by their numbers. The dead woman's family might be upstairs, and Schafer's presence had alerted several more of the dead outside. He had to get out of there.

Returning to the door where he had entered the house, he could see several of them on the street headed his way. He bent down and wiped his bat on the long grass, removing the woman's brains and blood. He saw a path through the dead to the other side of the road from where a smaller road would lead him toward the house on the hill and what he hoped would be their ticket out of Jeremy's to a safer place.

"Okay, Rilla, I hope you're right." Schafer hoisted the bat up high and started running to the road. He would have to take some of them down as he went, even if it meant coming back later to finish them off. He needed to scope out Attwood's house and get back to Rilla and Magda before the evening came. With little energy reserves to draw on he had to do it now whilst he still had the courage and drive. Taking down the woman had repulsed him, but he had no problem with it. These people were already dead. They had no options left open, no possible future, and he was only crushing the corpses left behind. Their souls had long gone, he knew that. There was a marked difference between them. Schafer had power, compassion, and motivation. Those that walked the streets were dangerous, but they were directionless, empty shells whose only ambition was to kill and undermine everything they had built. Schafer remembered the photographs and the woman smiling in them. That was what he was fighting for. He wanted to be able to give Rilla the chance to do the same, to raise a family and smile and laugh and make love. Schafer stepped foot on the road as the first zombie approached him and gritted his teeth.

"Right then, fuckers. Let's see what you got for Uncle Schafer."

CHAPTER 4

Charlie peeled back the top of the scab, forcing her fingernail right underneath the brown hard skin. She peeled back the top like it was the lid on a tin of tuna and exposed the soft pink flesh underneath. It was soft and felt moist to the touch, but it was refreshing; it was new, a part of her that hadn't been exposed to the zombies and the way the world was. She idly picked off the rest of the scab on her knee and let the breeze through the window cool the fresh new skin. Beyond the window was the garage where Kyler had been hiding all morning. They had argued ferociously last night about nothing in particular. It started when Charlie asked her father if they could spare anything for a dessert as she had not found the tinned hot dogs and rye crackers particularly tasty or satisfying. That in turn had led to a discussion on the merits of storing food long-term, which had evolved into how they were going to keep fed if no help arrived, and the zombies kept coming. They had gone from frustrated to angry in equal measure, and Charlie knew she couldn't win. He seemed to fluctuate between not speaking to her at all and picking a fight in which he always had to have the last word. Last night had ended with Charlie storming to her room, without dessert, while her father submerged himself yet again into a bottle of whiskey. She found it amusing how they had a seemingly never-ending stockpile of alcohol, yet their basic food stuffs were starting to run dangerously low.

Trying to take her mind off how uncomfortable and unwelcome she felt in her own home since her mother had passed, Charlie picked up the magazine from the kitchen table. She had read the article on The Hunger Games remake several times already, and her mind wandered as she tried to read it again. The pages were full of vibrancy and color, pretty young faces in borrowed jewelry and promises of new thrills just around the corner from amazing new films, all written with big, bold headlines and exclamation marks! Charlie had read all the magazines in the house over the past few months and was bored.

Last night had been the worst in a long time—possibly the worst since it was just the two of them. They didn't talk about Jemma anymore. It was as if she had joined a cult. Charlie couldn't understand how her father just ignored the fact that his wife was still out there, her ravaged body still wandering the streets where they had raised a daughter. At night sometimes Charlie would get up and look out at the dark night; at the shadowy silent figures that still walked around the house. Sometimes she caught a glimpse of her mother, a flash of red in the moonlight, yet some nights she couldn't find her. She didn't mind seeing her mother anymore; in fact, she found it reassuring in a weird way. It was as if she hadn't really left them. It was the nights when Charlie couldn't find her that were the most disturbing. Where did she go? Had she found someone to kill; to eat? In a way, the zombies were like a cult. Once you got in, there was no way out.

Charlie slapped the magazine down on the table and got up. Kyler knew how to hold a grudge, but she couldn't go on like this. It wasn't just the sitting around waiting for something to happen, or the unpleasant atmosphere they both lived in now, but the knowledge that eventually they would just end up dead, too, that worried her. It felt like a when, not an if. The food would run out eventually, and so, too, the water. It hadn't rained in a few days, and it wasn't going to get any better with the advent of summer around the corner. They had to do something. She knew if they didn't, they would both join her mother out on the dark streets of Peterborough, disappearing at night into another world.

Grabbing a bottle of water, she made her way to the garage. The water was just an excuse to see him; a pretense to make him talk. There was every likelihood that it would end in an argument, but she had to try.

"Dad?" Charlie walked calmly across the open yard and past the washing on the line that had turned hard and crusty in the sun. The zombies were still close. The fence at the driveway front still rattled in its hinges, and there was the occasional groan or mutter.

It was the call of the corpses; a sound she had become accustomed to.

"Dad?"

Kyler was bent over his workbench and looked up as Charlie entered the garage. He flashed his eyes over her quickly and then bent back over what he was working on.

Charlie could tell he wasn't in the mood to talk, but she had already resolved to talk to him. She had been thinking about how they were going to survive, and she couldn't do it alone.

"Hey, Dad." Charlie gently draped an arm around her father, and lowered her lips to kiss him on the cheek. He smelt bad, but so did she. It was something else she had grown used to over the past few months of captivity.

Kyler shrugged her off and kept working.

Charlie sighed. "So what are you working on?"

There was no response. Charlie tried to figure out what he was doing as he unwound a length of duct tape. He had a claw-hammer clamped in one vice and a short piece of wood in the other.

"Weapons," muttered Kyler, as if it was obvious to even an idiot.

Charlie watched as he began winding the duct tape around the wood and the handle of the hammer, creating a hybrid tool that would render it useless to anyone who didn't want to go out killing zombies.

"I brought you some water. Thought you'd need it. It's getting hot already." Charlie held the bottle out by the vice and put her hand on her father's sweaty back.

"Not thirsty." Kyler ignored the peace offering and continued taping up the hammer until the shaft was secured to the piece of wood that he had shaved down and smoothed off.

Resigned to an uncomfortable silence, Charlie unscrewed the cap and took a sip of water.

"You should save that." Kyler began to release the amalgamated tools from the vice.

"It's hot, Dad. We've enough for a sip." Charlie tentatively held the bottle out to him again, hoping he would at least take a drink. Even if he was still angry with her, he had to keep hydrated.

"Enough, Charlie." Kyler slapped the bottle from her hands, and she dropped it. The precious water immediately began to pour out over the hard floor, and Charlie quickly grabbed it. Half the bottle had gone before she could rescue it.

"What the hell, Dad? You don't have to be such a dick."

"I told you, Charlie. Save it. We're going to need it. You think while we're here, living comfortably in our own home, that we can afford niceties like dessert and snacks and drinking what little water we have left?"

Charlie screwed the cap back on the water bottle. She tried to resist the temptation to argue back. "I just thought you'd need a drink. You've been out here for a couple of hours and—"

"Save it, Charlie. Cuddles and trying to sweet-talk me aren't going to get you anywhere. I thought I'd made that clear enough by now."

When he looked at her, Charlie could feel the hatred. It certainly wasn't love in his eyes. Did he really hate her so much? What had she done to deserve it? Those brown eyes of his were alive now, and there was a part of her pleased that at least he wasn't just ignoring her anymore. It was almost better to feel his anger than suffer his apathy.

"Fine. So what are we going to do about it? It's obvious we don't have an infinite amount of water, as you made so clear, so what's the plan?"

Kyler took the hammer from the vice and examined it. He held it by the attached length of wood. "I'm working on it."

"Great." Charlie wiped her sticky blonde hair from her face. The garage was hot, and the breeze that had been so pleasant in the house didn't seem to flow in here. "Well, while you've been doing whatever it is you're doing, I've been thinking about Attwood's. We need to start thinking about exactly how we're going to get there. I figure we have a couple of weeks yet before things get serious, and the sooner we prepare for it, the better equipped we'll be."

Kyler looked at her with a puzzled expression. His eyes creased together, and then he began to laugh.

"What the fuck, Dad? I'm serious. You know he's still there. That place is like Fort Knox. I bet he's got enough food to live for years."

Kyler continued laughing. There was nothing funny about what she'd said, and his laughter was clearly unconcealed contempt for what she was saying.

"I really don't get the joke, you fucking asshole." Charlie put her hands on her hips and almost blurted out what she had been thinking for the last few days. "I wish you were…I wish you had gone out there instead of—"

Charlie stopped herself. It wouldn't be true if she said it. She was pissed at him and annoyed at herself for thinking he would listen to her. He valued her thoughts about as much as he valued sobriety.

Kyler's laughter began to turn to coughing, and suddenly he was bent over double as he tried to get it under control. He dropped the claw-hammer and used the vice to stop himself from collapsing completely.

"Dad?" Charlie could see he was struggling for breath, and she unscrewed the water bottle which he grabbed from her eagerly. He gulped it down quickly and soon the racking noises coming from his chest stopped. Sweat still poured down his face and body, but he seemed to be under control again.

"What was that? Are you okay?"

Kyler handed the now empty bottle back to Charlie. "Don't waste your time with that shit. I'll be fine. Just got a little hot in here. Forget it."

Charlie couldn't understand why he was being so dismissive. He clearly wasn't well. As much as they argued all the time, she still cared about him. "Maybe you should come inside and sit down for a while. We can talk if you like."

Kyler's expression made it clear he was not going to do that.

"Or not," said Charlie.

Kyler took Charlie's hand, and she thought that maybe he had reconsidered. Finally, he was seeing sense and going to rest. They could talk inside, really hammer out how to get to Attwood's place.

"Come with me. Put that bottle down. I've got a job for you."

Charlie left the bottle behind and let her father lead her away. The blue sky was nirvana compared to the dingy, hot garage, and the breeze a welcome respite from the stifling warm air. There was no wonder her father was feeling ill. As they crossed the yard, Charlie found Kyler dragging her away from the house.

"Wait, where are we going? I thought we were going to go inside? To talk?"

Kyler said nothing. They were marching down the driveway now, toward Peterborough, toward the fence, to the zombies at their door. Charlie noticed the stain on the ground and felt her father's hand gripping hers tightly. He was on a mission now, pulling her deeper into darkness.

"Dad, stop. What are you doing?" As much as Charlie tried to pull back, he only pulled her closer to the fence. He wouldn't relinquish his grip on her, and dragging her feet only seemed to spur him on more. As they neared the fence, he scooped up the crowbar that had lain undisturbed since the day her mother had died, and Charlie understood then what he wanted. "Wait, Dad, please?"

There were six zombies stood at the fence, their hands clawing at the metal, their mouths pressed up against it as if they could bite their way through.

"Go on then." Kyler thrust Charlie forward and held the crowbar out to her. "Go on. Do it. Dispose of that garbage and we'll talk."

"No way. This is ridiculous." Charlie looked at the six figures by the fence, horrified and terrified at being so close to them. It was one thing watching them from the safety of her bedroom and quite another being out here only feet away. "I'm not doing it," she said, refusing to take the crowbar.

"Like you said, Charlie, at some point we're going to have to leave. We may as well start thinning them out now. Not to go to Attwood's, but somewhere brand new, somewhere away from Peterborough and New Hampshire, somewhere far, far away where *they* aren't." Kyler looked at the zombies lined up against the fence and then at Charlie. He wasn't sure if she was more afraid of them or him. He had to make her understand. "Don't you see, Charlie? America is teeming with them now. They're like rats.

They infiltrated our cities and spread like a plague. Once there was one. Imagine that. The first one had to have come from somewhere. Then there were two, three, and a hundred; then a thousand until there were millions of them. And you know what? We can't get rid of them now. The government saw to that. Screwed us over big time. There's no rescue coming, Charlie, not ever. No, we have to leave. I don't know where yet. North or South. But I know we have to leave Peterborough."

"We can't kill them all, Dad. So you kill these six, some more will come along. We should leave them alone, Dad. This is pointless."

"That's what you think, is it? Leave them alone? Leave them alone, and perhaps they'll leave us alone? Maybe we should just let them take over, 'cause if we don't do something about them, they *will* take over. The streets aren't safe, Charlie. *Doing nothing is not an option*. If I had the ability, the power, I'd build a wall. I'd build the biggest fucking wall this planet has ever seen. Forget seeing it from the Moon, you'd see that fucking bitch all the way from Jupiter. I'd kill every last one of them, and then I'd erect a wall around the whole country. Nobody comes in, nobody gets out. It's the only way."

There was so much hate and vitriol when he spoke that Charlie feared he wasn't even joking. "You'd build a wall?" she asked, incredulous. "I think we're getting off topic here. We don't need to think about them, we need to think about us. It's what *we* do that matters."

"True, it does matter what we do. It matters what *you* do. You have to start thinking bigger, Charlie. If I could, I'd build that wall today. I'd start with our house. Then I'd protect our town, and finally the whole country. There's too much at stake to let it all fall now."

"So what happens when all the zombies are dead? What happens when other people need our help? You can't just block yourself in and close your eyes to what's happening out there."

"You're wrong, Charlie, that's exactly what I'll do. We need to separate them from us. We clearly can't live together. All we do is fight and kill each other. You want to try and live alongside *them*, then be my guest. You'll be dead in sixty seconds."

"Well, I guess it's a moot point anyway." Charlie wondered if he was truly serious. They barely had enough energy to get through the day as it was, and here he was talking about building walls. "You don't have the ability to build a wall."

"Not yet. Maybe I won't be able to. Maybe I'll be dead before we can get close to achieving anything for this sorry ass nation of ours. But I need to get it into that head of yours that you need to protect your own. You can't rely on other people; you have to do it yourself. So you put up a wall around yourself, got it? You find the biggest wall you can, and get yourself behind it." Kyler lifted the crowbar and looked the zombies. There were eight now. "Just let everyone on the other side kill themselves."

"I don't really think it's that simple. And besides, you seem to picture a world where the zombies are all gone. You think that's ever going to happen? There are way more of them than there are us."

"I'll agree with you on that. That's just what makes them so dangerous. You can't reason with them. You can't sit them down and talk it over. The only thing they understand is a damn bullet to the head."

"Dad, you know it's not that simple. They deserve a bit more respect than that. *They* are *us*. They were just unlucky enough to get this thing, but they're our family. They're human beings. Mom's out there. You want to put a bullet in her head?"

"You don't get it, Charlie." Kyler marched to his daughter, and twisted her around. He forced her to look at the zombies gathering by the metal fence.

"Kill them, Charlie. Take this crowbar, and kill them all. Put it through their brains. You have to fight, or die, Charlie. Do it."

Charlie struggled, but as usual her father was too strong for her. She wanted to turn around and slap him, to show him that he was being a fool, but he had hold of her too tightly for any chance of escape. "No, there's no point. They're already dead."

"No point?" Incensed, Kyler grabbed the back of Charlie's long, blonde hair and yanked her head back. She screamed at him to stop, but he began pushing her forward. Her slim frame offered little resistance to her father's bulk, and he easily made her walk over the last few feet to the fence.

"No, Dad, stop." Charlie screwed up her eyes. The arms and hands reaching through the iron railings strained to get to her.

Kyler stopped only when she was inches away. She squirmed in his grasp, but she wasn't going to get away that easily. "Fight or die. Which is it going to be?"

"Dad, you're hurting me. Let go." Charlie tried to twist away, but her father's grip on her neck only got stronger.

"No, Charlie, you have to decide. I'm not going to stop and neither are they. So decide: fight or die." Kyler prodded his daughter's head forward, only inches away from the gnarled and yellowing fingernails of a zombie, its thin skeletal arms waving and dancing in front of her face. "Well?"

Charlie gave up. There was no reasoning with him anymore. She couldn't fight him. If he wanted her to die, then she would. She closed her eyes and waited for the final push, for him to feed her to the zombies. After a moment the pressure on her neck eased, and she was suddenly free. She stumbled back and found Kyler behind her staring at the fence.

Charlie was about to leave him, to disappear into the recesses of the house, anywhere that he wasn't, when she realized he hadn't stopped because he had wanted to, but because he was distracted. She turned to the fence to see what he saw and found herself staring at her mother. The torn red dress was instantly recognizable although the battered face of her mother wasn't. She barely looked human anymore. They had eaten away so much of her before she had reanimated that she no longer resembled the beautiful woman she once was.

"Do it, Dad," said Charlie, turning back to her father. She rubbed her sore neck and glared at the man she once loved. "If it's that easy, then do it. Kill her."

Kyler gulped down his fear and lowered the crowbar. "This changes nothing. You should—"

"I should what?" Charlie stepped away from the fence. It was unnerving being so close to them, to the dead, *to her*. She was angry with her father and couldn't believe he had treated her like that, as if she was nothing but dinner for the corpses. "I should what? Fuck off and die? Is that what you want? You think I like living like this?" Charlie felt the sting of tears coming, but was unable to express how much she resented her father in that moment. She was tempted to grab the crowbar from him and smash it across his face. She hated how much he got to her, but there was no other way to live. One of them had to change soon, or it would end badly for one of them. "Peterborough is a good town to live in," she said. "We just can't stay here anymore in this house. It's too…painful."

"Correction, it *was* a good town. Now it's just a cemetery like everywhere else."

Kyler sighed. He looked defeated, but it was nothing to do with Charlie. It was the unexpected arrival of her mother that had changed him. He was calmer now, withdrawn almost, but he was standing his ground. He always had to have the last word.

"You suffer from a lack of ambition." Kyler said the words with such animosity that Charlie expected his next words to be, 'You're such a disappointment.'

"Your mother always tried to bring out the best in you, and God knows I pushed you too. Your grades were good, better than average, and you were a bright kid. *Are* bright. So what went wrong?"

It was a rhetorical question. Charlie knew Kyler was in the groove now, getting into the natural rhythm of his criticism of her. It happened occasionally, yet with more frequency since her mother passed. She knew there was little point in answering since it only seemed to spur him on. Any case for the defense was met with more criticism. Another minute, and he should get there. 'You're such a disappointment.' She almost wanted him to say the words, those four little words that he longed to express yet lacked the courage to say out loud.

Kyler looked down at the crowbar in his hand like it was an alien object. "I'll tell you where it went wrong: your last year you got involved with that Jackson boy. He let you think you would be happy here. He let you settle, let you think this was it, that you had achieved what you needed to; I think you fell in love with your first fuck and let him convince you that the outside world was your enemy. Stay in Peterborough, right? Settle down and have lots of babies? That about right?"

"Jesus, Dad, just quit talking like that. Jackson wasn't the problem." Charlie was still crying, and all the while her father kept talking she was aware that her mother was behind her. As usual she was stuck between them, unable to break free of the shackles they had thrown around her since she was a child. Why did it have to be this way? Why did everything have to be so hard?

"No, of course not," said Kyler. "You never could see anything wrong with him, could you? But he got into your head. Somehow he took away all that ambition, all that energy and drive you had, and turned you into this wet lettuce, devoid of any drive or character."

Charlie sighed and wiped her tears with the back of her hand. It was hard listening to him when he got like this. As much as she put it down to the drink, sometimes the truth came out, she knew that. And he hadn't started drinking today—yet—so she couldn't blame what he said on the liquor. She looked at him unable to recognize the loving father he had been when she was growing up. He was older and slower, but he was also bitter and angry. Why did he have to take it out on her? If she hadn't stuck around, he would probably have drunk himself into an early grave. She helped out around the house and looked after him, so why did he despise her so much? She had no response to his diatribe and vitriol. He could spout it all day long, it made no difference. It didn't change the fact that her mother was dead. Charlie had tried reasoning with him before, yet anything she said only seemed to make him angrier.

"Look at you. Even now when I'm insulting you you've got nothing to say. It's pathetic, Charlie." Kyler glanced at the fence, at his dead wife, and then back to Charlie with a startling clarity. He straightened his back as he looked at her. "Do you know what? Do you know what I think?"

Here it comes. Those four magic words every daughter wants to hear from her father. Charlie stared at him, her hands curled up into tight balls as if she was about to enter a boxing ring, her hands gripping the pockets of her jeans as if she was clinging onto the edge of the world.

"Do you want to know?" he asked.

Charlie knew she was going to hear it whether she wanted to or not.

"You're not the girl who I brought up. Where's the fighter I raised? Do you want to die, is that it? Where's all your fight gone? You're not your mother's daughter anymore. I don't know where our Charlie went. Maybe she's buried deep inside of you. Maybe you can find the key to the chains you put her in and get her out again one day, I don't know. But I can tell you this, Charlie. If your mother was with us now, she would say the same as me. You're a disappointment. Truly, you've not just let me down, but her too. That's what gets me. You would be *such* a disappointment to her."

So there it was. Finally, he managed to get it out. Charlie knew it was coming, yet when he finally said it out loud it felt like her heart was going to burst. All the time he had been talking she had been ignoring what he'd been saying. She had heard most of it before. At least once a week he would open a bottle of whiskey and get into something with her. It was a form of entertainment she supposed. Without TV or sports anymore, without anyone else to talk to, then what else was there to do but talk to each other? The problem was that her father didn't know how to talk anymore. All he knew how to do these days was bitch and moan, usually about her. That didn't mean she had to sit back and take it. As she looked at him in the sunlight, she looked into his eyes. They were red from the alcohol, yes, but there was life in them yet. He wasn't tired. Did he want to fight? Was that the only sport he could think of now, goading her into an argument that she knew she had no chance of winning.

"Feel better now? Feel better now that you've got it off your chest? What a relief, huh? Feel good about yourself telling your only child that she's *such* a disappointment to you?" Charlie considered for a brief moment of going to her mother, of letting her rip open her neck, and ending it all. She had no death wish, but there would be something satisfying about letting her father realize that he had failed her. He couldn't protect her all the time. There would be an irony in it if it ended up being her own mother who both gave her life and took it away.

Kyler scratched his nose and looked at Charlie. He folded his arms and sighed. The driveway fell into silence as they looked at each other, both waiting for the other to speak. There was no sound, and even the zombies seemed to hush.

"So that's it? We go to bed, I make you breakfast in the morning, and we carry on as before?" asked Charlie. She couldn't understand what he was trying to do. Another argument would get them nowhere.

"That's really up to you, Charlie. You tell me. You gonna fight now?" Smiling, he extended the crowbar to her. "Why don't you decide, right now? Fight or die? I've tried with you. I've done what I can. It's up to you now."

Charlie glared at Kyler. It was too much. She wanted to cry, to run away, to hit him and slap him and kick him until he saw sense, but as she pictured herself doing all of those things, she knew it was all pointless. He wouldn't change.

"I thought I was just a disappointment. What kind of fighter would I make, huh? And what about you? The great Kyler Gretzinger. The man. The one and only. What do you think you are to me?" Charlie ignored the offer of the crowbar and stared through her tears at her father. "What happened to us, Dad? What happened to my kind father? He disappeared when Mom died. Now I'm living with a drunken slob who hates me. You wonder why I'm so quiet, yet all you do is criticize me. Why would I bother trying to hold a conversation with you when I already know the answers? Charlie, you're so stupid. Charlie, why don't you listen to me? Charlie, your Mother didn't do it like that. Fight or die, Charlie. What the fuck is your problem? I'm sick of it. Guess what, Dad? *You're* the disappointment. You really think you're the man? You think this is the life I wanted? Living with you in this stinking house with no way out? Thank God she's dead, 'cause she would hate to see what we've become. Christ, if Mom could see you now she would hate you as much as I do."

Kyler threw the crowbar at Charlie and she ducked. It flew past her head and clattered into the fence, sending the zombies into a frenzy as the clanging noise reverberated around the still, warm air.

"Don't talk about your mother like that," said Kyler. "Don't you dare. You really believe it's a good thing she's dead? You happy with that situation?"

Charlie regretted her words as soon as she'd said them, but he kept pushing her. There was nothing more in the world she wanted than to have her mother back. She would never talk like this. She would never have let things get this bad between them. Her mother had been the glue holding them together, and now that she was gone the bond between father and daughter was gone too. It hadn't vanished overnight, it had taken a few weeks, but slowly it had gone. Her father had refused to talk about anything for a while, and by the time he came around to it, it was too late. There was a distance now that he and Charlie could never recover from. By the time Kyler had started talking again she could hear the bitterness in every word he spoke to her. Why did she have to be stuck here with him, with no future, with zero chance of making a future for herself? Was this all that life had left to offer: endless arguments with her father, never venturing beyond the walls of the house, and never seeing anyone else in the whole world but herself and the hatred in her father's eyes?

As the tears continued pouring down her cheeks she hated herself for it. No doubt he was pleased with his morning's work. He was right, she was pathetic. She was twenty-one. She knew she should be stronger than that, able to rise above the insults, yet she found that as every day passed she was getting weaker. She was giving up. She couldn't argue with him anymore. She couldn't see a way out of this mess. She wiped away her tears and summoned up what little energy she had.

"I wish it was you. I wish it was you out there instead of her." Charlie sniffed and rubbed her eyes. God, she was tired. It was barely noon, yet all she wanted to do was curl up in bed. "I wish Mom was here and you were dead."

Kyler strode up to his daughter, walking right up to her so that she could smell the faint residue of last night's whiskey on his breath. "And?"

Charlie looked at him, confused. And what? She had just told him she wished he was dead, and all he could do was look at her. Why wasn't he shouting at her? Why wasn't he berating her, telling her how ridiculous she was being or slapping her? Was this just a game?

"And what?"

"Well, I wish your Mother was here too. Every time I look at you, I see her. Every single minute that I'm conscious I wish she were here. Jemma was the best thing to happen to me until you were born. But she's gone, so wishing I was out there instead is pretty pointless, don't you think? Isn't it more realistic to think about what you can do about it, about your present situation, instead of dwelling on the past?"

"Me? But I'm pathetic. I'm a nobody, isn't that what you keep telling me?" Charlie shook her head. "What can *I* do about it, Dad?"

Kyler sighed. He brushed past Charlie and picked up the crowbar from the ground. Looking at Charlie, his large, brown eyes burned like fire. "Now *that's* a good question, Charlie."

CHAPTER 5

The plan was simple. Schafer knew which roads were best to take, which ones were clear of the corpses, and which to navigate to reach the house on the hill. That was the simple part. The hard part would be getting past the zombies that roamed through Peterborough at will. Schafer had found no evidence that anyone else was alive, although he had to admit he hadn't covered even as much as half of it. The excursion a few days ago had been quick and about gathering only what he needed. He had returned with a few cans of food, but very little else except the knowledge that the Attwood's residence was the only alternative to dying of starvation at Jeremy and Lyn's house.

"You sure about this?" Jeremy approached Schafer as they got ready to leave. They were making the last preparations before leaving. It was late in the day, and they wanted to get going before the dark. If they were stuck outside at night they would have severe difficulty finding, not just Attwood's, but anywhere safe to stay.

"Of course. As long as we are all ready, then we should get moving," replied Schafer. In the last few days his beard had seemingly grown even longer, so much that it was beginning to hide his voice when he spoke. With his clipped English and German accent, sometimes Jeremy found it hard to identify every word the man said.

"Right, right. It's just that I need to know that my family is going to be safe. I can't afford any mistakes with this. If you think there is any chance of this going wrong, then I need to know. It's not too late to back out. We can stay here. We can still make a go of it with the supplies we have. I'm sure if we just got the seeds to take and figured out an irrigation system we could—"

"Nein." Schafer had heard it before, heard all the excuses and reasons why they should stay. Jeremy had been the last one to agree to go, and convincing him had taken all of Schafer's efforts. Was it a desire to protect his home, fear of the outside world, or just blind naïveté that led Jeremy to think they were better off staying? Even his wife, Lyn, had agreed that they had to do something, go somewhere, and find help. They would surely die if they stayed at Jeremy's, and Schafer wasn't about to let him change his mind now, not when they were all ready to go. "We go today. Now. It's agreed, Jeremy. We will be okay. Do you think I would risk taking my wife and daughter out there if I thought it wasn't safe enough? I would do anything to protect Rilla, which is exactly why we are leaving."

Schafer saw disappointment in Jeremy's face. Surely he wasn't going to abort at the last moment? The man wasn't completely stupid. He and Lyn were intelligent people, teachers before the world stopped turning and became a dead zone. Victoria was well-educated and happy, she spoke politely, and they had taken in the strangers months ago without asking for anything in return. It seemed that being confined to the same building for months on end, though, hadn't brought them close but in fact driven them apart. They had very different ideas on how to proceed from here. Part of it, Schafer knew, was that this wasn't his home. This was Jeremy's house, and abandoning it for the uncertainty of the outside, with *them* out there, was no doubt unsettling. But it was the right thing to do. It was the *only* thing left that they could do.

"Look, Jeremy, if you want to stay, then stay. You, Lyn, and Victoria might be able to survive without us. Perhaps we have depleted your food reserves too much. I'm sorry. But I am very grateful that you took us in." Schafer put a firm hand on Jeremy's shoulder and smiled. There was no hidden agenda or anything sinister in it; he genuinely wanted the man to feel a part of the plan. "I can do this without you, but it will be much easier if you are with us, I think. We are also leaving. Now."

Schafer looked at the retaining wall he had climbed over a few days ago and remembered how it had been. At first, it had been quite easy. Until he had been forced to kill the woman in her own home, he had thought it would be relatively easy going from house to house. That first kill had almost undone him. It was only remembering how Magda and Rilla were relying on him that drove him on. He had killed more that day, more than he had wanted to, but it had been borne of necessity. He had passed through more houses, more streets, and eventually found a house where he had been able to look at the house on the hill that Rilla had urged him to investigate. The high walls around the estate and thick trees hid most of the property, but he could snatch glimpses of it. The house appeared quiet in the daylight, but he knew Rilla had seen lights at night. Schafer had stayed perfectly still in the upstairs bedroom of a stranger's house for the best part of three hours watching the house. The heat of the day had warmed the house, and he wanted to stretch his stiff legs frequently, but it was important to monitor the house for activity. Once he had found a good vantage spot, he had stayed there without so much as taking a sip of water. The dead still walked beneath the window, in the streets all around him, and so Schafer had remained quiet, motionless for hours. In all that time he had seen only one sign of movement at the house. A figure had emerged from a doorway once, though it was impossible to tell if it was a man or woman. They had brought out a bucket and thrown it on the ground then gone back inside. That was it. That was all he had seen. Had it been Attwood clearing away garbage? Nobody really knew if Attwood was married, but rich people usually had friends, so it wouldn't be outside the realm of possibility to imagine he had friends or relatives with him. It may have been a cook or servant throwing away dirty water. Whoever it was and whatever they were doing, there was nothing to suggest anything sinister was going on, and Schafer checked out how they would gain access. The high walls would be impossible to cross, and though the small moat could be crossed carefully, he could see some zombies had fallen in. They splashed around in the water, unable to climb the slippery banks out, and others wandered outside the walls, perhaps looking for a way in. The dead were thinner out there and more closely compacted in the town's residential area where Jeremy's house was. The only way in was to announce their presence and knock. Laughable though it felt, it was the only way.

There was a small roadway over the moat—which was no more than a glorified ditch—and it led to a building resembling a small warehouse. It adjoined the high walls and visibility was poor.

Schafer imagined the outer door could be raised to let in vehicles, and they were just going to have to go and ask to be let in. Whilst Jeremy and Lyn had told them that Attwood was slightly eccentric and obnoxiously rich, there was nothing that Schafer had heard to suggest he would turn them away. He had not made his money selling weapons to terrorists or by investing in hedge funds. He was a human, a man, and Schafer knew Rilla was right. He would help them, and now he knew how to get there.

"We all good here?" Lyn approached Schafer and Jeremy holding her daughter's hand. "Everything ready?"

Jeremy nodded but said nothing.

"Yes, everything is ready." Schafer noticed that Victoria looked nervous. It wasn't usual for her not to be smiling or laughing, and she clung to her mother's side. Schafer bent down so his eyes were on the same level as hers. "What do you think, Vicky? You all set? This is just a vacation. It'll be fun, just—"

"Thanks, Schafer, I've got it," said Jeremy stepping in front of him.

With Jeremy blocking his way, it was clear that Schafer wasn't welcome. Lyn began fussing and cooing over her daughter, telling her to pull up her socks and ensuring she had her bag packed, as if she were about to head off to school.

"Ja. Okay."

Schafer began walking to the wall, feeling Jeremy's eyes digging into his back. Even now there was a lack of trust between them. Perhaps the men knew that if it came to it, both would sacrifice the other, even their families, if it meant living. Both kept trying to take the upper hand, but they were locked in a stalemate, thrusting forward pawns in search of an answer, only to find their way blocked.

"Problem?" Rilla zipped up her light blue jacket. Even though it was warm, she wanted to take it with her, knowing there was every chance she was going to spend another winter in Peterborough. She carried a bag on her shoulders, as they all did, but kept her arms free. She held the brass base of a lamp in her hands, its cord and shade removed so as to allow her to move it freely if needed. They had had to improvise when it came to defending themselves, fashioning crude weapons out of whatever they could lay their hands on. Jeremy had no guns in the house and only a couple of large knives which he and Lyn held.

"No, it's fine, they're coming. Just a little nervous."

"Nervous? I'm scared as hell." Rilla drew in a breath and then puffed out her cheeks as she exhaled. The wall they were about to cross was the point of no return. They had packed as much as they could take with them and were going to end up at Attwood's house. Rilla was excited, pleased at the knowledge they were finally taking action instead of waiting for something to happen. She was also scared. She hadn't been outside since the motel, and that experience had been terrifying. Having corpses attacking them and having to literally run for their lives had been the hardest thing she'd ever done. Now they were willingly going out there again knowing what they were going to have to face. Rilla looked at her father with admiration. He had already been out there, already faced them, and returned to do it all over again. He was the strongest man she knew. "Let's do this."

"Magda, remember to stick close to me and Rilla," said Schafer as he tightened the straps on her backpack. He tugged the bag on tightly and then turned her around so he could look into her eyes. "We'll be fine. I've already been out there once. This time is no different. If anything it'll be easier. We have strength in numbers. We'll be at the house on the hill in no time."

Magda bit her lower lip and stared up at her husband. "Okay. So we go now. It will be okay. It will be all okay, yes?"

Schafer grabbed her face and kissed his wife's firm lips. "Vertrauen Sie mir."

Magda carried a long-handled screwdriver, but Schafer knew she was unlikely to use it. His wife wasn't a fighter, and whilst he carried the baseball bat he intended to make sure that neither she nor Rilla were obliged to use their own weapons. He grabbed the ladder they had placed by the wall. There was no secret about what they were doing and no need to take any chances. The ladder was cold, but its feet dug into the ground and would hold them all as they ventured over it far more securely than the garbage bins. He climbed up the first rung and turned around. Five sets of eyes stared at him with hope, but each with their own secrets too. Jeremy held bitterness in them, as if he didn't want to accept that all of their fates now resided in what Schafer did next. Lyn had anger in hers, though Schafer could not know if it was directed at him or at her own husband for failing to stop him from taking them away from their home. Victoria was sad, too young to fully understand what they were doing but old enough to know they weren't just going on vacation as they had tried to tell her. Magda tried to hide her terror, but was managing to convey to Schafer that she was completely out of her comfort zone and failing to hide her fear at all. When Schafer looked at Rilla, he felt pride rising inside of him. There was hope there but determination too. She was just like Magda had been years ago, before motherhood and age softened her. He saw himself in those eyes of his daughter's. She would fight to her last breath, he had no doubt, yet he hoped it wouldn't come to that. He was going to try to lead them down the clearest streets so that they didn't have to fight. Killing them wasn't easy. It was like killing a real person; something nobody should have to do. He didn't want Rilla to be put in that position, yet they had no choice but to leave. They had barely gathered up enough food to fill their six bags, which was a timely reminder of why they were leaving.

"Keep close." Schafer smiled and lifted his baseball bat to the blue sky. "Today is a beautiful day. Tonight we will eat and sleep in a stranger's house. But we will be safe. We will be happy. It will be beautiful."

He climbed the ladder quickly and dropped down the other side waiting for Magda to follow. As Schafer planted that first foot on the neighbor's property, he felt exhilarated. It was as if he were marching to war and should be waiving a flag above his head with a bayonet in hand, singing songs about a great leader. Instead, he was armed with just a baseball bat about to face an army of walking corpses with his family behind him. His exhilaration quickly evaporated when he realized the enormity of what they were doing. Lives were depending on him and what he did next, and not just his own. He did not doubt himself, but he also recognized the perilous journey they were about to undertake.

They all made it over the wall without encountering any problems and then to the end of the row of houses with relative ease. They reached the house where Schafer had killed the woman and waited. Schafer saw the street was clear which was unusual considering how he had left it. The dead bodies were still there where he had left them, but the walking ones were absent. He made everyone stay silent as he crept out onto the street on his own. Looking up and down, he saw nothing. He was surprised but wasn't complaining. The fewer zombies they were confronted with then the quicker they would be. He beckoned the others out to join him.

Rilla looked at the motionless form of a dead boy in the gutter. His skull was caved in, his arms covered in infected cuts and bite marks. He wore pale blue pajamas with smiling teddy bears on them, and his feet were bare. She was thankful she couldn't see his eyes and turned to her father.

"Where are they?"

Schafer could see the base of the lamp in her hands was trembling. She was brave, but that didn't mean she wasn't afraid as well. "I don't know. They probably aren't far away. We should keep moving," he replied.

"What's going on?" Jeremy looked around nervously clutching a steak knife in his hand. Lyn and Victoria were the last to join them. Victoria refused to run, worried that if she did so her footsteps would be too loud and bring the nasty people.

"Was ist los?" asked Magda.

"Is something wrong?" asked Lyn, noticing the concern etched across Magda's face. "What's she saying? I knew we should've—"

"*No.* Everything is fine." Schafer had only waited for Lyn and Victoria to catch them up, not wanting to leave any kind of gap between them. If they got separated, they would be in trouble. Now they were all together, they could move on. "It's okay."

"Where are they?" asked Jeremy. "Where are all the dead people? I thought once we crossed that wall—"

"Does it matter? Let's just keep going." Rilla urged her father on, ignoring Jeremy's questions. She had learnt that he was a narrow-minded and cautious man who needed to know everything about something before doing it. He wouldn't eat something without knowing what was in it and had refused to agree to the plan to relocate until Schafer had told him everything about the outside world. Jeremy was irritating her already, and a part of her wished he had stayed behind. If he had, then Victoria would've stayed, too, and Rilla loved her like a sister. So if putting up with Jeremy's whining meant Victoria was safe, then so be it.

They left the open street and headed for a smaller road that was flanked by single storey homes. Rilla could tell exactly where her father had been by the dead bodies they skirted past. It was just as he had described it, the houses, the open road, and rotting corpses that cooked slowly in the sun. There were two differences to what he had told her. The obvious one was the lack of zombies. There should be at least a few corpses wandering about. Not that she wanted to face them or deal with the dead, but it was unnerving at just how quiet the streets were. She half expected them to all jump out from behind a wall and yell 'Surprise!'

The other thing that he hadn't fully conveyed to her was the smell. It was the stench of death; an almost overwhelming foul stink that made her eyes sting and her throat constrict. It made the air taste warm and sticky, and she wished the corpses would hurry up and rot away to nothing. It was obscene. Every few feet there was another corpse, sometimes undistinguishable from the one she had just passed. Arms and limbs were scattered about the road ,too, as if left by a passing mortician who had decided to throw them out like confetti. As she passed a dead man, she noticed the skin drawn tight around his neck, his hands and fingers curled up as if clawing at the ground. He looked like a waxwork model, adorned with dirty clothes, and thin black hair slapped crudely around a balding head. There was a hole in the side of his skull just above the ear. Somebody had shot this man. As they continued, she saw another body with a bullet hole in the side of the head. At one point, someone had been here with a gun. It didn't really matter. Once a zombie was put down, it stayed down as long as it was in the head. That was as much as they had learnt before the world went black.

As they rounded an empty hearse, Rilla noticed a wreath tied with brittle string to a lamppost by the curbside. The once crisp, yellow flowers were wilted and pale, the green stalks now a faded gray as if the effort of grieving so publicly was too much. Rilla noticed her mother bow her head as they passed. Strangely, the wreath for the dead was the only thing she saw that reminded her of how alive the place had once been. The silent cars, the overgrown lawns, and the stiff clothes that still hung on the line were symbols of a life long gone, yet there was something poignant about those flowers. They were a symbol for mourning, something they no longer did. Everything was black and white now; everything was a matter of life and death.

"Through here," said Schafer.

Two buses lay ahead at an intersection, each left as they were on the day the dead rose, abandoned in the road. The cars that had piled up behind them had created a funnel effect, and as they passed between the two buses Rilla found herself imagining that they were passing between two giant metallic statues. It felt like they were entering not just a foreign land but another time, a time when things like cars and electricity didn't exist, and all that mattered was living through another day; the only way to achieve that was with your own bare hands and the will to live. Rilla knew she and her father had it but wasn't convinced by Jeremy and Lyn. They kept lagging behind, using Victoria as an excuse.

Rilla looked at them fussing over their daughter who was perfectly capable of running. Jeremy's eyes kept darting around nervously, whilst Lyn hardly looked at where they were going, so preoccupied was she in molly-coddling Victoria.

"Hey, hurry up," said Rilla as she paused for them. "We have to keep going."

Schafer and Magda were just ahead, and Rilla had passed the buses wearily. The heat sapped her energy, and they had not had to run anywhere in a long time. Taking the opportunity to catch her breath, she noticed Jeremy furtively glance behind him. He urged Lyn and Victoria on, but as he reached Rilla, it was obvious something was playing on his mind.

"What?" Rilla really didn't care what was behind them as long as it stayed there.

"It's nothing, just a zombie. It's on its own. I think we left it back by that convertible."

"Go on." Rilla made them move on to catch up her parents and stared at the deserted road they had left behind them. She couldn't see anything. Jeremy may have been mistaken. Still, it would pay to watch their backs. She let them take Victoria ahead, and decided to follow so she could monitor the road for any zombies that may decide to sneak up on them.

"Everything okay"? yelled Schafer.

Rilla smiled and waved. "Okay."

Alerted by the noise, a corpse from the nearest house suddenly appeared in the doorway. It saw the figures running down the street and then Rilla waving her arms above her head. It opened its mouth, letting an almost silent groan escape its rotten lips.

Rilla began to walk slowly, keeping an eye on the others up ahead, and another on the road behind. She forgot that they could be anywhere and ignored the houses on either side of the road. They seemed empty and posed no threat. It was the vehicles she was more worried about in case anything came at them from the cars. They could be hiding any number of zombies who might appear in a second.

A gurgling noise caught her attention. It sounded in her left ear and grew louder very quickly. Turning around sharply, her eyes widened in shock as the corpse came running at her, its stiff arms reaching for her, its dead mouth impossibly wide.

"No!" Rilla uttered a brief scream and then instinctively dodged to the side as it tried to grab her. It missed her body, but one hand caught hold of her arm, and it whirled around to grab her again.

"Dad!" Rilla raised the heavy lamp base and froze. The dead man leering at her was hideous, but he had been well preserved inside his house for several months. His eyes were white, and his skin had become almost mummified. It felt like she was attacking an old man, and her hesitation allowed the zombie to close in on her.

She tried to use the lamp to defend herself, to hit the zombie around the head as her father had taught her to do, but it was too close, and all she succeeded in doing was dropping it as her wrist bumped against the zombie's shoulder.

The zombie got both its cold hands on Rilla, and her blue jacket ripped open as the corpse pulled her towards it. Suddenly she was in its embrace and staring into the face of the man about to kill her. Although he was dead, he appeared very much alive, and if it wasn't for the stench of rotting meat she would've been fooled into thinking he was a survivor in need of help. The zombie's white eyes rolled back in its head, and it brought its face up to hers. Staring into its mouth, Rilla felt revulsion rise in her gut. Shivers broke out over her forearms and neck as it pulled her closer. She saw the dull silvery fillings in the back of its mouth, and the swollen purple tongue that was covered in a moldy growth of some sort. Sores and blisters permeated the thing's face, yet they had dried up and cracked open making the dead man's face all the more disgusting. Rilla felt the zombie's cold hands digging into her arms, and though she tried to repel the corpse, it wouldn't give up. As its deadly teeth neared her supple skin, she tried to turn her head away, but she succeeded in merely exposing her neck, which spurred it on.

Rilla screwed her eyes shut and tensed up, preparing herself to feel the pain of its teeth ripping through her jugular, when her face was drenched in something wet. It was cold and sticky, and Rilla opened her eyes again as the zombie let go of her. It fell away in slow motion, and she saw Jeremy plunge the knife into its skull again, ripping it out and plunging it back in, twisting it around inside the man's skull like a corkscrew through a cork. Rilla spat the foul blood from her mouth and watched as her father appeared through the red mist swinging his bat. As Jeremy removed his knife, Schafer made the sure the zombie went down once and for all. The bat cracked the skull into pieces, and the man's head resembled a bloody broken vase. The corpse lay motionless on the ground, and Rilla felt hands grab her again. This time was different. They were warm and comforting, and they were pulling her toward her father.

Schafer stood in front of her shouting something, but she heard nothing. Her eyes were transfixed on the dead zombie as if she had been hypnotized by it. Blood dripped from her face and filled her ears, and the warm hands on her shoulders began to shake her as Schafer continued shouting something. Rilla could see his mouth opening and closing, but it was as if no sound was coming out. Her eyes were drawn back to the man on the road. He had been going to kill her. He was going to *eat* her. Piece by piece, bite by bite, he would've *eaten her alive*. Rilla felt faint, her head swimming with a million thoughts that all ended up with her being eaten alive. The red in her eyes was giving way to a fuzzy gray that devolved into darkness, and it felt like a thousand bright stars were shimmering in her vision.

Schafer slapped his daughter's face and caught her as she fainted.

"Jeremy, help me," he said as he dropped his bat. Jeremy helped to carry Rilla to the side of the road as Lyn picked up Schafer's baseball bat now smeared with brains and hair.

"What do we do now?" asked Jeremy, as they lay Rilla gently on the sidewalk.

"Just give me a minute." Schafer began to wipe the blood from his daughter's face. She had been brave, but she had also taken her eye off the ball, and it had almost cost her everything.

"Schafer, we can't just hang around here. There'll be more. The screams... They'll have heard the—"

"Back off, Jeremy. Give me some space," said Schafer, not trying to hide the venom in his voice. Jeremy had saved his daughter's life, undoubtedly, but he was still an asshole.

"Rilla?" Magda sank to her knees beside her husband. "Meine Tochter! Is she okay?" she wheezed. "Is she—?"

"She'll be fine." Schafer had cleared her face of most of the blood. The corpse had failed to bite her, and Schafer knew it was just the shock. He had protected Rilla from the worst of it back at the motel. She deserved better than that. He should've warned her what it would be like. He knew he could've done more to prepare her.

"Magda, we need-"

"Here they come. Fuck, here they come." Jeremy pointed at the buses, at the narrow funnel they had caused in the road. Four zombies appeared, and another two behind them.

Schafer picked Rilla up carefully. "Let's go. Nothing's changed. We keep going."

Ignoring the increasingly frantic Jeremy, Schafer marched down the road away from the zombies. Magda kept by his side, and Schafer heard Jeremy, Lyn and Victoria follow. If they kept moving, he saw no reason why they couldn't make it to Attwood's before the zombies caught up with them. Some were faster than others, but the ones behind were slow.

"Which way?" asked Magda. "Welche richtung, Schafer?" They neared another intersection. A gas station lay across the road, and a tanker blocked the road to the left. To the right lay rows of shops and houses with a few distant corpses ambling through the ghost town in their direction.

"Left," announced Schafer without pausing. "Behind that tanker there's another road that will take us almost all the way there."

"Schafer, this is madness." Jeremy scuttled up beside him. "Victoria is tired, and you can't possibly hope to carry on all the way carrying Rilla. What if we're attacked? What if those zombies catch us? What if—"

"Save it, Jeremy." Schafer approached the tanker and refused to look at his companion. "We can't go back, so we go forward. Even when you can't see them, they're all around us. If you think you're safe anywhere out here—or back at your home—then you're an idiot. I'm getting my daughter somewhere safe. You should be focused on doing the same instead of worrying about your own neck."

Schafer was sweating profusely. The effort of carrying Rilla was taking more out of him than he had expected. The lack of food and the draining heat of the sun made him slow down more than he wanted to.

"Now, hold on, Schafer." Jeremy grabbed Schafer's arm forcing him to stop. "You said you knew what you were doing. I put my daughter's life at risk because of you."

Schafer glared at Jeremy. He didn't have time for this. The zombies behind were getting closer and growing in number. They had drawn others, and there were almost twenty now. Schafer blinked away a droplet of sweat from his eyelid. "*You* do what you like. *I'm* going to carry on. Magda and Rilla are coming with me to Attwood's."

Lyn dragged Victoria to the shady side of the tanker that offered a little shelter from the sun. "Are we there yet?" she asked. "I can hear them. Can't you hear them?"

The zombies were making a lot of noise and Schafer realized the noise wasn't just coming from the ones behind them.

"Now, hold on, Schafer," said Jeremy as he turned away. Jeremy tried to grab Schafer's arm again, but he shrugged it off and walked past the rear of the tanker.

"Magda?" Schafer stood in the road with his daughter lying in his arms, wondering suddenly if Jeremy wasn't right.

Magda joined her husband's side and looked at him. "Was ist—"

"Oh, Lord." Jeremy rounded the tanker to find Schafer and Magda staring at the path ahead of them. The road to Attwood's was full of corpses. There had to be at least a hundred or more filling the road, blocking any route through to the far end.

"Now what do we do?" asked Jeremy. "We can't go back and we can't go forward; just what the hell do we do now?"

Schafer looked at Rilla and was reminded of how he used to carry her up to bed like this when she was younger. She would inevitably fall asleep whilst watching TV, reluctant to go upstairs to be on her own. He would carry her up gently and place her in bed without even waking her. She looked the same now: carefree, relaxed and innocent. He couldn't let anything happen to her, he *wouldn't*.

"We have to... to..." He couldn't actually think what to do. They were almost surrounded. Going back to Jeremy's or forward to Attwood's meant a fight, and he wasn't going to be any use carrying Rilla. He could see that Magda was struggling with the heat, and even Jeremy and Lyn looked exhausted. Victoria was silently sucking two fingers in her mouth, her eyes downcast. They were all relying on him, waiting for a decision, for an order.

A zombie suddenly appeared at the back of the tanker, its body clattering into the axle and arms scratching against the hull. It stumbled forward toward them, its intent all too obvious. Magda screamed, and Lyn pushed Victoria behind her while Jeremy began to back off.

"What do we do, Jeremy, what do we do?" Lyn shouted hysterically.

"Take it out, Jeremy," said Schafer, calmly.

The zombie approached, its feet scraping across the tarmac, and pustules around its mouth oozing dark slime. The woman had worked in the garage once, and her slim figure had drawn many admiring glances. Now her ravaged body was riddled with maggots and blow-flies, and her arms were missing large chunks of flesh.

"What the fuck?" Jeremy stepped back again. "What the…?"

Schafer knew then that they had no way of fighting their way anywhere. They were scared. All of them were scared. He couldn't risk giving Rilla to Jeremy to carry. He would dump her as soon as they got into any kind of trouble. Lyn had Victoria to take care of, and Magda simply didn't have the strength. Schafer sighed.

"We have to go. There's a narrow alleyway over there behind that station wagon. It'll double-back to the buses, but we'll have to take it and find somewhere else to hold up for now. Attwood's will have to wait."

As they all backed away from the advancing zombie, another appeared from behind the tanker, then a third, and then a fourth.

"Schafer?" Magda looked at her husband who was gently lowering his daughter to the ground. Ignoring her, he grabbed the baseball bat from Jeremy and pointed it at them.

"Go. All of you. Down that alley."

"What are you doing? Are you coming?" asked Jeremy as he began to trudge away toward the alley, his eyes locked on the party of zombies.

"Oh, I'm coming all right and I'll bring Rilla with me." Schafer turned back to the zombies, his face set in grim determination. The plan had been shot to shit, but they would make it another way. He just had to figure out a way around the horde ahead of them. He had to figure out a way to get Jeremy on board. As it was, he was just as much of a liability as his little girl. Schafer lifted the baseball bat in both hands and gripped it firmly as his eyes focused on the nearest zombie. "I've just got to take care of business first."

CHAPTER 6

The last lock of hair fell to the floor silently, and Kyler held up a mirror in front of his daughter's face. She looked at herself blankly, and it was obvious she hated it. She had gone along with him reluctantly, but ultimately he had not given her a choice. The whole process had taken less than ten minutes, and Kyler felt relieved when it was over. He was more nervous about cutting his daughter's hair with the scissors than he was the end result.

Charlie shrugged and looked at her father in the mirror behind her. "Happy now?"

Kyler shook his head. "This has got nothing to do with me being happy, and you know it."

Charlie got off the stool and brushed herself down, thick clumps of blonde hair cascading to the ground and joining the hair already there. They had arranged to cut her hair outside so at least they didn't make a mess inside.

"Here." Kyler passed her the mirror, and she took it to look at hew new haircut once more. "Clear that up," he said as he trudged back inside.

"Yes, Sir," muttered Charlie. She had known he wouldn't offer to help clean up afterwards and already prepared herself for it. It was the end of another warm day, and little strands of hair had fallen down her top causing her back to itch.

"Very…" Charlie searched for the right words to describe her new haircut. Nothing came to mind. Kyler had effectively turned her into a boy, chopping off her long blonde hair that her mother had used to tell her was her best feature. Now most of it was blowing around the garden, and she looked more like a young man than a girl. Her father refused to explain why she had to do it other than to say it was more practical. She had tried to counter him by arguing that it was practical to stay sober, to be on guard with the increasing zombie activity outside the main fence, but he had refused to be drawn on his drinking and insisted they cut her hair that day. He had muttered something about how the zombies would be able to grab her long hair if they ever went outside, so she may as well get used to it being short now.

Sighing, Charlie went to the garage to put the stool and scissors back. Kyler hadn't even used a decent pair of scissors when he'd butchered her hair and used a rusty pair from the garage. She was surprised he had any since he spent most of his time fashioning weird weapons from what tools he had. As she placed the stool down quietly, she noticed something new on the workbench, and suddenly realized where the steak knife set had disappeared to. There was a pair of gardening gloves with a knife neatly bound to each finger. They reminded her of the glove from an old horror film, though these would no doubt be more comfortable to wear. She picked one up and slipped her hand inside. The glove was a size too big, but it remained in place, and she swished it through the air, imagining herself decapitating a zombie. She had never struck a person in her life, nor had she had to deal with one of the dead. Still, it was interesting to pretend. Kyler obviously thought about it a lot more than her; he had spent all day making these gloves.

Charlie slipped the glove off and put it back. As she went back outside, she noticed the warm air carried the strong moans of the dead clearly today. Either there were a lot of them close by, or something had piqued their interest. Carefully, Charlie walked to the driveway and looked at the fence. There were no more than three at the fence, rattling on it like caged prisoners. She wasn't sure if they wanted to get in, or if she wanted to get out. The moaning sound was further off, carried to her by the gentle breeze. Shrugging, Charlie returned to the house. Whatever had drawn them away wasn't her problem. Since the screaming woman had arrived and died on the day that her mother had been taken away from her, Charlie had wondered if there were others. The woman might have been living with her family, although that didn't explain why she was on her own. Surely nobody would leave their family behind? If the woman had been with others, then perhaps she had been the one who had been forced out to look for help. Perhaps it was her family who were being slaughtered out there, forced to leave their house in search of food. Perhaps the thousands of zombies around Peterborough had found them.

Charlie shuddered. Her own morbid thoughts were too depressing, and she locked them away as she made her way into the downstairs bathroom. She put her hands on the cold rim of the sink and stared into the dusty mirror on the wall. She looked not just tired but terrible, in fact. It wasn't just the drain of living alongside the dead that took all her energy, but living with her father. Either side of the fence there were problems and pressures, just different ones.

She rifled a hand through her cropped hair. Maybe she could do something with it. She picked up a hair clip and tried to pin a length of hair back from her fringe, but the short hair wouldn't hold.

"I need to accessorize." Charlie went to the laundry and perused her father's fishing gear. Several rods were leant up against the wall, a cobweb stretching between them. He hadn't been out for months now, and Charlie wondered how big the fish would be. She could just imagine a nice fat trout, its juicy white meat filling her belly. As her stomach groaned, she began to rummage through the drawers along the wall. There were old jackets and scarves that rarely saw the light of day. Her hand touched a soft felt cap, and she pulled it out, recognizing her father's old fishing cap. It had blue and green checks on it and smelt a little musty from being in the drawer for so long, but as soon as she dropped it onto her head she felt better. She turned back to the mirror and looked at it. It was at least two sizes too big for her, and she couldn't help but smile. She hadn't seen that hat for years. The last time she could recall seeing her father wear it was on her fifteenth birthday when he had returned home late from taking some tourists out on Edward MacDowell Lake. He had come home stinking of fish and oil, and she had been so happy to see him that she had hugged him and got the smell all over her party dress. The memory of her party brought back other memories, too, of her friends, of laughter, of the dreams of a bright future, and of her mother. Charlie's smile faded.

"Dinner's ready." Kyler called out from the kitchen.

"Coming." Charlie rubbed her hands on her thighs and walked through to the kitchen where she found Kyler sat at the table and two plates of cold spaghetti waiting.

Kyler frowned as she took her seat. With her jeans and UCLA sweater, Charlie was beginning to look more like the son he'd never had than his daughter.

"Take that hat off while we're at the table," he said gruffly. "You know the rules."

"Of course." Charlie slipped it off and put it beside her plate. She had hoped it might draw a comment from him; maybe elicit an old memory like it had in her.

"Elbows?"

Charlie forced a smile upon her face. "Sorry, Dad, forgot," she said removing her elbows and arms from the table. Couldn't he just let it slip this once? Charlie very much doubted that God was watching, and if he was then elbows on the table were the least of his problems.

She waited for Kyler to say grace and then picked up a fork. She spun it around on the plate, reeling in a strand of spaghetti. It wasn't much of a meal, but she knew they hadn't much choice. They had to make what they had last as long as possible. She held up the fork and sucked the spaghetti in, savoring the cold tomato flavor before returning her fork to the plate and twisting another piece around it.

"What should we do tonight?" Charlie sucked another piece of food from her fork. "Monopoly? You haven't won in a while now." The truth was they hadn't played in a while. Not since the day her mother had died, in fact. They hadn't played anything since then, and the tedium of watching her father drink until he fell asleep wasn't riveting entertainment. She had read every magazine from cover to cover three times over and wanted to try and entice her father out of his shell. She watched him chew his food and then place his fork down on the table. He said nothing, and she wondered if he was even going to answer her at all or just sit in silence.

Kyler swallowed heavily and then rested his hands on the table either side of the plate. He stared at his food, at the cold spaghetti that he had so carefully emptied from the can and poured out onto the two plates.

"You want to play games?" he asked, quietly.

Instantly Charlie knew she had said the wrong thing. Of course he wouldn't want to play a game. *Of course* he wouldn't want to do anything with her. She was so bored of it all, of everything, of knowing exactly what he was going to do or say before he'd even thought it.

"Okay, maybe not then. How about a run? The park's lovely at this time of year." She couldn't resist it. Her mother had always encouraged her to speak up, and now there was no stopping it. Charlie knew she would piss Kyler off for being so flippant, but she seemed to piss him off anyway, so she might as well enjoy herself.

Kyler looked at Charlie. "No, I don't think—"

"The cinema then?" asked Charlie, keeping her tone light and irritating. "You know, popcorn, big fat sugary drinks, and lots of—"

"NO!" Kyler banged his fists on the table causing the plates to jump, and his fork fell to the floor.

Charlie bit her lip. Too far. Oh well. So, he was angry with her—what else was new?

"This isn't a game, Charlie. This isn't what you think." Kyler looked at her, his face red from anger. "Those games you used to play with your friends are over. You have to grow up. You can't act like a little kid anymore."

"I think I got that, Dad," Charlie said as she slipped another fork loaded with spaghetti into her mouth. She looked outside at the fading sunlight. Another hour and it would be dark. "The only games I could play with my friends now would have to involve a Ouija board, right?"

Kyler leant back in his chair and a shadow fell across his face as the sun dipped behind the horizon. "You want to talk about that?" he asked Charlie.

"Talk about what?"

"Your friends. Them." Kyler's eyes were hidden in the shadow, but he was looking at his daughter carefully, watching how she ate slowly. He brought his chair forward again so that she could see him, that there was no misunderstanding that he meant it seriously. This was no game to him. "*The dead.*"

"Oh, Dad, don't be so melodramatic. No, I don't want to talk about my dead friends. That's hardly going to solve anything."

"Very true. I'm glad you understand that. In the old world you would've been booked in to see a shrink if one of your friends died. In this new world we've dispensed with useless things like psychiatrists and—"

"Shaving?" Charlie muttered as she finished her food.

Kyler looked at his daughter as she pushed her empty plate away. "So, this is just a joke to you?"

"Do you see me laughing?" Charlie reached for the bottle of water on the table, but Kyler snatched it away before she could reach it.

"Really? What's that for?" Charlie went to tuck her long blonde hair behind her ears and then remembered there was nothing there anymore. She brushed the side of her head with her fingers and pretended to scratch her ear. "I'm not allowed a glass of water now?"

"You can have a glass in a moment. I just want to make sure that you comprehend what is happening here. You seem to still think you can get back to the way things were; that one day this will all be over."

"It will, Dad. Sooner or later, it will."

"Oh, yes, Charlie, but you seem to think that things will go back to the way they were."

"Well, I think—"

"You have to see that they won't ever be the same again. Those things out there won't allow it. We let them take control. The time for change has gone. We let them grow, let them spread, and now they have complete control. We can never get back to what we were, not with *them* out there. How do you think you'd cope if you were on your own?"

The question shocked Charlie. She had been prepared for a lecture, even considering trying to answer back, but this was a question she hadn't been expecting.

"I'm not on my own, Dad. I'm not going to be. You're here."

"Your mother was here too. You can't rely on others for the rest of your life. Our situation is far too perilous for that kind of naïve attitude."

"Yeah, but what happened to Mom was an accident." Charlie felt her cheeks flush at the memory. Why should he make her feel guilty about it? "It was just an accident, Dad."

"An accident? Perhaps. But that implies an event that occurred without warning, an unforeseen turn of events that was outside the realms of control. I don't buy that. Do you? Do you think what happened was a random act of nature or God or something that we couldn't have controlled had we been more prepared?"

Charlie looked at the blue and green cap on the table. Her father hadn't always been like this. The tourists used to love him, they all did. He was fun to be around, and she refused to believe that man had gone. "I guess not. We didn't know that woman was going to come."

"Yes, but we weren't prepared, Charlie. We weren't prepared anywhere near enough. I should've thought through what could happen, made you and your mother understand—"

"Yeah, well, I understand now, Dad. It's going to be a long, hot summer. And those poor people outside our gates are going to stay there. I get it."

"Do you?" Kyler sighed. "I'm not sure you do. Would you have done what your mother did? Would you have opened that gate to help?"

"I don't know. I mean what happened can't be undone so there's no point dwelling on it. It's in the past now."

Kyler picked up his plate and carried it to the sink. He shook his head as the dying sun bathed his face in an orange glow. He turned around and leant against the counter looking at Charlie.

"What?" Charlie felt uneasy with him staring at her like that. It felt like he was judging her; as if sizing her up to enter a pageant. Why did he have to make her feel so uncomfortable in her own home? "Well?"

Kyler didn't answer, but continued staring at her. Exasperated, she stood up and carried her plate to the sink. Greeted with nothing but silence Charlie went back to the table, got the bottle of water, and poured herself a small glass. All the time she moved about the room his eyes never left her. Charlie drank the water quickly, deciding she would just go upstairs and read in her room. He was in one of those funny moods again. Sometimes he would challenge her, and sometimes he would argue. This appeared to be one of those times when he was going to ignore her. She could deal with that. It was better than fighting.

"How was the water?" he finally asked, just as Charlie was about to leave the kitchen.

Charlie looked at her father who was still at the sink and shrugged. "Watery."

Kyler nodded. "You realize that it's not going to last forever, don't you?"

"Yes, Dad." Charlie headed for the exit and then stopped. She hadn't talked about it for a while, but now felt as good a time as any. "You know where we can find plenty of water?"

Kyler opened a cupboard beneath the sink and pulled out a bottle of whiskey, the contents sloshing about as he unscrewed the cap. "No, tell me," he said as he took a dirty mug from the sink. The mug was still encrusted with dried coffee at the bottom.

"Attwood's. Up on the hill. You know they have fresh water running through the property. What about Attwood's, Dad? I still think we could go there. He'll help us. You've seen the light at night. We should—"

"No. Absolutely not." Kyler filled the dirty mug with whiskey and swished it around. He carried it and the bottle back to the table and sat down. "No, Attwood is an eccentric old man. I've already told you that, and we've already had this discussion. So save your breath."

"But he's still alive. You've seen the lights at night, I know you have. So—"

"So what? So what if he's still alive? We're better off on our own. We don't know anything about the place. It's far too dangerous."

"Dangerous? More dangerous than staying here and running out of water? More dangerous than waiting until the zombies figure out a way in, and kill us while we're sleeping? More dangerous than what, Dad?" Charlie heard the frustration and anger rising in her voice, but was powerless to stop it. Why couldn't he see it?

Why did he insist on staying in this place? "I'm sick of it, Dad, sick of it all. I can't just go on living here, with you, like this."

"Good. I'm pleased to hear it. So what are you going to do about it?"

"What am I... ?" Charlie rolled her eyes and then looked at her father as he took another sip of whiskey. "What the fuck do you mean? I just told you what we should do about it. Christ, Dad, how many times do I have to tell you? Attwood's. It's our best chance of—"

"And you really think that's our best option? You think if we make it to Attwood's everything will be *fine*?"

Charlie knew he was being sarcastic. "No, everything isn't going to be *fine*. I'm not an idiot. But I know that living here with you isn't *fine* either. One day we'll run out of water and you'll run out of whiskey, and then what will we do?"

"You're missing the point, Charlie."

"I give up." Charlie grabbed the fishing cap from the table and shoved it down on her head. "I'm going to pack. Seven days and I'm leaving. I'll go on my own. I'll go to Attwood's."

Kyler began to chuckle, and his hollow laughter echoed around the kitchen. Charlie watched him until the laughter faded away. The tears were coming again, and she hated herself for it. This is what he did to her. He made her hate herself even more than she hated him.

"I'm sorry, I shouldn't have laughed. But you have to admit that you going out there alone is a little. . . unrealistic."

"Right, because I'm pathetic. Just a child, right Dad? I couldn't possibly do it on my own because I'm *such* a disappointment. That about right?"

"Charlie, you can't even break a defenseless bird's neck. How are you going to kill those zombies? What are you going to do when one is on top of you and you have to thrust a knife through its skull? What are you going to do when it's about to take a bite out of your arm? Fight back? Cry? Run to your room?"

Charlie loathed her father. When he began drinking he became spiteful. He talked to her as if she were still a little girl holding his hand. He couldn't see her for what she was now. The death of her mother had changed her, changed everything; now it was ripping them apart, and she couldn't find a way to make him see. "Let's be honest, Dad, the truth is you're coming with me. I don't want to go out there on my own. So the question is, what will you do when a zombie is about to bite me? 'Cause right now, I'm not so sure. I'm not sure that you wouldn't just let it take me, and you can be done with me. That'll be a weight off your mind, huh? Finally, Charlie will be out of the picture, and you can just drink yourself to death in peace. Happy days."

Kyler stood up and angrily flung his mug against the wall behind Charlie. It narrowly missed her head but showered her in drops of whiskey. "Happy? You actually believe I could be happy without you? First your mother, and then. . ."

Charlie began crying, unable to stop herself. Her hands were trembling though she didn't know if it was fear or shock. She looked down at the floor, at the black and white pattern on the vinyl, and waited for the next explosion. Was he going to throw the bottle next? Was he going to hit her? When nothing happened, she looked up and found him sat down again, his head in his hands. He had done it again. She felt guilty for pushing him like that, for making him react the way he did.

Kyler mumbled something through his hands, but Charlie couldn't hear it and stepped closer to the table wearily. Part of her told her this was a trick, a ploy to get her closer so he could grab her before she could run. Maybe he wanted to snap her neck and put her out of her misery too.

"Fight or die, Charlie. That's all that's left now," Kyler said quietly.

"What do you mean?" Charlie heard the words echo around her head. "Fight or die?"

"You have to have more ambition than that," replied Kyler. "They will do anything they can to stop you. There are thousands of *them* out there. I'm not sure that any wall is going to be big enough to keep those fuckers out. You have to see that Attwood's isn't going to work. Peterborough will kill us if we stay here. They'll come for you, and eventually me too. They'll just walk right on in and take this place from us; take everything I worked so hard for. You have to realize how much potential you have

Charlie, if you could just see past the end of your damn nose. There's so much more for you out there, Charlotte."

Charlie wiped her eyes and sniffed. The room was eerily quiet and dark, and her father hadn't called her Charlotte since she was a little girl. He wasn't as strong as he made out to be. He was scared, too, and she could see that now. She didn't know it was possible to love and hate someone so much at the same time, but she found as she looked at him sat at the table with his head in his hands, that there was no way she could leave him. Going to Attwood's on her own was a pipe dream. She needed him as much as he needed her. After everything that happened, they still needed each other.

"This can't go on," Kyler said as he finally looked up at his daughter.

"Why do we have to fight all the time? We should be working together, Dad." Charlie took the cap off and held it in her hands, twisting around nervously. "Why are you doing so much to drive us apart? I feel like sometimes you wish I were dead."

"Never, Charlie, never. I know I'm hard on you, but that's because I have to be. I see you and I see Jemma. I see where it all went wrong and how I let her down. I need to do better with you. I'm doing what I do precisely because I do love you, because it's my job to bring you up and teach you how you're going to live your life. That's what a parent does, and God willing, I hope you get the chance to do the same one day."

Charlie had to admit she hadn't thought about her future like that for a long time. She had wondered about when she would have children, and she had thought that Jackson would be the man she spent the rest of her life with. But he had left her and was probably just another corpse now. The thought didn't cause her any concern. What worried her was what was running through her father's head. Did he think about that kind of stuff; about the future? She thought all he thought about was fighting and drinking. Maybe she had misunderstood him.

"Look, Dad, let's—"

A short scream interrupted her, and she looked at her father. "Did you hear that?"

Kyler got up and nodded slowly, a frown spreading across his face. His eyes went to the window when they heard another scream.

"Christ, Dad, who is it?" Charlie felt afraid again and walked to the window to join her father. They couldn't see the road from there, but there was no mistaking where the screams had come from: Mr. Riley's house next door. Whoever was out there wasn't on the road. They were in the neighbor's property. Who the hell was it?

"I don't know," said Kyler as he took his daughter's hand. "It is *not* happening again," he said firmly. The anger in his eyes masked his fear, but Charlie heard it in his voice.

Charlie pulled her hands free as she understood. "I'm *not* leaving them out there to die." Even as she said it, she could hear her mother's voice in her head saying much the same thing. It was the last thing she had heard her mother say.

Kyler nodded. "I know. You're just like her. Too damn kind for your own good. She didn't have a mean bone in her body. Jemma would run across a busy street if it meant helping someone." Kyler sighed and looked at his daughter. There was no way they could stand by and listen to someone die. "Okay, if we're going to do this, we're going to do it right this time. You follow my instructions and stay behind me, got that? And if I see any sign of trouble, I'm pulling the plug."

"Got it."

Kyler lead Charlie outside into the cool evening, and they stood there waiting for another signal. There were voices, shouting, but no more screams.

"They're inside Mr. Riley's aren't they?" asked Charlie. "What the hell are they doing? Is it the military? You think they're going house to house?" Suddenly Charlie began to hope that this was the rescue; that this was a sign that things might get back to normal.

"No. It's not help. Wait there." Kyler ran to the garage and returned a moment later with tools. He handed Charlie a crowbar and held a hammer in each of his hands.

"What are we going to do?" asked Charlie as she looked at the huge brick wall separating them from the neighbor's property. "There's no way into Mr. Riley's except through the front gate."

As her father looked at her, Charlie understood. "Fuck."

They ran down the driveway and approached the fence. Three zombies were banging on it, their hands wrapped around the metal. Kyler dropped the first one by smashing it over the head with a hammer. He dropped the second in the same fashion, but the third was standing too far back and couldn't be reached without opening the gate. Kyler put his hands on the lock and prepared to unlatch it so they could get out and around to Mr. Riley's. He looked at Charlie.

"Ready?"

Charlie looked at the zombie at the gate, at the dark road outside, and then her father. She held up the crowbar and steeled herself.

"Do it."

CHAPTER 7

"We weren't prepared. We didn't have enough weapons to fight them off," said Schafer. "I had planned the route, but I hadn't expected to encounter such a large group of them. It was almost as if they were waiting for us; as if they knew we were coming. I know it's ridiculous, but. . . Look, I take full responsibility for what happened. I can't promise you anything or offer you anything, but I know how to get there. If we could just find some more weapons, maybe even a gun. . . "

Charlie stood up. "We have weapons."

Kyler glared at her. "Sit down, Charlie. This doesn't concern you."

"Shut up, Dad, of course it does. And we *do* have weapons. No guns unfortunately, but we have plenty of things we can use out in the garage."

"Fuck, Charlie, why don't you just give them the house keys while you're at it? Sit down and be quiet. We don't know these people. We certainly don't want to go telling them about everything we have. For all we know—"

"I know that they came to us for help, *Dad*." Charlie remained standing. She wasn't going to back down, not from this fight. "Schafer knows how to get to Attwood's, and we have the weapons. What is it, three miles? We can do this. You're not going to keep me a prisoner here anymore."

As Charlie and Kyler stared at one another, Schafer decided it would be best to stay quiet at this point. He was indebted to them for his life, for saving his family's life, and didn't want to cause a fight between them. They had been lucky enough to come across them, and if they hadn't have randomly picked the house to hide in when they had, then they would probably not be here now. Schafer reached across and put his hand on Magda's lap.

"Listen, Schafer, just tell me again how the fuck you all ended up in my neighbor's house." Kyler wished he had a gun, but refused to have one in the house while Charlie was at home. It was something he regretted now, especially with *them* at the door, but he couldn't change the past. Next time he knew who he would be voting for.

"Of course." Schafer felt Magda squeeze his hand. She was nervous, but Schafer felt confident that these two people were okay. They had helped them and, if anything, they seemed to be interested in how to get to Attwood's. Jeremy and Lyn looked uncomfortable sat opposite him in the darkness with Victoria wedged between them, but they were keeping silent. Schafer just hoped Jeremy would keep quiet long enough to get Kyler on side. They were all sat in Kyler's kitchen around the table. Rilla was awake but still felt sick. She was sipping on a glass of cool water letting her father do all the talking.

"Have you been out there, Kyler?" asked Schafer. "Do you know what it's like outside of these walls?"

"I saved your ass, didn't I?"

"Then you know what it's like. Facing them isn't as easy as I thought. We were vastly outnumbered, but if we go now, this minute, then we have the advantage."

"You want to go out in the dark? Have you lost it?" Kyler paced up and down, his eyes casting suspicious glances over all of the new guests. "Let's just reassess the situation. So you were all tucked up safely in *his* house, right?"

"Correct," said Jeremy.

His black shirt clung to his sweaty body, and Kyler could tell the man was nervous. It was obvious that Schafer led this little party.

"And you left it to go to Attwood's?" asked Charlie.

"Correct again." Jeremy whispered at Victoria to stop fidgeting. "Schafer thought we should go."

"Nice," said Kyler. "You going to throw him under the bus, just like that?"

"It's okay," interjected Schafer. "We're okay. I get it."

"So how did that work out for you? I'm guessing not so well as you're sat at my table instead of sipping champagne with Attwood out of a crystal glass."

Charlie sniggered, and Kyler threw her a glare. "Well, let's hear it." Kyler's question was aimed at Schafer.

"We had some trouble out on the road. My daughter, Rilla, encountered some trouble, and we narrowly avoided some zombies. I took care of them, but our path was blocked. Something caused the dead to converge in one place which cut us off from the route I had planned. We couldn't get back to Jeremy's place, so we had to find somewhere else. I guess we got lucky and ended up at your neighbor's."

"Lucky? Is that what you call it?" Charlie refilled Rilla's glass. "I don't think Mr. Riley saw it that way. He was about to—"

"Yes, I know, thank you." Schafer remembered all too well the encounter with Mr. Riley and did not need any reminders. After breaking into the house with Jeremy, they had gone from room to room downstairs to ensure they were alone. Rilla had taken Victoria and started to barricade the front door while Lyn and Magda went upstairs to check they were in the clear. That's when the screams had started.

Mr. Riley was still in the bathroom when Magda had first come face to face with him. As she rummaged through the mirrored cabinet looking for some pain-relief tablets that she could give to Rilla, his bloated body rose from the bathtub and was on her before she had time to react. Lyn had screamed seconds after Magda and uselessly stabbed her knife into Mr. Riley's back. There had been a brief struggle before Schafer had come to the upper floor and finally put Mr. Riley down with a swift blow to the side of the head. The old man had been in the tub for months and his reanimated, fragile body hadn't put up much of a fight.

"I'm feeling a lot better now," said Rilla. "Thank you for helping us, Charlie."

It was the first words that Charlie had heard the girl say. She seemed to be of about the same age yet was quite different. It wasn't just the accent. Rilla wore a light blue jacket that looked expensive even though there was a tear in one arm. Her brown hair was tied up in a bun, and she looked a lot like a slimmer version of her mother. Rilla had been quiet and withdrawn, but Schafer had mentioned how she had fainted and felt sick in the subsequent escape that had ended up with them next door.

"Do you want anything to eat?" Charlie saw her father glare at her again, but ignored it. "I can find something, I'm sure."

Rilla smiled sweetly. "No, I don't feel much like eating."

"Actually, I do think we should be leaving," said Schafer.

"After what we've just been through don't you think we should rethink our strategy?" asked Jeremy. "I think poor Victoria has had quite enough for today. Your route is compromised, Schafer, and if it weren't for Kyler and his daughter then, quite frankly, we'd be history right now."

"Hold on, hold on. By the time we got to you, you seemed to have things under control." Kyler approached the sink and looked out of the window at the black night sky. He could see stars forming through the twilight.

"Exactly." Schafer pushed his chair back and rested a hand on his wife's shoulder. "You cleared the path between these two houses which is precisely why we should stick to the plan and go now. This is a perfect opportunity. We're close to Attwood's, and that crowd of corpses is on their way here. If we go now, then the road to Attwood's should be clear. We can be there very soon and hopefully not encounter any of those things."

"Those things don't sleep, Schafer," said Jeremy. "Look, you can't just tell us what to do. Kyler, listen to me: *it's not safe out there*. We have to stay. We need to stay here tonight. I'm sorry, but I'm not putting my wife and daughter through that again."

Kyler knew he had a decision to make. Things had come to a head much sooner than he had hoped. He had expected to have more time with Charlie, more opportunity to make her understand. There didn't really seem to be much of a choice. The hundreds of zombies that Schafer had reported were on their way here. Drawn by the others and the screams, they would surround the house, and then there would be no way out. If they went outside, they risked everything. But staying put was playing a long-term game that he wasn't sure they could win. Whatever they were going to do, they were going to have to do it fast. Suddenly going out in the dark didn't seem like such utter madness.

"Charlie, come here." Kyler waited for his daughter to join his side. "You did well out there earlier."

"I didn't really do anything, Dad. You did the hard work. I didn't even have to kill any of those. . . people."

"Still. You didn't freak out."

"So... " Charlie wondered what her father was looking at. It was dark outside, and with the street lights not working, the town was no longer bathed in that eerie orange glow. The stars were bright but somehow she didn't think they held much interest for her father. She also wondered why he was paying her a compliment. It wasn't like him, at least not recently.

"So, I think we should make up the spare rooms. These people need a bed for the night." Kyler was thinking about the garage and the poor array of weapons inside—that and the bottle of whiskey he craved so much.

"Are you serious?" Charlie had been waiting for him to give the go ahead for them to leave. "But you heard Schafer. This is our best chance of getting out of here."

"Why, Charlie? This place is safe. Just like Jeremy's. And you see what happens if you go out onto the streets ill prepared. It's a war out there, and you can't face *them* without being armed."

"But—" Charlie couldn't believe he was blowing it.

"Kyler, if I may say so, I think you're making a mistake," said Schafer from the table. "I appreciate your offer of hospitality, but do you have enough food and water for eight people? How long do you think we can make it before we turn on each other? How long before those people outside are inside?"

"With respect, Schafer, I'm only offering you a bed for the night. I didn't say anything about long-term. Tomorrow you'll be on your way. Charlie and I are just fine here."

"You're throwing us out?" Jeremy stood up and pointed at Kyler angrily. "You can't do that. What are we supposed to do?"

"Jeremy, calm down," said Lyn. "Victoria is stressed out as it is."

"Listen to your wife. Sit down." Kyler faced the table. "This isn't a democracy. This is my house and my rules. You will do what I say. I'm the President here, and if you don't want me to kick you out right now, then you need to start listening to me."

"Dad, just listen for a moment. We have an opportunity for change here, to make our lives a little bit better; not just for ourselves but all these people too." Charlie felt bad for siding with the others. She felt like she was betraying her father, but she couldn't agree with him. He would have them close up their house, and they would die in it. He was so stubborn he would rather do that then open their doors and consider helping these people. If they worked together, they stood a chance. All Kyler wanted to do was build a wall around them. He thought if he built it tall enough and strong enough they would be all right, but he misunderstood that walls could be broken down. "Attwood's is achievable, Dad. It's right there. I know we can do it. I know it. Please?"

"Attwood doesn't care about you, Charlie. He doesn't care about any of you." Kyler began to raise his voice and talked over Jeremy's whining protests. "That house he built on the rise is just a rich man's playhouse, somewhere to keep his sports cars and do some organic farming. Fuck, he probably paid cash for it and avoided the tax. I know how they work. I know how people like Attwood think. I used to see rich people like him come up all the time from Boston. They would come out here to fish, and I would have to listen to their inane stories about how they *only* made a million last week, or how they were fucking the maid behind their wives backs because she'd put on too much weight. These people live in a different world to us. You think he's going to let us in? If you believe that he'd even give us the time of day then excuse me, but you're all going to die out there at his front door. A world of zombies, and you think he's going to risk opening the door to his mansion to let a few hicks in? I don't think so. You want to go on your suicide mission then do it. Leave. I'm not stopping you."

The room fell into silence. Charlie watched as the girl, Rilla, slowly got up and walked around the table to her parents. She leant over her mother and kissed her on the cheek then took her father's hand and made him stand up. She leaned into him, and as they embraced, she whispered something in his ear. Charlie saw Schafer's face change. Even in the darkness she saw the edges of his lips curl upwards into something approaching a smile. Beneath his bushy beard lay a kind face, a face that she trusted. His clothes were splattered with blood. He understood what it was like to be out there, and yet still wanted to go.

"Kyler, thank you for getting us out of a fix back there," said Schafer as he approached Kyler. He held out his hand. "We'll be going now. My family, Magda and Rilla, don't want to inconvenience you. I understand your thoughts. I don't want to force anyone to do anything. I think if we stay here we would probably starve to death or end up hating and killing each other. I don't want to contemplate such a thing. We'll be out of your way in a moment."

Kyler looked Schafer up and down and then shook his hand. "Okay. Well, if you're certain."

"We are. It's best we go now. By morning the streets will be full of those corpses again."

As they released hands, Charlie saw Lyn stand and drag her daughter to her feet. The younger girl, Victoria, looked scared and tired. How long had they been dragging her around?

"Come on, Jeremy, let's go."

Charlie watched as Jeremy shuffled his feet nervously and drew in a deep breath.

"You still want to go? With *Schafer*?"

Charlie understood that these people, these two families, were together only out of necessity. There was clearly no love lost between the two men.

Lyn looked like she was about to slap her husband, but Charlie watched as she simply pushed her daughter around the table and joined Schafer. One by one, they filed out of the kitchen. Schafer, Magda, Jeremy, Lyn, and Victoria walked past Charlie and Kyler silently. It felt like they were being led out to a hanging; as if they were on death row instead of going to fight for their future.

"You're still welcome to join us," said Rilla. "I can see you're both good people. You helped us when you could easily have ignored us. I wish you would come with us. My father is right about Attwood's. He can get us there. He *will* get us there. It was my fault that we stopped. I hadn't seen them up close like that before. The dead were... were not how I imagined."

Rilla stepped forward and shook Kyler's hand. He said nothing and stayed by the sink. Then Rilla turned to Charlie. "Thanks for the water. Good luck." Rilla leant forward unexpectedly and hugged Charlie, wrapping her slim arms around her.

Suddenly the tears welled up in Charlie's eyes, and she hugged Rilla back. This girl who had only been in Charlie's life for half an hour at most had shown her more compassion in the last thirty seconds than she had known or felt for the last thirty days. Her father would never dream of holding her or comforting her. Even on the day that Jemma died he had kept his distance. Rilla didn't know her, didn't know anything about her. Even with her family and friends gathering outside, she had stayed behind to thank them. Charlie's feelings changed as she hugged Rilla back. The pain and regret were gone, the animosity she felt toward her father turned into pity, and she knew she had to change her life.

Rilla was the last to leave. Charlie had heard how she had fainted before, but she seemed better now. She was nice, friendly even, and it was rare to find that. Charlie had spent so many days cooped up in her room since her mother had died that she had forgotten what it felt like to see genuine warmth on someone else's face and to feel a loving touch. Kyler hadn't exactly made them feel welcome, and Charlie felt like Rilla was actually talking to her instead of at her. It was rare to find someone who cared—about as rare as it was to find anyone alive—and Charlie suddenly felt very alone. Once Rilla left the house it would be just her and her father again. How long would it be before they had another chance? How long would it be before her father lost his temper and did something he would regret? Charlie knew what she wanted, and her mind was made up.

"Dad, I'm going too," said Charlie, as Rilla walked to the doorway. Charlie had nothing with her except her father's old fishing cap and the crowbar he had given her earlier. Her room was full of photos and books and CDs and a ton of stuff that meant nothing to her now. She didn't need to pack anything. She just wanted to leave. She wanted to find herself again away from the hatred and tension that living with her father brought. "I'm sorry, but I have to."

Rilla paused in the doorway and waited for Charlie. "You realize that we are going right now? Don't you want to get your things? Shouldn't you discuss this with your father?"

Charlie looked at Kyler. He remained by the sink and said nothing. In the darkness she couldn't see his face or read what he was thinking. Why didn't he say something? Why didn't he shout and curse and tell her how disappointed he was in her? Why didn't he hit her or do something, do *anything*, to let her know that he still cared?

"No, let's go. There's clearly nothing here for me now," said Charlie. She couldn't believe he was going to let her go just like that. No matter what had happened between them, no matter how bad things got, underneath it all she still loved him. They had too much history to throw it all away like it was nothing. "Jesus, Dad, did you hear me? I'm leaving. I'm going with these people, and you can't stop me."

Kyler calmly bent down and opened the cupboard beneath the sink. Charlie heard the chink of glass and then watched as he drank straight from a bottle of whiskey.

"Rilla, come on, hurry up." Schafer's voice outside was muffled, yet the urgency was clear. It was time to go.

"Um, look, I need to go. Are you coming?" asked Rilla gently. She understood that the situation was serious and hadn't intended to cause any kind of rift between them. Charlie was kind, and even though Kyler had his defenses up, she could see kindness in him too. She wanted them both to come, but didn't have the time or energy to fight about it now. They had done all the talking that needed to be done. Now it was time to go. Rilla slipped her hand into Charlie's. "Are you coming?"

Charlie looked at Rilla, her eyes welling up with tears, and then looked back at her father. "Will you come too? Please, Dad. Don't let it end like this. Come with us. With *me*."

"Take care," said Kyler, as he took another gulp of whiskey. It burnt his throat as he swallowed, and he let out a small cough. He remained standing by the sink. "Just remember everything that I've taught you."

Charlie wanted to laugh but knew if she did that she knew she wouldn't be able to stop. Her father was behaving absurdly. This wasn't just stubborn; this was plain old mean. She wasn't just a disappointment to him, she was nothing. The only thing worse than being hated was not being cared about at all.

"Remember what you taught me? What's that, Dad? Misery? Hate? How horrible you are to me? Fine, stay here and rot. See if I care." Charlie sighed. "Let's go Rilla."

"What about your father?" asked Rilla.

Charlie looked at Rilla and the open door and shook her head. "He's dead. He died when my mother did."

Charlie left without looking back and followed Rilla outside. The stars were out in force now. The fresh air wrapped around Charlie's face, and she saw the others looking at her.

"Okay then," said Schafer. He nodded warmly at Charlie. "You take care of my daughter now, you hear?" Charlie knew he had accepted her without judgement and appreciated him not asking where her father was. He obviously understood what was happening and may have overheard some of the conversation.

Quickly, they made their way down the driveway, and Charlie kept hold of Rilla's hand. It felt comfortable and natural. She felt more secure than she had for months. A part of her kept screaming to go back, to go home, and that her father needed her to look after him. Yet the stronger part of her mind told her to go on; if she went back now she would never leave that house, at least not alive.

The gate was open and the road clear. Charlie could hear faint groans on the wind from far away. The others ahead were on the road looking back at her through the fence. Once she stepped out onto the street, there would be no going back. She couldn't believe it had come to this. She couldn't believe that her family was gone, that her mother was dead and her father as good as. These people were her future now. She was putting everything she had on the line to join them, and they were strangers. As she looked at them, she realized she couldn't even remember Jeremy's wife's name. She had hardly spoken more than three words to her or to the little girl. Yet she was journeying out into a world full of walking corpses and relying on them to get her to safety. The world was far different to the one she had grown up in. Peterborough used to be a nice small town that grew in summer when the tourists came for the fishing, hiking and cycling. Half of those tourists were still there, their dead bodies unable to go home. Although there was doubt in her mind, Charlie knew she was doing the right thing. The house she had called home was her past, and everything in it was of no use to her anymore. It had stopped feeling like a home a long time ago. She squeezed Rilla's hand as they stepped through the gate and onto the sidewalk.

"Charlie?"

Footsteps came running down the driveway, and suddenly Kyler appeared at the fence. "Wait up."

Rilla slipped her hand out of Charlie's and watched as Kyler stood before his daughter. The half crescent moon gave her enough light to see that he carried a hammer in one hand.

"I'm sorry," said Kyler as he faced Charlie. "I've fucked up a lot of things in my life, but I'm not about to fuck you over. You want to go, we'll go. I've got your back. *Always*."

Charlie was pleased he had come out to her. It didn't even matter why; she was just grateful that he had come to his senses. "Fight or die, right, Dad?"

"So you do remember what I taught you?" Kyler turned to Schafer. "Right then. Let's go pay Attwood a visit. Let's turn this fucking road red."

CHAPTER 8

The streets of Peterborough were unnervingly silent as the disparate group made their way through them. Charlie thought she heard dogs barking somewhere in the distance and the occasional groan of a zombie, but it was strangely beautiful in a way. When she had been in her room and looking out on the zombies at the gate she had seen how horrible it was out there and assumed the town was full of them. Yet the quiet streets were as charming as they were dangerous. She hadn't seen Peterborough like this for a long time. She hadn't seen the town itself for months, not since they had barricaded themselves in at home, and as they crossed an intersection she wondered if anyone else had made it out.

"Mind out for that truck," said Kyler.

"I got it." Charlie passed the abandoned truck cautiously, avoiding its closed doors for fear of alerting anything to her presence. The windows were smeared with dirt and as she looked up at the mirrors she thought she saw blood splattered on the passenger seat. She moved on quickly.

"You doing okay?" she asked Rilla.

"Yeah, I just want to get there. I don't like being out in the open like this."

They passed in front of a grocery store and Charlie paused by a baby stroller. It had a large brown hood with penguins on the side and a teddy bear tied to the handle with a red ribbon. The stroller was jammed up against a low brick wall and one of the wheels was missing. It felt surreal to see it abandoned like that and Charlie felt like she had to make sure there was no baby inside. There was no way a baby could still be alive, but Charlie was drawn to the stroller and wanted to make sure, to know for certain they weren't leaving a child behind.

"Don't," said Rilla, putting an arm over Charlie's.

"I just thought, you know, there might be a chance. . . " Charlie stared at the stroller and reached a hand out to it. As she wrapped her fingers around the handle she thought she heard a faint gurgle from inside. She looked further under the hood and saw a pile of blankets and a cream cardigan stained with blood. Something moved underneath the pile of blankets.

"Just don't." Rilla shook her head and pulled on Charlie's arm. "Let's catch up with the others."

"Yeah. Yeah, of course."

"It's gone," said Rilla quietly. "Whoever she or he was, they're gone. They're in a better place now."

"I guess," said Charlie, mourning the child she never met, and never would.

"And so will *we* be soon. Come on. We shouldn't let ourselves lag behind." Rilla took Charlie between two parked cars. It looked as if they were taking a short cut through a parking lot. There was a huge shopping mall to the east, and her father had weaved a path between the vehicles to a side road on the other side of the parking lot. "I don't think it's too far from here."

"I'm glad we didn't come across that group of zombies your father told us about. I don't think I could handle it. It's weird just being near the shops and houses. I keep thinking we're being watched, you know? It's so quiet that it feels like I'm trespassing or something."

"This place is not nice. It's not how it used to be. But my father knows where he's taking us. We'll be fine."

The tall glass doors to the shopping mall were open and a zombie ran out into the lot. A second followed it, and then half a dozen more followed behind. Most were women, but some were children. Some ran, some walked, and some just seemed to lope lazily along, but one thing united them: all were dead. Charlie opened her mouth to scream but Rilla slapped a hand over her mouth.

"No. Be quiet." Rilla shoved Charlie roughly against a blue transit van. She poked her head around the rear of the van. "Shit, they saw us. They're heading this way."

Charlie's palms felt sweaty. "All I've got is this," said Charlie holding up the crowbar. She wanted to run back home, but knew that it wasn't a real option. "What do we do?"

"My father is coming. He saw them too. We stand a better chance with the others." Rilla kept one arm across Charlie's chest, as if she could protect her by just holding her away from the zombies.

Charlie pressed her back against the side of the van and closed her eyes. *They* were coming. The dead were coming. She could hear them; hear their footsteps, their moaning and their deathly march across the parking lot. Yet as she concentrated on listening she heard the others. She heard her father calling for her. She heard people running. Rilla was right. They would be better off fighting as a group. Charlie was terrified and yet Rilla was there. She hadn't run or left her. Rilla had stayed and given her some hope.

"Dad?" As the first zombie came running toward them, Charlie thought momentarily that Kyler had reached them first. The man wore a loose-fitting shirt and was of a heavy build, like her father. Unlike Kyler, though, his lower jaw was missing and his rubbery tongue hung uselessly over his bleeding gums. His pale eyes looked directly at Charlie and she raised the crowbar in her hands that she had last used when entering Mr. Riley's house.

"I can't. . . I can't. . . " Charlie froze as the dead man lumbered toward her.

Rilla swung the brass base of the lamp and hit the approaching zombie in the face, dismantling the rest of its jaw. Teeth scattered around the tarmac and the zombie smacked into the side of the van as Rilla pushed Charlie out of the way.

"Quick, get to the others," shouted Rilla as she swung the lamp at the man's head. He was already getting to his feet and clawing at the side of the van.

Charlie turned around and saw a woman meandering toward her, long strands of golden hair swaying in front of her face, her murky eyes appearing from behind the curtain of hair only intermittently, her teeth bared and clacking together. Charlie stepped back, afraid of the woman, and lifted the crowbar again. She had to do it. She had to defend herself and Rilla. But it wasn't what she had expected. These people, these shoppers, were real and present. Unlike the baby she hadn't seen, these people were in her face and all too real.

As the dead woman reached out a hand to grab Charlie a hammer struck the woman on the side of the head, and the zombie crumpled to the ground.

"Charlie, get out of here," yelled her father.

Charlie watched as Kyler grasped the hammer and sunk it into the back of the zombie's head. He smashed its skull open until it stopped moving and then whirled around as another zombie appeared from behind the van. A girl, no more than six or seven, stumbled straight for Kyler. The dead girl wore a pretty light blue dress adorned with large white spots. There was a hole in her stomach and a gaping wound in her neck. Charlie saw her father smash the girl's head open with the hammer and she took another step back. Blood flew around everywhere and as Charlie turned to run the other way she found Magda thrusting a screwdriver through the temple of another zombie. A tall, thin girl, no older than Charlie herself had her arms around Magda, but as the screwdriver penetrated her brain the zombie let go and fell to the ground.

"Come, quick," ordered Schafer. He and Jeremy had opened up a pathway through the cars to the far side of the lot. Magda was already running through it toward Lyn and Victoria who were waiting safely in the distance. Charlie saw Rilla follow her mother and then she heard footsteps behind her.

"Dad, thank God, come on, Schafer's got a way through." Charlie spun around to take her father's hand and found a small boy grasping it. His black eyes looked up at her and his grin revealed a row of rotten yellow teeth. His cold fingers intertwined with hers and Charlie only had a moment to take in that he was wearing a superhero costume with a massive tear in one side. There was a raw gaping hole in the side of the boy's neck and his hand was cold to the touch.

Charlie screamed as the boy lunged forward and wrapped both small hands around her wrist. His teeth neared her skin and she knew that if he succeeded in biting her then she was as good as dead. In a second she raised the crowbar and smashed it across the boy's face. His cheekbone cracked as the boy's head whipped back and the crowbar gouged out a large chunk of his forehead. The boy's hands slipped off her and Charlie swung again, bringing the crowbar down on the boys' fragile head. The skull imploded with a popping noise and Charlie staggered back in shock. The boy fell to his knees and raised his hands to his face. Blood and brains spilt from the top of his shattered head over his face and his black eyes seemed to look at her accusingly, as if she was to blame for his death.

A moment later and Charlie saw Kyler crack his hammer around the boy's face, sending the zombie into oblivion.

"Come on, Charlie, take my hand." Kyler grabbed Charlie and pushed her away, toward the others. "You have to fight. You *have* to," he said as they ran together through the parking lot.

When they reached the far side Charlie glanced back. More zombies were spilling out of the mall and spreading throughout the parking lot. They had been drawn out, away from hunting for bargains and into the hunt for man.

Schafer helped Charlie over a wooden fence and then she found herself back with Rilla.

"Are you okay?"

Charlie looked at Rilla feeling sick. "I think so." Charlie rubbed her wrist where the boy had grabbed it. "Yeah, I am. I'm okay."

"Great." Rilla put an arm around Charlie's shoulder.

"Hurry," said Schafer. "We need to hurry. If we can get around the other side of that building we're almost there." He pointed to an apartment block opposite where they were standing. "They won't be able to see us and if we can stop those zombies following us to Attwood's then we might just have a shot at making this work."

"You'd better be right," said Jeremy, the frustration evident in his tone.

As one they all followed Schafer, pleased to be leaving the mall behind. Charlie kept glancing over her shoulder, worried that they were being followed, but it seemed to have worked. Once they were on the other side of the apartment block she lost sight of the zombies. At one point her father and Schafer worked together to kill a couple of zombies who had wandered out from one of the many quiet shops. At an intersection Kyler took out another zombie, one crack over the head with his hammer doing the trick. After the horrors of the mall they were pleased to encounter fewer zombies and their path became clearer the further they got away from the center of Peterborough.

As they reached the edge of town, Charlie noticed the house on the hill and forgot about the dead boy who had almost killed her. With Rilla beside her she felt better and she knew Kyler was watching out for her too. She had frozen back there but as she looked at Attwood's house she began to feel better. The end was in sight. Their destination was dark, the house obscured by trees, but she knew Attwood was there. He would let them in despite what Kyler thought. When it came down to it, having money didn't necessarily mean you were an asshole. Nor did not having it mean you were scum. She had read about Attwood's generosity and philanthropy. He had donated a lot to the area over time, and she saw no reason why he wouldn't help them.

Schafer lead them down a small tree-lined road. They passed a couple of abandoned cars and suddenly stopped. Schafer held up his hand, and they clustered around him.

"What is it? Trouble?" Jeremy looked but couldn't see anything. "Zombies?"

Schafer nodded slowly. "Ja. There, to the side of the road."

Charlie squinted and finally saw what Schafer had seen. The small rise where Attwood lived wasn't completely clear of zombies, but it looked manageable after what they had just been through. They were close to the entrance to the house, and she could see the small bridge that took them to the only way in. There was a tall metal fence with barbed wire at the top and surveillance cameras perched at regular intervals along it, although she didn't expect they still worked. Under the bridge ran a small creek, a moat, providing a natural barrier that made it even harder to climb the fence if anyone had the inclination. Thrashing about in the water were several zombies. Evidently over time they had fallen in and couldn't get out. The banks of the creek were slippery and muddy, and tall unattended weeds grew along it. The moat around the property was dark, the water almost black, and Charlie did not want to go falling in.

"You think it's okay?" Kyler ambled up alongside Schafer. "I think they're all stuck. I don't see any on the road."

"I think you're right. As long as we stay clear of the water we should be fine." Schafer turned to face the others. "Okay, listen up. Stay behind me, and don't leave the road. There are dead people in that ditch, and if you go in, you're not coming out. We need to get over that bridge, and then we're home free. You can see the outline of the annex they built to the garage there. There is a door in it which I'm hoping is open. If not, we just have to knock and hope they hear us. It might take a while. We may even have to wait for someone to find us, but as long as we're careful there's no reason to worry or panic. Those zombies can't get to us, and the road is clear. I'll lead the way."

"What if the door is locked? What if Attwood is asleep and some zombies do come along?" Jeremy asked. "I'm just being practical about this. We can't sit out here all night."

"Look up there through that ash tree," said Kyler. "To the left of the annex there's a small window in the house."

They all turned to look and saw the light on. It was faint, but it was on, and that meant somebody was probably awake.

"Maybe Attwood has a weak bladder, or maybe his girlfriend forgot to brush her teeth. All I know is someone is there." Kyler clutched his hammer firmly. "Let's not worry about problems until they present themselves. Have a little faith. They *will* let us in."

Charlie joined the procession directly behind Rilla. She thought she heard a dog whining, but whatever or wherever it was didn't matter and was soon drowned out by the zombies by her feet. Some clutched at the grass as they walked past, and some increased the splashing as they fought to get out, but none could reach them. Charlie saw one reach up for her, its arms stretched up to the sky as if in prayer. The figure still wore a cycle helmet and tight fitting Lycra. A black hole in the corpse's neck told Charlie how it had ended up the way it had, and she saw a glimmer of metal flash in the moonlight under the water. There was something circular and dark attached to it, and she figured it probably belonged to the cycle the man had been riding before being attacked and killed. That's how a lot of people had gone. They were going about their business when it happened—just out shopping or going to work. So many people had gone out and never returned home.

"Hey, you okay?" whispered Rilla.

"Yeah, I'm good," replied Charlie. "Thanks for looking out for me back there."

"It's okay. One day you might have to do the same for me."

"I hope not." Charlie almost smiled as she spoke with Rilla. Getting through Peterborough hadn't been easy and if Rilla hadn't helped her back at the mall, then she wouldn't be here now. Rilla was almost like a sister to her, and her family was nice too. It was better this way, better than if it had been just her and Kyler.

They kept walking over the bridge, and Charlie felt her heart beating faster. This was it. This was what she had been hoping for, dreaming of for so long now. Attwood simply had to hear them. She didn't know if she could wait for hours out there with the zombies splashing around. She could picture one of them managing to get out, climbing up, and slithering over the road in the darkness, on them before they even saw it coming. Charlie shivered. If there was any comfort to be had it was that her father was with her. They had a lot to talk about, but the main thing was that he hadn't left her. Although it was her leaving their home, he had been the one about to abandon her. She felt better knowing he was there. She was still angry with him, but at least they were together and would have plenty of time to go over things once they got inside. It felt like they had turned a corner.

Reaching the end of the bridge, Charlie stared up at the building blocking their way. Through the moonlight Charlie sensed it was a solid construction with both walls connected to the fencing that stretched around the border of the property. There was a small door to one side and an even smaller window above it. There was a roller door in the center that could be raised to let in cars or small trucks, though she doubted they would be lucky enough for it to be open now. Attwood wasn't stupid. He would have the place locked down tight. She watched as Schafer tried the handle in the center of the roller door. Nothing happened. There was a faint rattling as the metal jostled under his weight, but the door stayed shut. He moved to the side door under the window and tried the handle, pushing and pulling, yet it refused to budge even an inch.

"Should we try calling out for help?" asked Lyn. "Victoria's getting cold. She doesn't want to be out here."

"Yeah, hurry up, Schafer, I don't like this," said Jeremy. "I thought this was going to be simple."

Charlie watched as Victoria looked at her parents with disdain. Even in the darkness it seemed like Victoria was unhappy, yet it wasn't the cool night air or the presence of the zombies. Victoria looked at Rilla who looked back, and the two smiled. Charlie looked at her father for reassurance, but he was preoccupied in monitoring the road behind them.

Schafer rattled the door again, but it wouldn't open, and he let out a curse.

"Schafer, how long is this going to take?" asked Kyler. "There's movement in the field over there. I can't tell from here what it is, but I'd prefer not to find out."

"I'm not sure," said Schafer. "I think—"

"Jesus, look at that thing." Jeremy pointed at the bridge behind them.

A woman was crawling up the side of the creek using the tall grass to haul her body out of the water. The dead woman had no legs, and her naked torso had been ripped up and carved open. Her head hung so low down between her shoulders that her neck must be broken and Charlie wondered how she managed to know where to go. Did they use sound or smell to find their way around? The woman slipped back a few feet when a clump of grass came free from the loose dirt holding it in, but that did not deter her. The corpse resumed its quest to escape the creek, and Charlie noticed its body was covered in mud and slime. There was a faint smell of sulfur, but mostly it just smelt like shit. It smelt like the whole creek was full of it, and Charlie tugged on her father's sleeve.

"Dad? Dad, what should we do?" It was partly a rhetorical question. Charlie knew exactly what had to be done, but didn't want to admit it. She also knew that her father would take care of it, and by asking him she was letting him take responsibility for it, just as he had done with the bird.

Kyler waited a moment until the dead body had found the lip of the bank, and then he smashed it over the head with his hammer. It took three strikes before the back of the woman's head caved in and she stopped moving.

"Right, Schafer, decision time," Kyler said, returning to Charlie's side. He put an arm around his daughter as he wiped the bloody hammer on his leg. "What now?"

Schafer looked at Magda and Rilla. "Okay, well I guess it isn't going to be as easy as we thought. I guess it was too much to ask for the door to be unlocked. Here's what we need to do. I'll go—"

Suddenly a powerful, bright, white light from above the annex illuminated the bridge. It was so strong that it blinded them all. Their eyes had grown accustomed to the dim moonlight, and it took a moment to adjust. The whole area around them was bathed in light and Charlie saw more clearly the zombies thrashing around in the moat. She looked across at the field where her father had indicated earlier that he had seen movement, and she saw a black horse bolt. Half a dozen zombies were in the field with it, and with the horse galloping away they had seen the light flick on. Now they were heading towards the bridge, and Charlie knew they had to get the door open soon or face a fight with them.

"What is this, Schafer?" asked Kyler as he rubbed his eyes. "Did we trip something?"

"There could be a motion sensor up there. Perhaps me trying the door set off a security system."

"Well, that's great, but what are we going to do now?" Jeremy looked at Rilla. "You. You wanted to come here. You said you'd seen lights at night, so there must be someone in there. What do you know about this place?"

"As much as you, Jeremy."

Charlie saw that Rilla was looking nervously over the edge of the bridge. From the groaning noises coming from beneath it, there had to be a few zombies trying to reach up.

"Look, if the security light still works then they have power. They might—"

"Hey, let us in," shouted Jeremy. He looked up at the roof of the annex scanning for a camera or a sign that somebody maybe watching them. "Attwood, you hear me? Let us in right now!"

"Look, just be quiet a moment and wait," said Schafer. "We can figure this out, but if you go shouting your mouth off you're going to drag a thousand zombies here."

"My husband is trying to *do* something about this fucked up situation that you got us into," said Lyn firmly.

Victoria pulled her hand free of her mother's, not that Lyn seemed to notice. Charlie watched as the girl grabbed Rilla's hand. They obviously shared a bond like sisters even though there was a large age gap between them. Rilla caught Charlie watching and smiled at her.

"It'll be okay," mouthed Rilla silently.

Charlie suddenly felt like a small piece of a jigsaw. The people around her all had their own motivations and relationships; they had a history together that wasn't as simple as she had first thought. She wasn't sure how she and her father were going to fit in with it all, but it had to work. They simply had to make it work. Charlie knew they were running out of time. The figures in the field were getting closer, and the light that shone over them all would make them stand out for miles. She saw Schafer getting angry as Jeremy continued shouting.

"Attwood, you asshole," shouted Jeremy, ignoring Schafer. "Open the door!"

"Jeremy, calm down."

As Schafer and Jeremy started arguing, and Lyn chipped in with barbed comments about how Schafer was going to get them all killed, Charlie heard a click. It came from the garage, and then the side door slowly creaked open. The door that had been so clearly locked when Schafer had tried to open it was now ajar.

"Dad?" Charlie pointed to the door. "Dad, look."

Kyler actually let a half a smile spread over his face. "All right, ladies, cut it out." He pushed his way through to the door and pulled it open. "Seems Attwood heard you."

"I knew it," said Jeremy. "That rich asshole was just playing with us. He's probably been watching us the whole time. Come on, Lyn, let's get inside. Thank God I started shouting at him and made him listen. You can't treat people like that and just leave them to die. You can't do that anymore."

Schafer tugged on his beard and frowned. "If he was watching us the whole time, then it wasn't your shouting like a fool that got us in then, was it?"

Kyler nodded for Charlie to follow him, and he stepped through the doorway into darkness.

One by one they stepped through the doorway, and Charlie watched them all disappear until it was only Rilla left.

"You know he's not always this bad," said Rilla. "Jeremy, I mean. He's a dick, but he can be okay. He saved our lives a long time ago. You don't need to worry about him."

It was as if Rilla had read Charlie's mind. She was more concerned about Jeremy right then than facing Attwood.

"Where are you from, Rilla?" asked Charlie. "Your accent. You were on vacation, right?"

"Yeah. Some holiday it turned out to be. We're from Germany. I'm sure we'll go home one day. I think so anyway. Maybe you can visit me." Rilla crossed the threshold to the annex. "Come on. Let's see what this Attwood is really like. I've never met a millionaire."

Charlie followed Rilla into the cold building and found everyone standing in the center of the room. A single bulb hung from a tall ceiling which gave them little light. There wasn't enough energy coming from it to penetrate the gloom, and Charlie couldn't see the walls on either side of the building, which made her feel uncomfortable. The ground was solid concrete like the garage at home but was stained and filthy. There was a bad smell to the room as well, almost as if the room had been used as a toilet. She assumed it must be because of the building's proximity to the creek. With so many decomposing bodies in it then it made sense that the smell would find its way in here.

"Attwood, turn the damn lights on. We can't see anything in here," said Jeremy.

"Do you think you could just hold your tongue for a minute," said Kyler. "I don't think we're in any position to start making demands. We got this far. If he wasn't going to help then he wouldn't have opened the door, would he? So chill out."

Charlie smirked as Jeremy eyeballed her father. She knew from experience that doing that would get him nowhere. Kyler stared back until Jeremy backed down.

"You think he's watching us now?" asked Rilla, quietly.

"I guess so." Charlie saw Victoria come up to Rilla's side again. "Maybe he's got a camera up there somewhere. Probably how he keeps an eye on the door and knew to open up for us."

"This is your party," said Kyler to Schafer. "You do the talking."

"Hello, Mr. Attwood," said Schafer, loudly, his voice echoing around the annex. "Thank you for letting us in. We're just looking for help and a place to stay. You can see we're not armed. Can we talk?"

They waited patiently, but there was no reply. After a few seconds of silence there was a clicking noise, and Charlie whirled around to see that the side door had closed on them.

"Must have a self-closing mechanism," said Rilla.

"Uh-huh." Charlie heard a faint whining sound but couldn't quite place it. It sounded like an animal, but with the zombies out in the creek, it could easily be one of them. She dismissed it and took Rilla's hand.

The three girls stood in a line waiting for someone to do something. There was still a nervous tension in the air. Even with the door closed behind them and the zombies behind the wall, they couldn't feel completely safe until they knew that Attwood wasn't just going to throw them back outside.

"Can we talk, please?" asked Schafer again. He was prepared to wait as long as it took. They were relatively safe in the over-sized garage, and diplomacy was now the name of the game. Making threats or shouting like Jeremy could potentially scare Attwood off. They were guests now and needed to respect the fact that they were asking a lot of a complete stranger.

"Can we—"

Another light flickered on high above them revealing a man stood on an upper gantry. There was no obvious way up there as the light was only enough to see the man's face and a few feet around him. The man wore a black hooded jacket, and the lower half of his face was covered in a thick black beard. When he finally spoke he had a much younger sounding voice than his face suggested.

"Good evening." The man smiled as he looked down at them all. "How are we all doing this fine night?"

"Attwood, stop messing around and let us in." Jeremy spoke with anger in his voice. "My daughter is only ten. Let us in, and we can talk inside."

"Damn it, Jeremy, just shut up." Schafer wanted to punch Jeremy, but he knew he had to keep himself calm. He shouted up to the man on the gantry. "Attwood, I'm sorry, we don't mean to be rude. It's been a long journey here, and we're all stressed out. You can imagine, right? We don't mean any trouble."

"Of course, I understand completely. I have to apologize about all the cloak and dagger stuff, but you can imagine how many people have come here trying to take this place from me. I have to be very careful about who I let in."

"Absolutely," replied Schafer. He turned to Magda. "You see, my love? It's going to be all right."

"Okay, let's do this. I don't know you, and you don't know me, so we're going to have to start by trusting one another. This is my place, and I have certain rules that make sure it stays that way."

"But you're going to let us in, right?" asked Jeremy. "My wife has been through a lot. I just want—"

"Who are you?"

"Jeremy. I'd feel a lot more comfortable if you'd just let us in, Attwood."

"Jeremy? If you know anything about me, you'll know that I am a very generous man. I take it you know all about me? I don't seem to recognize any of you though."

"We all know of you, Mr. Attwood," said Schafer. "Obviously, we haven't met you before, but we are so grateful for your kindness. I appreciate it's dangerous to just open the door to anyone, so tell us what you want, and we'll do it."

"Well now, that's just what I wanted to hear."

"Attwood?"

"Yes, Jeremy?"

"Can you stop the bullshit and just open the door?"

"Okay, okay, I'm sorry. Look, do me a favor and toss your weapons over in front of you. I can see you don't have much, but I can't in good faith let eight armed people in just like that."

"Do it," said Schafer as he saw Jeremy tuck his knife into his belt. "Don't be an idiot, and just do it."

Reluctantly Jeremy tossed his knife away as the others did the same.

"Thank you. One of my associates will just clear those up for you."

Charlie watched as a door opened up ahead of them, and a man came through it carrying a gun and a sack. He wore a black jacket similar to Attwood's and a beanie pulled down low over his forehead. Through the gloom she saw a white goatee and marks on his hands, like tattoos or scars. The man didn't speak or acknowledge them at all, but simply scooped up the meagre pile of weapons into the sack, and then went back out the same door as he had entered through. It closed softly behind him.

"So we can go now? That the way?" Jeremy made to go to the door, but Schafer held him back.

"Take your time, Jeremy. Attwood's on our side. Don't rush this, and we'll be fine," said Schafer.

"Wonderful. Well, I guess we can get things settled now. Sorry about the welcome. I know this doesn't look much, but I can assure you the house is amazing. I've got so much food and fresh water I hardly know what to do with it all. The walls extend all around the property, so you'll be quite safe here."

Schafer hugged Magda and looked into her eyes. "You see? We did it. We're going to be fine."

Jeremy grinned as he took his wife's hand. "You were right, Schafer. I'm just pleased this is all over."

Charlie looked at them all smiling and felt relieved. It was amazing to think that Attwood had been here the whole time. They could have come here months ago and saved themselves a lot of heartache. Maybe now they could get back to being a family again. Her father had suffered and struggled when it was just the two of them, and this was a chance to start afresh. Charlie was so glad she had decided to come. It was over. They could actually live here without having to worry about where their next meal was coming from or if the dead would break in at night. This was going to be paradise compared to what they were used to.

"Vicky, come here, darling," said Lyn, beaming. "It's all right, Vicky, Mr. Attwood is going to help us. It's all okay."

Charlie watched as Victoria nervously approached her parents. "You took good care of her," Charlie said to Rilla. "I can see she trusts you perhaps more than anyone else."

"She's a great kid, really. Usually she's very bubbly and fun. I guess today's been hard on her. You'll see the best of her tomorrow when she relaxes and gets to know you."

Rilla smiled as she heard her mother laughing. Schafer held her in a bear-hug and was kissing her on the side of the head.

"I guess it's been a long time since you saw your parents like that?" asked Charlie.

"Yeah," replied Rilla. "A long time." Rilla's smile made Charlie feel safe. There was something natural and warm to the girl. She had no pretenses or affectations.

"It'll be good to get to know all of you," said Charlie. "I can see—"

The door in front of them automatically opened revealing the house beyond. It was the same door the man had come through earlier to take their weapons, and he was now stood in it again blocking their exit.

"Charlie," said Kyler approaching her. "Tug your cap down, quickly."

"Why?" Charlie smiled at her father. She still wore the blue and green fishing cap, and on top of the baggy sweatshirt she wore, she felt distinctly unfeminine next to Rilla. Charlie reached up to take it off. "I thought I'd get rid of it actually, it kind of makes my head itch. Rilla, could—"

Kyler yanked it down hard on Charlie's head, hiding her short blonde hair.

"What did you do that for?" asked Charlie.

Above them, Attwood smiled and reached out to a switch on the wall behind him.

"Don't say a fucking word. If they ask, then you're my son," said Kyler quickly and quietly as light flooded the room.

"Dad?" Charlie didn't have time to take in her surroundings. Her father was standing right in front of her, and when he put his hand on her arm, she could feel him shaking.

Kyler leant in closer and whispered in Charlie's ear. "That's *not* Attwood."

CHAPTER 9

As Charlie's eyes got used to the brilliant light in the room, she heard voices talking but paid no attention to what was being said. After the gloom of the roads and only moonlight to see by, the dazzling white light that illuminated the annex made it difficult to see clearly. She stared at her shoes with one hand on Rilla's shoulder. Squinting through her reluctant tears, she noticed the stains on the concrete. There was an odd odor to the room, something mixed in with the smell of shit that reminded her of hospitals. As she stared at the floor, she realized it was some kind of bleach, as if the floor had been scrubbed with it to remove those stains.

She wiped the tears from her eyes and looked to her right. The wall was painted a dark green, almost black, and had those same stains on it. As she looked around the room, she noticed that there were scratches on the wall, too, deep cuts that ran through the paint into the fabric of the metal. They were all around her and more by the two doors. She looked back from where they had entered the annex and saw a small red light on a panel above the door indicating that it was locked electronically. She also noticed that there was no door handle, and the frame of the door was silver copper overlaid in more scratches. High above the door and well out of reach was the upper gantry, a single walkway that stretched around all four walls of the room but with no way down. There was a door behind the man who had said he was Attwood and a green light above his head.

"Charlie, what are they?"

Charlie looked at where Rilla pointed, noticing the four small panels on the wall closest to them. Above each one was another small red light.

"I don't know, Rilla." Charlie felt all of the fear and terror back in an instant. This wasn't right. Suddenly she felt trapped. There was no way out. If Kyler was right about Attwood, then they had just stumbled into a trap.

"Listen, Attwood, I don't know what kind of stupid game you're playing, but I'm not laughing," said Jeremy. "I demand you let us in. This place stinks, and I'm not going to stand around here all night while my wife and daughter catch some disease. Get your man out of the way."

Attwood leant over the gantry and called out. "Conan, you want to move aside, and let these folk in?"

The man with the white goatee remained in the door ahead of them and shook his head slowly. He raised a gun and pointed it at the group, singling out nobody in particular.

"Now hold on Attwood, there's no need for any of this," said Schafer. He held both hands out to indicate he was unarmed and looked up. "Please. We came to you with good intentions. We don't have any weapons, just a little food and water. All we ask for is a little kindness. Surely, with everything that's happening on the other side of that wall, you can understand why we needed to come here? Surely you can understand what we're doing here? We're not like them. We're not infected; we just need a decent place to spend the night in safety without worrying about the war going on around us."

"Save your breath," said Kyler. "This guy's not listening."

"Attwood, you let us in *right now*!" shouted Jeremy angrily.

"Hush, hush, it's late. You don't want to go waking the whole neighborhood, do you? Those people you just passed on your way here are not too friendly. In fact, they're a little snappy." The man on the gantry clacked his teeth together. "No? Nobody? Tough crowd." He cast his eyes around the group. "Okay, so there's just the six of you? You're the largest group we've had stop by in quite a while. What do you think, Conan, gotta be a few months?"

Conan said nothing and kept his gun focused on them.

"Forgive him," said the man on the gantry, "he doesn't say much. The big man's just a pussycat really. Aren't you, Conan?"

Again the man said nothing.

Schafer looked at Magda and felt like he had betrayed her. All her hope and happiness had evaporated, replaced with abject fear.

"Look, Attwood," Schafer said, "we can figure this out. Whatever it is you want, we'll do it. We can help you."

"You help me? Thanks, but no thanks. I've got everything I need right here. That's why you've come crawling to me asking for *my* help, right? Look, let's start over. It was interesting to begin with, but the truth is it's late and I'm tired. So, how about a few introductions? Mr. Attwood is otherwise engaged right now, so—"

"Is he even here?" asked Kyler. "I bet Attwood's not even at home."

"Oh, he's here. But like I said, he can't come to the door, so you're left with me."

"And you are?" Kyler was pleased Jemma wasn't here with him. He had a bad feeling about this. He flexed his fingers ready for a fight. If it came to it, he would rush Conan and risk being shot rather than wait here to die.

"Well, my name isn't really important, but you can call me Butcher." The man on the gantry smiled and then stifled a yawn.

"Well, Butcher, how about we continue this conversation inside? Like my friend said, we'll do whatever it is you need. It's late, and everyone is tired. There's no need for any... trouble." Kyler didn't think it would be that easy to gain access to Attwood's, but he had to try for Charlie's sake.

"Oh, you'll do what I need, I know that," said Butcher. He drew a gun silently from his jacket and pointed it down at Kyler. "Now, let's start this again. Names. Go."

"Kyler."

"Schafer. This is my wife, Magda."

Jeremy was increasingly anxious and jittery. He kept looking at the gun pointed at them. "Look, Butcher, I don't see—"

"*Names!*" Butcher's scream echoed around the annex shocking them all.

"Just tell him," said Schafer quietly. "It'll be okay."

"Jeremy. My name is Jeremy. My wife is Lyn. And my daughter, Victoria," Jeremy said softly.

"And you two at the back? Don't think I can't see you there. Names?" asked Butcher, straightening up and reaching for a panel of controls in front of him.

"Rilla. And you can kiss my ass."

"Charming. And you?" asked Butcher, pointing at Charlie.

"That's my son, Charlie," said Kyler quickly. "Since we lost his mother, he doesn't say a lot. He's what you would call simple."

"Nice." Butcher sighed. "Okay, let's get this over with. If you're half as tired as I am, then you'll want to do this as fast as you can. So you, Rilla, the one with the potty mouth, go on over to Conan."

"No way," said Rilla firmly. "I'm not going in there on my own. What about my family? My friends? You're letting us all in, right? You have no idea what we've been through, how far we've come, and what we've had to cross to get here. I'm not giving it all up now."

"Darling, I don't have time for your sob stories. I only need people I can use. So hurry the fuck up and get over to Conan, please? He'll take you inside. No messing about, please. My friend has a Desert Eagle semi-automatic aimed at you, so I encourage you to do what I say. Get over to Conan, *now,* and don't fuck with him."

Rilla folded her arms. She knew what kind of man Butcher was. He was interested in her because she was young and pretty. She had learned about that kind of man a while ago and wasn't about to become some piece of meat passed between him and his friends. "Fuck that. We all go, or we all stay."

"Butcher, this is insane." Jeremy strode forward toward the open door ahead of them. Attwood's house lay just beyond it. "I don't care what you think you're doing, but you tell your buddy Conan to let us by this second. I've had enough of listening to your shit. I demand that you let us go and speak to Attwood. This is his place, not yours. My daughter is ten. Ten! How dare you treat us like this? I'm going to—"

The sound of the gunshot bounced around the annex like thunder, and Charlie watched as Jeremy turned around to face his family. The left side of his head was gone, and his jaw hung open in surprise. A flap of skin draped loosely around his chin, and a chunk of brain plopped out onto his shoulder. Warm red blood flowed from his head and streamed down his neck. Charlie heard Lyn scream as Jeremy's lifeless body collapsed to the ground. Then she saw her father grab Schafer's arm and hold him back. As the blood spewed from Jeremy's shattered skull, Charlie noticed how it formed a large pool around his head. It was going to be just another stain in this dirty, horrible place. Then she knew: how many times had they done this before? How many times had someone come to them for help only to be turned away or killed?

She caught her father's eye and tugged her cap down tight. She hadn't understood why he had lied about who she was, about why he had said she was his son and that she was simple, yet as she saw Victoria cry and the disbelief in Lyn's eyes, she understood. He was protecting her. Even now, he was doing what he could to protect her.

"Oh fuck," said Rilla gently. "Oh fuck, oh fuck, oh fuck."

Charlie shivered.

"Right, let's just try this again, shall we?" The impatience in Butcher's voice was evident. "You. Rilla. Step forward. Trust me. You really don't want to piss off Conan. You can see how he acts when someone doesn't listen."

Rilla slowly pushed her way through to the front of the group and stood beside Jeremy's body. She glanced down and saw a lifeless eye stare back at her blankly. At least he wouldn't be returning. Rilla knew that she had no choice, yet couldn't help but think that this might be the last time she saw her parents alive.

"No, Rilla, don't," said Schafer. "You can't go."

"You heard him, Dad. I have to."

Rilla, listening to her mother crying, crossed the floor and reached Conan. She turned around to look at them again, to see if she could convince Butcher to let the others in, when Conan pushed the gun between her shoulder blades. His warm breath tickled her ear when he spoke.

"The girl too."

Rilla looked at Charlie, confused. But Kyler had told them she was his son. It was a good move considering the circumstances, and may just have saved Charlie's life, so how did Conan know? How could he tell that underneath the fishing cap and baggy sweatshirt she was female? There was no way from back here that he could know. Rilla didn't want to be on her own, but she was afraid of what would happen to them if she let them take them both. Charlie stood a better chance with her father.

"Look, Mr. Conan, I don't think—"

Conan pressed the gun between her shoulder blades and then raised it up to the back of her neck.

"Don't think. Just do it. The little girl. Victoria?"

Rilla realized he hadn't meant Charlie after all, but then stopped herself from going to get Victoria. What could they possibly want with her? What could they need with a young girl? It hit Rilla then exactly what they could do to her.

"No way, I'm not letting you take her too. You just killed her father, and now you want to drag her into this sorry mess?"

Conan pushed Rilla forward, and she fell to the ground. Her hands felt the cold hard concrete and slipped into the blood pouring from Jeremy's dead body. Shaking, Rilla scrambled desperately to her feet.

Conan looked at her blankly and pointed the gun at her head. "Five. Four. Three. Two—"

"Okay, okay!" Rilla wiped her hands on her legs and turned to Lyn. "I'm sorry. I'll take care of her."

"One."

Rilla heard Conan behind her and raced forward. She grabbed Victoria's hand and pulled her away from her mother. The girl tried to hold onto her mother's leg, but Rilla couldn't afford to let her get away, and she held Victoria in a bear-like hug.

"I'm sorry, honey, I'm sorry," said Rilla as she marched back to Conan with Victoria struggling in her arms.

"Butcher, stop this. You're not going to achieve anything by splitting us up," said Schafer. "Let my daughter go. The girls have nothing to offer you. I'm strong. Kyler too. We can help you build this place, make it stronger. Think about it."

There was silence, aside from Magda and Lyn crying, and Schafer wondered if Butcher was thinking it over. There had to be something else, something he could do to make this right. Butcher and Conan were insane. If they kicked Schafer and the rest of the group back outside, then he would do anything to get back in to rescue his daughter. Butcher had to know that. Butcher surely would know that a father would do anything to protect his children.

"Don't you have a child?" asked Schafer. "You know I love my daughter. Rilla is my only child. I would do anything for her, and I can't let you hurt her. You *know* I can't. You understand that I'm offering to do anything right now, but if you hurt her or Victoria, then I'll kill you. You kick us out now, and I'm going to come back for her."

"Yeah, I get that." Butcher sniffed. His silence hadn't been because he was thinking about Schafer's offer, but because he was distracted. "Sorry, I was just figuring out the controls here. It's been a while since I had to do this. Anyway, you said something about coming back for her?"

"Jesus, Butcher, what do you think is happening here? You can't send us back out there, not to face *them*."

Butcher peered over the gantry. "Conan, if you've got them, then take them both back up to the house, and close the door behind you. You can come back later to clean up. Get them to Verity. If the older one gives you any shit—just shoot her."

"No!" Schafer pleaded, but as Conan shoved Rilla and Victoria through the door, it closed behind him, and the light above it turned red. There was no time for goodbyes, no time to promise her that he would come back for her, and no time to do anything but watch her leave.

Lyn sank to her knees and reached out for Jeremy. She put a hand on his leg and then collapsed over him, sobbing. Kyler glanced at Charlie who had been watching in horror the whole time.

"Whatever happens, stay behind me."

Charlie nodded. She felt like this couldn't be real; that she was dreaming this. Rilla and Victoria were inside, but were they safe? What were those two men going to do with them? Jeremy was dead, and now she was stuck in this foul room with just her father, Schafer, Magda, and Lyn. It didn't make sense.

"You fucking animal," snarled Schafer. He pointed his arm up to Butcher. "Fine. Send us back out onto the streets and see what happens. You think I'm going to forget about Rilla—about *you*? You're making a mistake. We could've done so much together. This place you have is a haven. The corpses out there are killers, but there's something natural about what they do. They hunt and they kill, but without feeling. You have a choice, and you act like this? You're just plain fucking evil."

"You done? Great." Butcher hit the control panel, and a whirring noise started off to the side of them behind the wall.

Charlie turned to the exit but the light above the door was still red. The machinery making the noise was coming from the side of the annex and was hidden from view. What was he doing? What was Butcher playing at?

"You see, I'm not that stupid. Evil maybe, but not stupid." Butcher hit another button, and the lights switched off save for the lone bulb that swung high above them. It was the light that had first come on when they had entered the place. Being back in near darkness was unnerving. Charlie felt for her father's hand and took it, wrapping her fingers through his.

Ice cold fear hit Charlie. "Dad, what's happening? Daddy?"

Kyler spoke through gritted teeth. "Stay behind me. Just stay behind me." The chance of taking on Conan was gone. The opportunity to fight had never arisen, and now events were spiraling rapidly out of control.

"He's letting us go, right?" asked Charlie. "Are we going back home? What about Rilla?"

"I love you, Charlotte."

Even in the dim gloom Charlie could see the tears welling in her father's eyes, and that scared her more than anything. Even when her mother had died he hadn't broken down. The look in his eyes told her that this was serious.

Schafer barged past them suddenly and started pounding his fists on the exit. The door barely even moved in its frame despite the battering he gave it. He turned around, his face full of rage.

"Butcher. The door's not opening. Let me out of here, or I'm coming up to get you. I'll climb these fucking walls with my bare hands if I have to."

Butcher's laughter started out small and quiet before developing into a hysterical laugh that echoed around the room.

Schafer looked at Magda and it hit him. He had lost. He had been fooled into thinking he had a chance. They were at the point where they had reached the end, and the King was in sight. Attwood was the goal, and Schafer had forgotten about how people could manipulate and trick him into constantly moving forward. The game wasn't always played in black and white. Schafer felt so miserable at losing, knowing he had just lost everything: Rilla, Magda, and himself. Schafer licked his lips and then looked up at Butcher.

"You're not letting us go, are you?"

Butcher opened the door behind him and the whirring machinery suddenly stopped. A metallic crunching noise reached Charlie, and she realized the sound was coming from behind the wall to their left. There was another sound too. It was like a faint whining sound accompanied by scratching. Was it whatever had caused all those scratches on the floor and walls? What was behind those panels in the wall?

"Sorry I can't stay, but I've got a couple of new house guests to see too. Nice to meet you folk. I've got what we need now. You've got about two minutes. They're on a timer, so make the most of your time together. You five aren't going anywhere. You ain't nothin' but zombiekill. My Verity always said if you ain't good for nothing, then you ain't good for anything but feeding to the wolves." Butcher smiled maliciously and then disappeared through the door which closed shut behind him. The light flickered to red, and the door electronically locked as Butcher left.

"Checkmate." Schafer looked at Magda. The lone bulb shone directly above her, and he went to her. As he embraced his wife he saw Lyn still holding onto Jeremy's body. There was nothing she could do for him, yet she still clung to him. He was all she had now. Her daughter was gone, like Rilla. Schafer knew there was no way out of the room. He had been caught in a trap, and whatever happened next wasn't going to be nice. They had two minutes at most. What exactly did that mean? Were they to be kept prisoner here? Was somebody else coming to get them?

"Dad?" Charlie looked at the wall opposite them, and the four red lights turned green. Her father backed away keeping Charlie behind him as the panels began to swing forward. It was slow at first until the first one appeared. Finally, she understood. When the first one appeared Charlie knew what was going to happen and she grabbed her father, wrapping her arms around his thick body.

"Just stay behind me," said Kyler nervously. "Charlie, I need to tell you something. I don't blame you for what happened to your Mother. I was horrible to you, and I know things went bad for us, but-"

As the first panel swung open, the barking began. Another dog howled and then appeared from behind the second panel. Finally, a third and fourth appeared. All four dogs were ferocious and bared their teeth as they faced the five living people in the annex. Saliva dripped from the dogs' jaws, and their black fur was matted with excrement and blood. Some of the dogs had deep infected cuts on their bodies, and one appeared to have been deliberately blinded in one eye.

"Dad?" Charlie gripped her father's shoulder. "What happened to Mom was a horrible accident. I don't want—"

"It's okay," said Kyler. "Be quiet now. We'll talk later."

The single bulb above them was enough to see what was happening, though the corners of the rooms were still in dark shadows. Charlie knew it was impossible to hide from them. There was nothing left to do, no way out. The dogs were pitiful, horrible creatures who had long since lost any kind of attachment to man. They were feral animals with a thirst for blood and a hunger for meat. They only knew one thing now. Man was their enemy, and Butcher had them for good reason. It was a cowardly thing to do, but effective. He had left them to die and would probably be sleeping soundly by the time it was all over. It crossed Charlie's mind to try and placate them, but these dogs had been treated badly and had one thing on their minds. She wasn't sure exactly what breed they were although one was definitely a Rottweiler and the other three appeared to be Doberman's. Now that they were free of their cages they intended to feed, and Charlie's eyes widened in horror as they sprang forward.

The first dog leapt forward effortlessly and took Lyn's head in its jaws. Its teeth clamped around her face, ripping off an ear and digging through her cheeks into her soft flesh. Lyn screamed and grabbed the dog's neck as they rolled onto the floor, but the dog was unrelenting. It shook her head around and clawed at her until the screaming stopped and her arms went limp. An incredible amount of blood pooled around Lyn as the dog savaged her, ripping apart her face in seconds and reducing it to nothing but a bloody mask for her broken skull.

Instantly two more dogs raced forward and jumped up at Magda and Schafer. The sheer power of the dogs knocked Magda off her feet, and Charlie heard the crack of her skull as she hit the ground. She held her arms up to protect her head and the dog attacking her kept snapping at her, digging its teeth into her fleshy arms. Her hands were bitten, and Charlie saw several fingers break off to be gobbled up quickly by the dog. Schafer tried to get to his wife but had problems of his own. The dog attacking him was huge, and its shiny black coat shimmered in the dim light. It wrapped its jaws around his leg, and blood was pouring through his jeans as he beat on the dog's head.

"Dad?" Charlie's eyes were drawn to the fourth dog that was walking toward them. Its black eyes were locked on hers, and Kyler pushed Charlie behind him. Shivers of fear raced up and down Charlie's spine, and she felt her bladder weaken as the dog picked up its pace, going from a walk to a jog to a run in a split second.

As it neared them the dog jumped up and Kyler pushed his arms up defensively. Charlie screamed as the dog latched onto her father and dragged him down to the floor. They rolled around like wrestlers as the dog tried to get its sharp teeth into Kyler. Charlie saw Kyler smack the dog on the side of the head two or three times, but it had no effect. The dog kept twisting its head around, nipping at Kyler's hands and arms, and Charlie saw that her father was bleeding. She looked around frantically for a weapon, for anything they could use to defend themselves, but there was nothing. The room was completely bare.

With her heart pounding in her chest, she looked over at the others for help. Magda was dead. The dog that had attacked her was gorging itself on her as it thrust its jaws deep into her neck. The dog's face was covered in Magda's blood, and Charlie looked to Schafer for help.

"Schafer?" He was lying on his back holding a dog above him. His arms were trembling with the effort, and the dog's jaws were only inches away from taking off his face. The dog pawed at him and was gouging out a huge amount of flesh from Schafer's torso.

"Oh, God, what do I do? What...?"

Charlie noticed that the dog that had killed Lyn was padding toward her, its tongue hanging out as it panted. Blood dripped from its mouth and it ignored Schafer, Magda, and Kyler. Its aim was clear as it walked toward her. Charlie pressed herself up against the cold wall. She was afraid to take her eyes off the creature, but found herself drawn to it as if hypnotized. As it neared her it snarled and revealed a row of dirty sharp teeth. It barked rapidly and approached her cautiously.

"Dad?" Charlie glanced at her father who was still fighting off the dog. His fist was hammering the belly of the dog, but he was losing the fight.

Kyler stretched his head back and his eyes met his daughter's. He pushed the dog up and put an arm around its neck. Kyler's face was covered in sweat and drool from the dog, and blood splattered his neck. "I love—"

The dog whipped its neck free from Kyler's grasp and buried its teeth into his neck, ripping out his jugular, and destroying any last chance he had of telling his daughter what she meant to him.

Charlie screamed as she watched her father torn apart. He was the strongest man she had ever known. How could this be? There was a sharp jolting pain in her leg, and she felt blood trickle down her ankle through to her sock. The dog had bitten her shin and was jumping up to bury its teeth into her belly. Darting backwards, Charlie reeled from the attack. The snarling vicious dog snapped at her, and she grabbed the dog's head with her hands as they sank down to the ground. The dog stank and was more powerful than she had imagined. Its face hovered above her as she tried to hold it off, but it was too heavy. It scrambled to get to her and managed to rip open her cheek as its upper jaw sliced through her skin.

Charlie screamed in rage knowing that her father was dying right beside her. She ignored the blinding pain and jammed her thumb into the dog's right eye. It burst and sprayed warm blood over her as she screamed and pushed her thumb into the socket until she felt bone.

The dog howled and backed off leaving Charlie prostrate on the floor. She rolled over and saw her father next to her, his body twitching as another dog jumped up on top of him and ripped open his stomach.

"Dad, please." Charlie felt a weight on her legs and looked down to see a snarling dog climbing over her. This was not the one she had just blinded but another one. It had killed Magda and been drawn to Charlie; to fresh meat. Its black eyes poured hatred over her, and it peeled back its lips to reveal an array of broken yellow teeth all jagged and sharp, its gums lined with pieces of flesh and dark blood. It let out a series of barks that silenced the others and made the hairs on Charlie's neck stand up.

As it lunged, Charlie rolled to her side. The dog narrowly missed her, and as she attempted to get up, the blinded dog ran back at her, clamping its jaws around her thigh. Letting out a scream of rage she yanked the dog's head back, thrusting her fingers into its slavering jaws and pulled it off. The dog's teeth ripped through her flesh and tore her leg, but she managed to pull it off her, and she hit the dog with as much force as she could, aiming for its bloody eye.

The dog wheeled away but was instantly replaced by another one which charged at Charlie. She turned and ran, jumping over her dying father as she made for the door through which Rilla had left earlier. She banged on it furiously, but there was no way through and no one to answer her. She turned just in time to see the dog flying through the air. It hit her full on, its massive head barreling into her chest and winding her. Charlie fell and raised an arm which the dog gleefully sank its teeth into, shredding her left forearm as it pulled back and forth. It ignored her screams and dragged her away from the door like she was just a chew toy.

The dog relinquished its grip, and Charlie's bloody arm fell uselessly. She saw it look at her as it prepared to bite her again, and another dog in the background was coming up behind it. All her energy was gone, and Charlie couldn't do it anymore. Her father was gone. Her mother was gone. Everyone she knew and loved was dead.

"I'm sorry, Dad, I—"

The huge Doberman lunged, and then Charlie saw a boot kick it in the side of the head.

"Get up," said Schafer. "Quickly."

Charlie felt him lift her to her feet, and in the rush her head swam.

"What are you...?" Charlie looked at him, at his bloodied ripped body, and was surprised he was still standing. His grey beard was covered in blood, and his eyes were sad. His soul had been shattered, and he looked ready to drop to his knees and give up. "Schafer, I thought—"

"Go. I killed one, but I can't hold them off for long." Schafer thrust a piece of bone in her hand no more than seven inches long. It was covered in matted fur and dripping with blood. "It's from one of the dogs. Go, Charlie, go to the kennels and hide. Get away from here. Get Rilla for me. Please, make sure she is—"

The huge Doberman jumped on Schafer's back, and he howled in pain as the dog's claws dug into his skin. Charlie ran for the panels and pushed one back. The foul stench coming from the dark tunnel that lay ahead of her made her want to vomit, but the fear of staying drove her on. She looked back at Schafer as she silently lowered the swinging panel. All three dogs were on him, tearing and ripping his flesh with abandon as he succumbed to their power. Slowly, Charlie closed the panel. With blood dripping from her wounds, she crawled forward into darkness.

CHAPTER 10

Butcher threw back his hood and saw the expression on Rilla's face. He suppressed a smirk and remembered the first time when he'd met Conan face to face. There was a certain degree of bemusement then too. It seemed he just had that effect on people. "What did you expect, a monster?"

Rilla had anticipated someone looking at least a little more sinister than what was revealed from underneath Butcher's hood. The thick black hair that grew over his chin and neck also sprouted from the top of his head and flowed down to his shoulders. Yet his skin was pale and blotchy, as if it hadn't seen sunlight for several weeks. Butcher had small brown eyes that appeared to be sunken into his skull and a bony nose that had probably been broken a few times. Despite his appearance, he was young, much younger than Rilla had expected, and she guessed he could barely be thirty years old.

"I might be young, but I know that monsters come in all shapes and sizes," replied Rilla. "I wonder how you got to be like you are when you don't even look old enough to grow that beard."

Butcher smiled. Conan had delivered the two girls as ordered and left them with Verity, and Butcher had joined them in the house soon after. He needed to know just who he had let in. Presently they were in one of Attwood's many sitting rooms. It was beautifully decorated with pieces of modern art on the walls and eclectic furniture spread throughout the spacious room. Rilla and Victoria were comfortably sat in an eggshell leather sofa whilst Butcher stood before them. Conan was in the door to the atrium, and Verity was in another corner of the room watching. There was no way out.

"Never mind me," said Butcher. "It's you two I'm interested in. How old are you?"

Rilla glanced at Conan. He had his arms folded and his handgun was tucked in a pocket from where but he could get it out quickly should the need arise. Conan was staring at Victoria intently. It wasn't the look of a man who wanted to protect her, but to do something else, something that no man should want to do to a ten-year-old girl. Rilla turned and looked at Verity. Since arriving in the house, the woman had said nothing to them. Rilla guessed from her age that she might be Butcher's mother. Her face was wrinkled and weathered from too much sun, appearing quite the opposite from Butcher, and she wore a velvety pink dressing gown. Evidently she hadn't been awake, and the old woman's bleary eyes suggested she wasn't happy about it either.

"What does it matter how old I am? You don't care about me or Vicky." Rilla put an arm around Victoria who was silent. The young girl moved up the sofa to be closer to Rilla. "Just let my family in. Let Victoria's mother join us. They're good people. Please, just drop the tough guy act. Can't you show a little humanity."

"Humanity? You hear that, Conan?" Butcher laughed, but Conan just kept on staring at Victoria, his face blank but his eyes focused. "Rilla, I just saved your life. How about that for some humanity? We could have left you out there. We could have kept the door locked and waited for those zombies to take you all. But after we spotted you on the camera I opened the door, and now you're sat here on this *nice* soft sofa in this *nice* house, and you're asking me about fucking humanity?"

"So you saw us out there? You were watching?" asked Rilla.

"Yeah we were watching. What, do you really think that we'd still have a place like this if we weren't? There's a camera above the door. We can't get the perimeter cameras working, but at least we've got the door covered. Anyone shows up we can flick a switch and let them in. Conan saw you heading here and got me long before you dumb fucks started bouncing around that annex."

"Right, well then you'll know that we can't cause you any trouble. We don't have any guns." Rilla glanced at the gun in Conan's pocket and wondered if that was all they had. She hadn't seen Verity produce anything, and if Conan was the only one armed then there might be a chance of getting out of this. "You have to know we're just ordinary people. We just wanted to see Attwood. This place is the best chance of surviving this nightmare. Where is he anyway? I want to talk to him."

"That's not possible right now." Butcher reached across to a glass table where a decanter and six crystal glasses were.

As he grabbed a bottle of Scotch, Rilla noticed a gun under his jacket. She also saw a set of cutlery next to the decanter including a sharp knife. She had no doubt she could reach it before Butcher even realized what she was doing, but with Conan there she couldn't risk it. He had already proved he wouldn't hesitate to kill when he had shot Jeremy, and she wasn't about to risk Victoria's life. She also wasn't about to wait all night for Butcher to get to the point. Her parents were still in that annex, or even worse had been thrown back out onto the street to face the zombies. She had to push things and get Butcher moving.

"Is he asleep?" Rilla stood up. "Attwood, you here?" she shouted. "Attwood, you hear me? Your *caretaker* is making an ass of himself." She looked at Butcher directly. "Or maybe he's just the guy who cleans out the septic tank?"

Butcher drank straight from the bottle of scotch and then put it back on the glass table. He ignored Rilla and walked to the sofa where Victoria sat.

"Hey there. You tired, darling?" Butcher looked up at Rilla and gave her a withering look as he continued speaking to Victoria. "You want to go to *bed*?"

He deliberately emphasized the last word knowing it would antagonize Rilla. She thought she could wind him up with her acerbic comments about him working for Attwood, but he had all night to play games. He could tell that Rilla was strong and not truly afraid of him. She hadn't understood yet what she had gotten into. She still thought her family was safe, alive; she needed to understand just who was in charge.

"I think—" began Victoria, before Rilla cut her off.

"You leave her alone," said Rilla grabbing Butcher's arm. "Victoria, ignore him. Don't listen to him."

Butcher had been expecting Rilla to try something, and as she grabbed his arm he whipped around, forcing her arm around her back.

"Let go of me," protested Rilla as she struggled to get free.

Forcing her back against the glass table, Butcher grabbed the gun from underneath his jacket and shoved it under Rilla's nose. "Now just listen to me you fucking bitch. I will do whatever I want. I don't work for Attwood. This place is *mine*. You want to talk to him, sure, I'll take you to him. But first I need to know you're going to behave." Butcher drew the gun from under Rilla's nose and pointed it at Victoria who remained on the sofa crying. "You going to behave?"

Rilla knew that the knife was right behind her almost within reach. The arm that Butcher had pinned was brushing against the decanter, and she could almost feel the knife. Yet there was something in his eyes that told her he was serious. He would shoot Victoria just to make a point. His breath reeked, and those brown eyes of his were hard and full of anger. He believed himself and thought he had all the answers. Rilla had to wait, find that one moment when he let his guard down, and then she would do whatever it took to get her family and Victoria to safety.

"Yes, I'll behave." Rilla said the words calmly and coldly. She didn't want to give him the satisfaction of knowing he was scaring her. "I'm...sorry."

Butcher pushed Rilla back down onto the sofa. He pinched the top of his nose and sighed. "Let's start again, and quit the messing about. How old are you?"

"Seventeen," said Rilla, defiantly. "Vicky is ten, almost eleven."

Butcher seemed pleased with the information. He looked across at Conan who was nodding his head. "Right then. I guess you don't add up to much. I think we can get some use out of you though."

"Wow, thanks a lot. I'm so lucky that you think so highly of us." Rilla rubbed Victoria's back and held her. The girl was withdrawn and scared, yet Rilla had no way of getting her out of there. "Mind you, Butcher, I get the impression you don't think a lot at all."

Butcher clapped his hands and let out a little laugh. "Hear that, Verity? This one's got some fight in her."

Rilla looked around the room, but there was nothing she could use to fight them off. She was outnumbered and outgunned, and as much as she hated to admit it, was going to have to go along with Butcher. Not that she intended to make it easy for him. Her father had brought her up to not be a pushover, and with Victoria in her care, she wasn't about to cave now. "So can we go let my family in now?"

"Verity, I think it's time little Victoria got to bed," said Butcher looking at Rilla. "Take her up and make sure she's tucked in tight. I don't want any more surprises tonight."

"Where are you taking her?" asked Rilla. "I'm not letting her go anywhere without me."

"She'll be fine," said Verity. The old woman approached the sofa, dragging her bare feet across the expensive carpet. A limp unlit cigarette dangled from her mouth, and Verity held out her hand. "I'll make sure to take good care of her. You can look in on her later."

Rilla looked at Verity and knew she had no choice. At least Victoria seemed to be in better hands with her than with Butcher. And Rilla didn't trust Conan as far as she could throw him.

"Vicky, go with this lady. I'm going to talk to Mr. Butcher, okay? I've got to go with him and get my parents. Your Mom too. Okay?"

Reluctantly, Victoria let go of Rilla's hand and stood up. She looked at Rilla for reassurance.

"I want to go home," said Victoria, shyly. "I just want to go home."

"Go on. Verity will take you to your new room. I'll be up shortly."

Rilla hated not being able to reassure Victoria, but her home was as far away now as Rilla's. As Rilla watched Victoria nervously take Verity's hand, she wondered if her parents were still in the annex or had been thrown outside yet. How long would they survive out there at night without any weapons? How long *could* they survive? She had no option but to trust that Verity would look after Victoria, painful though it was to let the girl out of her sight. Perhaps they should've stayed at Jeremy's. Perhaps seeking out Attwood's had been a mistake after all.

Verity led Victoria out of the room, and then Rilla stood up to face Butcher. "You promise she'll be okay?"

"Conan, you can go back on watch now. Keep an eye out for any more unwanted visitors, though I think we've had all we're due for one night. Don't forget to clean up the cages in the morning and wash down the garage. Then Tad can take over on watch."

Rilla felt relieved knowing that Conan had to go back out on watch. That meant he couldn't do anything with Victoria. There was an uneasiness that crept through Rilla as she watched Conan silently leave the room. Butcher had mentioned someone else. She had assumed that it was just Butcher, Conan, Victoria, and Attwood here, but now there was someone else.

"Tad?"

Butcher smiled. "Don't worry, you can meet him in the morning. I'm sure he's going to *love* you. For now, we need to go get your parents, right? Maybe give you a little tour of the place?"

Butcher took Rilla's arm sharply and held the gun to her back. "Just remember, no more games. Otherwise Victoria is going to have a very short stay here. I can assure you, though, it'll be one she remembers."

As Butcher led Rilla out of the room, a hundred thoughts swirled around her head. The smile that spread across Butcher's face when he mentioned Tad had elicited disturbing thoughts about why he would 'love' her. She was putting a lot of faith in Verity about whom she knew nothing. She was worried about all the others she had left behind and even felt guilty for being in the house when they were still behind her in danger. Why was Attwood employing such assholes as his security?

"So the zombies can't get in here?" asked Rilla, as Butcher led her back into the cool night air.

"No chance," said Butcher confidently. "The walls running around the property, combined with the natural moat we have, mean we have had zero incidents. Zero. The only way in or out is through the garage and annex that you came through earlier which we have under constant supervision."

"You've got it all worked out," said Rilla. As they walked back from the house to the garage she tried to look around the property.

It was dark, too dark to see clearly, and other than a few trees and a couple of vehicles, the place was apparently deserted. Attwood was probably sleeping soundly letting his henchmen take care of everything. "Of course, if you take it all for granted then one day it'll all come crashing down around you. Those zombies will find a way in eventually. They're not dumb animals."

"Oh, I know," said Butcher. "I'm quite impressed by them. Truthfully, they show a lot of resilience if you think about it. They never give up, never stop—not for nothing. Some of them have walked miles and miles across all types of terrain and through all kinds of weather. Yet they keep on coming. Nothing stops them. You can't talk to them, make them turn around, or do anything. They don't worry about visas or passports. None of that shit applies anymore. The only thing we can do is stay behind these walls and wait it out. One day something else will come along and wipe the scum out: a plague or a disease or something. Fuck, I don't know. Maybe they'll do us all a favor and kill each other, just turn on themselves instead of coming after us and bringing their problems to my door. Poor fucks."

"Or maybe they'll take a bite out of your ass, and you'll be just like them, wandering around out there looking for your next meal."

"Not likely, sugar." Butcher shoved Rilla down the path to the garage and stopped her short of the door. "I've got Conan watching my back, not to mention the others. Plus, now I've got you."

As Rilla waited for Butcher to unlock the door, she heard the sound of dogs barking coming from inside. "What's going on? Did you send my parents back out there? Whose dogs are those?"

Butcher put one hand on the door and pointed the gun at Rilla. "You really want to know?"

Rilla nodded. She wasn't confident that she did, but she had to. She couldn't just abandon her parents or the rest of them. She had to know what was going on, even if the worst had happened, and he had thrown them outside unarmed. Rilla worried about Charlie, even though she barely knew her. There had been a connection between them from the outset, and she would hate to lose the chance to get to know her better. As Rilla watched Butcher punch a code into a panel on the wall, she saw how contented he was. He enjoyed the power he held over her; relished it even. He was a sadist and probably got off on others' pain. When he had finished entering the access code for the upper level, he waved the gun in Rilla's face and ordered her to go up.

"Up there. I'm not going to waste what power we have turning the rest of the facility on, but you can see from the upper gantry what you need to. You'll figure it out."

With Butcher behind her, Rilla climbed the flimsy metal staircase to the door at the top of the garage. The light above the door was green, and she cautiously pushed it open as the barking of the dogs grew louder.

"What is this?" she asked, as she stepped over the threshold onto the flimsy metal walkway that offered a viewing platform above the annex. "It's pitch black in here."

Butcher stayed in the doorway and held the door open. "Let your eyes adjust. You'll see in a moment."

It took a few seconds before Rilla could understand what she was seeing. The room was still locked, and the barking and grunting noises of the dogs below echoed loudly around the smelly room. She thought there were probably three or four dogs, but couldn't be sure, and as she watched she saw shapes appear on the floor. There were six in total, large dark blobs that remained motionless no matter how much the dogs pulled at them with their teeth.

Rilla put a hand over her mouth and nose. The smell was almost overwhelming, and it wasn't just the smell of dogs, but of something more, something base and evil. It was the smell of death. "What have you done?"

Rilla looked at Butcher in the doorway behind her, her hopes and fears washing over her as she saw the glint in his eye. Surely this wasn't what she thought? Surely he was playing a trick on her?

"Where are my parents? Kyler? Charlie? Did you throw them out?" Rilla wanted Butcher to say yes. She wanted him to tell her that he had let them go back onto the streets with a chance to get home. Five minutes ago she had hoped they were still here, but now she needed to know they weren't. The dogs below were huge and ferocious, she could tell that much, and the longer that Butcher didn't answer her, the more her fears grew. Rilla's throat closed up, and she started shaking.

"Tell me," she demanded. "Tell me right now."

"No. I didn't throw them out. Once you come through that door it doesn't open again," said Butcher.

"But..." Rilla looked back into the dark room and peered at one dog in particular. Its coat was jet black, and its eyes seemed to almost glow in the darkness as if it were a hound released from Hell. It was gnawing on something, and as Rilla looked closer at the object in the dog's mouth she saw the object was an arm. Three pale fingers adorned one end, and the other abruptly came to a halt in a bloody stump. The dog chewed on it as it if was half starved.

"No, this isn't... this can't—"

"Sorry, Rilla, but your family is right where I left them," said Butcher. He peeked over the control panel into the room and saw the motionless shapes on the floor. It was a sight he was familiar with and was becoming bored with. At first it had been entertaining to watch; amusing to see how people tried to fight back, to claw and hammer and bludgeon their way out of a locked room. He had lost a couple of dogs over time, but very rarely did anyone get the better of his pets. If they ever did, he made sure a bullet to the head took care of it.

"Jesus, no." Rilla's knees buckled, and Butcher caught her.

"Okay, time to go. Say goodbye to Mom and Dad."

With Rilla sobbing hysterically, Butcher carried her back down the stairs and watched as the green light turned red. Back on solid ground, he let her go, and she fell to her knees. Rilla clutched the earth and brought great mounds of dirt up in her hands. It was cold and dry, and she let it fall through her fingers.

"Why?" Rilla couldn't believe her mother and father were gone, just like that: Lyn, Kyler, and Charlie too. All of them gone, all of them dead; and not just dead, but murdered by this madman.

"Why?" Rilla screamed. She jumped up and began to beat Butcher's chest. "Answer me, God damn you!"

Butcher grabbed Rilla's wrists and looked at her tear-stained face. "You came to me with *nothing*. You offered me *nothing*. A couple of knives, some tins of food, and eight hungry mouths. You would've bled me dry. You think this place is paradise, but once I start letting people in, I have to let everyone in. Fuck that. No fucking way am I doing that. This place is a paradise precisely because I *don't* let people in. If I let your family and friends in, then more would come. Then soon they would want to make changes, want me to adapt to *their* ways, *their* culture. No way is that happening. I've got it good here, and it's staying that way."

Rilla tried to pull away from Butcher, but he had two strong hands holding her close. She looked up at him. This man had killed her parents, and she wanted him dead. If she could get that gun off him she would shoot him dead right then, right there, without hesitation. But all she could think about was that Butcher had made a mistake. He had let her live. So obviously he thought she had something to offer. If she could understand his thinking, then maybe she could get him to talk and let his guard down. The second she got a chance to take that gun, then she would end it all and gain some sort of vengeance for what he had done. "Why me? Why Vicky?"

Butcher pulled Rilla closer so she was forced to look right into his eyes. "Me and my boys get lonely. You can understand that, right? The only woman here is Verity, and I'm not into doing my own Mother, no matter how insane you think I am."

Rilla tried to pull away, but Butcher had her wrapped up tight. Verity had raised this psychopath? Did she know what he was up to? Did she know what her son did to people unlucky enough to come here? Rilla could feel the gun nuzzled against her chest. She grabbed one of Butcher's arms and held onto it like a life raft. She felt like she wasn't just lost, but drifting out over a burning ocean into Hades. "This place is Hell. I thought it would save us, but it's the opposite. You're fucking mad. You've destroyed everything. All you've done with this place is create Hell on Earth."

"Hell?" Butcher stared at Rilla with cold hard eyes. "This place is fucking pearly gates and angels compared to life out there. I'm surprised Jesus himself hasn't paid us a visit yet. This place allows you to govern your own lives and not be dictated to by anyone else. Those fuckers outside these walls can't get to us in here. Don't you see how much stronger we are for being in here? Those zombies—once you let one in, you may as well let a thousand in.

You are royally fucked. One by one they keep on coming, insidiously, any time of day or night with no warning, with no thoughts but getting what's yours. This life we have is ours to protect, and by God, I'm going to do whatever I have to."

"By killing innocent people?" Her parents were dead. Everyone that Rilla knew was dead except for Victoria who thankfully was safely in Verity's company. Rilla was all alone with this madman.

"Casualties of war," said Butcher calmly. "I didn't start this war, *they* did. All I'm doing is protecting my own. This is *my* land, *my* country, and one day it will be great again. Until then you play by *my* rules, or—"

"Or what?" asked Rilla. She knew the answer. It was what had made him murder her family.

Butcher grabbed Rilla by the back of the neck. "You really want to know the answer to that question?" he snarled. Butcher twisted Rilla around and shoved the gun into her back. He frog-marched her back up the incline toward the house, but before they reached it he pushed her toward the parked vehicles.

"Where are we going?" asked Rilla as they approached a black sedan with tinted windows.

"You wanted to know what happens when you don't do what I want."

Butcher pushed Rilla past the car, and on the other side was a rose garden. Surrounding it were ash trees and what appeared to be pieces of wood on the ground. They passed under a ramshackle trellis covered by ivy and through a pergola before reaching the center of the rose garden. Something tall and dark reached up into the night sky, and Rilla couldn't understand what she was looking at. As they got closer she could see movement and heard the familiar sounds of the dead.

"What is this?" Rilla wondered if Butcher was about to feed her to a zombie. It was too soon. Victoria was still in the house. Rilla wouldn't go without a fight and got ready to tackle Butcher. If she had to wrestle the gun from him she would. "What are you doing?"

"You wanted to talk to him, go ahead. Talk. Ask him anything you want."

Butcher pushed Rilla forward causing her to fall to the ground once more. On her knees she looked up at the strange object that had been erected in the middle of the garden. A tall piece of wood stretched vertically up in front of her with another section nailed horizontally across the upper half. A body was nailed to the cross, its arms outstretched and guts ripped open. The body twitched but couldn't free itself.

"Oh my God." Rilla put her hands over her mouth in shock as she looked at the crucified corpse that hovered above her. "Is it... is that Attwood?"

"Bingo." Butcher stood next to Rilla. "That asshole deserved nothing less. He wasn't going to let us in either. My mother, Verity, worked for him for years. She did all sorts of work for him. She cleaned this place from top to bottom, and when the shit went down he turned her away. If it wasn't for me and Tad, we'd still all be out there. So don't go feeling sorry for him. He got what he deserved."

In her peripheral vision Rilla saw Butcher's gun. She could try now. She could spring up and grab it while he was off guard.

"So you just took his house and killed him. Why leave him here? Like this?"

"A reminder, so that people like you realize this is all mine now. If you cross me, you'll end up next to him. Or worse I'll feed you to my dogs to be eaten alive."

Rilla jumped up and grabbed Butcher's arm. He dropped the gun and together they fell to the ground. Rilla quickly punched Butcher in the face and in the gut, and then spun around looking for the gun. It lay next to an overgrown rose bush, and she reached for it. But with her hand only an inch from it, she felt a stinging pain in her leg and screamed out. Another pain erupted in her other leg, in her calf, and Rilla turned over to find Butcher kneeling above her with a long knife in his hand. Blood oozed from his broken nose, and he looked angry.

"You think it's gonna be that easy? Have you not heard a single fucking thing I said?" Butcher plunged the knife down and stabbed Rilla at the top of her leg just below her hip.

"Stop!" Rilla cried out and clutched her leg. She felt blood flow freely through her fingers, and white hot pain racked her body. Butcher crawled up her body and shoved her arms beneath his knees, leaving her powerless to break free from underneath him. "Please."

Butcher brought the knife to Rilla's throat. She could feel her own blood dripping from it onto her skin and closed her eyes. She wished she had died with her parents. She couldn't take on Butcher on her own. She should've have stayed with them and fought with them. She had let them down, and now she had let Victoria down. If Butcher didn't kill her right now she was going to bleed to death.

"You think you know everything. What were you going to do? Shoot me, shoot Conan, and Tad and Verity? Then what? Cut Attwood down and give him a nice burial? You're wasting your time. You're never getting out of here. *Never.*"

Butcher lowered his face and let his soft lips kiss her cheek. Rilla felt his breath caress her neck, and she could feel his beard on her skin, his breath mixing with hers as he leered over her, all the while holding the knife to her neck.

"Please don't hurt me, don't—"

"What?" Butcher pressed the knife firmly against her neck, nicking the skin. A thin line of blood trickled out.

Rilla screwed her eyes shut. "Don't rape me," she whispered. "Just kill me. Get it over with. Do it."

Butcher laughed. "Why would I do that?"

Rilla said nothing. Whatever answer she gave would be the wrong one. Her arms and legs were going numb, and she could hear Attwood moaning above them.

"I can't very well fuck you right now, can I? If you bleed out in the garden you could change right when I'm—well, you know." Butcher sat up and took the knife away from Rilla's throat. "So here's what we'll do. Verity can see to your wounds. I'm sure she can stitch you up. When you're better, we'll see if you've come around to my way of thinking. Me and Tad have been waiting a long time for someone like you to come along. Conan, well he's a little different. He prefers his women a bit younger. It's not my cup of tea, but who I am to argue with him? I think he and Victoria will get along just fine." Butcher got up and stared at Rilla. He put the knife back in his jacket and scooped up the gun. He pointed it at Rilla. "Well. You want to come inside or stay here and talk to Attwood a little more?"

Rilla had no choice. If she fought back now, then Butcher would kill her. If she didn't go with him, then she would surely bleed to death. The only way out was to go along with him. For now.

Rilla raised an arm. Her head swam with pain, and her leg was numb. She felt cold and scared. "Take me inside. Take me to Verity."

"And you're not going to fight me anymore?"

Rilla shook her head. The night sky was suddenly blacker than she remembered, and she couldn't see the stars anymore. "I just want..."

As Rilla passed out, Butcher looked up at Attwood and sighed as he wiped his bloody nose. "Looks like it's just me and you, buddy. Want to give me a hand getting her inside?"

Attwood's dead body twisted around, but the nails held it firmly in place on the cross. His teeth clacked together, and he uttered a low moan.

"Is that a no?" Butcher reached down for Rilla and put his hands under her body. He lifted her up and threw her over his shoulder. "Fine. I guess it's just you and me then, girl. Verity would tell me you ain't good for nothing, and I should feed you to the wolves. I reckon there's some use in you before we get to that."

Underneath the moonlit sky, Butcher carried Rilla back to the house. Verity would have the younger girl tucked up in bed by now and would be able to stitch up Rilla's cuts. Then they would finally be able to get some sleep. Tomorrow was going to be an interesting day, and Butcher didn't doubt he was going to need all the energy he had.

CHAPTER 11

It occurred to Charlie as she curled up into a ball that the dogs might kill them all, but would they *kill* them all? There was no doubt in her mind that her father was dead. She knew that Schafer and Magda were dead, that Jeremy and Lyn were dead, and that the dogs would eat large parts of their bodies. There was nothing she could do about that, as much as it horrified her. It was undignified and undeserved. But what if they came back? What if Kyler or Schafer came back? If they found her, they would kill her too. There was no way she could repel any attack from a zombie; certainly not one from her father. How could she kill him? How could she defend herself against anything? The cage was small and cramped, and the wire mesh cold against her skin. As she backed up into the corner, she stared down the long dark tunnel through which she had crawled. The dogs' kennels led directly into the garage, and now she could hear them yelping and barking and running around, having killed everyone. The darkness was absolute. Blood and sweat kept dripping into her eyes, and even though she blinked it away, she knew she was covered in it. The smell of her body was like a beacon to them, and she knew it probably wouldn't be long before the dogs finished up and returned for her. What would she do then? How could she get away from them—from any of this? Her left arm was numb, the bone broken, and the skin a shredded mess. She was bleeding badly, and the bites to her leg stung as she brought her knees up to her chin. She tried to control her breathing and focus. She had to focus on finding a way out. If the dogs returned, or if those men did, then they would finish her off one way or another.

One thought kept racing through Charlie's mind: *Why*? Schafer had offered to help. He and her father had both been able to help, they all had. They were of no threat, and yet those men had taken in only Rilla and Victoria. It made no sense. The house offered protection from the dead, from the world that offered only death, and yet they had been turned away. Charlie hated them all. She hated everything the world had become, at what those men had become, and what had made them that way. Was it the corpses and the zombies that had twisted their minds into such hatred, or had they always been that way before the walls went up? Charlie was beat. Mentally and physically she just felt like curling up into a ball and giving up. Her energy levels were at zero. Charlie lifted her right hand to her face and gingerly felt along the tear in her cheek where one of the dogs had ripped it open. A hunk of skin flapped around loosely, and when she touched it the raw nerve endings sent shockwaves of pain to her brain.

"Fuck." Charlie rested her head back against the metal cage. She kept seeing Schafer in that last moment before he succumbed to those dogs. She kept seeing his face and hearing his pleading voice.

'Get away from here. Get Rilla.'

He had been a tough man; maybe as tough as her father. Yet those creatures had still taken him down. What chance did she have when they discovered where she was? Could she get away? Was it even possible?

Charlie drew in a lungful of oxygen and almost retched. The air tasted of shit and rotten meat. It left a bitter taste in her mouth, and she knew she had to find a way out. Staying here meant certain death. If the dogs didn't get her, then the infection would. Her cuts ran deep and needed treating. She ran her hand over the wire and began to search for an exit. The kennel was in complete and total darkness. She felt around, and the wire cage was no more than four feet high, yet stretched as far as she could reach. Along the bottom of the cage ran a gutter. It was full of stale water and discarded food. She had hoped to find an exit of some kind, perhaps another lock or opening where the dogs got out for exercise. But she found nothing, and knew she was going to have to move. She inched forward and winced with every movement that sent shuddering waves of pain through her bites and mangled left arm. Using the wire for support, Charlie dragged herself forward, staying close to the edge of the kennel. The ground was cold and damp, and her clothes became sodden as she crawled slowly forward.

'Get away from here.'

She wanted to stop, to rest, to grieve, and let the dogs take her into oblivion; yet something drove her on, and inch by painful inch she managed to crawl the length of the cage. In the corner she found the wire was looser at the base and she could even wiggle a few fingers underneath. The concrete was cracked, and she guessed that the dogs had attempted a breakout and dug the ground away. The gutter led to a drain in the same corner, and she ran her hand over the grate. It was slimy and dripping with the dogs' waste. Charlie slumped back against the wire. There was no way out, no secret door, no passage to anywhere else; she could hear the dogs barking and waited. It wouldn't be long before they found her. Was the best she could hope for a quick death? She remembered the dog she had half blinded and the others that had attacked her. She remembered how they had attacked so viciously. It wasn't their fault. Butcher had clearly trained them to behave that way. He probably tortured them, and they didn't know any different. He had raised them to be killers and done a good job of it.

Suddenly Charlie heard a creaking sound coming from down the tunnel. One of the panels was lifting up, and as it swung back into place, she heard the unmistakable padding steps from a dog. One of them was coming back already. She heard panting and wheezing, and then the footsteps stopped. It had realized she was in here in its home.

Charlie held her breath and waited. She waited for the inevitable attack and curled her right hand into a fist. Her left arm was useless, and the hand was a mess. But as she sat there waiting to die, she knew she could put up a fight, maybe even try to blind another dog. She vowed she would fight to the end and not give in. Would Schafer give in? Had her father given in? Had Rilla meekly surrendered to these evil men? No, they had fought back. It dawned on Charlie that not only could she do the same, but that she should do the same. Why should she be forced to die like a pig? Why should she let some evil bastard take everything from her—take her family, her friends, her life? Charlie brought her fist up to protect her face as the invisible black dog came closer. She was going to fight if it took her last breath.

'Get Rilla.'

A growling sound came from somewhere up ahead, and Charlie tried to find the dog but it was impossible. Her eyes found nothing. The cage was devoid of light. The dog was closer. She could smell it just as she knew it could smell her.

"Come on then, you bitch. Let's see what you've got." Charlie pushed herself back into the corner of the cage and prepared to fight. As she did so, the grate beneath her legs moved. She had dislodged it from the opening below, and she realized she was sat almost directly above the drain. The huge dog was running now and barking. Quickly, Charlie turned over and pulled at the grate. She sensed there was still time to remove the drain cover and perhaps slip into it and avoid the dogs. It could be a way out, but as she removed the drain cover she felt the slavering jaws of one of the dogs rip into her back, and she screamed in pain.

The dog ripped open a huge chunk of her shoulder, tearing through her clothes and skin as if they were made of feathers. Charlie screamed and brought the grate up with her hand, cracking the dog over the head with it. She didn't know where she had connected with the beast, but it seemed to stop it, even if only for a moment. The pain surging through her back was indescribable, and it felt like she had been hit by a truck. She lifted the grate again and held it in front of her face just as the dog attacked again. Its jaws snapped at the metal and clamped around the grate, threatening to pull it from her grasp. She knew that if she lost it then she would not physically be able to stop the dog. Charlie roared at the dog to back off and pulled the grate from its mouth. Before the dog could back away, she smashed the heavy grate over the dog's head again, and it yelped in pain. Charlie knew she had hurt it and whipped the grate through the air again, hitting the dog once more on the top of its head. She became aware that the dog had fallen to the ground just in front of her feet. She could hear it breathing and whining pitifully.

"That all you got?" Charlie smashed the grate down on the dog's head again and again and again. She could feel the bones in its head breaking, and the soft fur eventually gave way to the hard ground. She obliterated its head completely, and when she was sure the dog was dead, she dropped the steel grate. Her arm ached and yet it wasn't over. The barking from the other dogs was still echoing down the tunnel from the other room, and she didn't have the energy to fight more of them. If they attacked all at once, she would have no way out and knew there was only one chance now.

Charlie climbed to the lip of the drain and reached down. The walls were wet and oily, and she couldn't reach the bottom. The opening was about two feet across, just about wide enough for her to squeeze through. There would be no going back, and she had no idea if it would lead anywhere, but she knew if she waited any longer, then the others would come. She pulled herself over the lip and lowered herself head first through the opening. The foul smell was worse than up top, and she kept her mouth closed as she lowered herself into the drain. It was better to breathe through her nose than have the taste of it in her mouth.

With her right arm in front of her, Charlie felt her waist on the lip and reached out. The ground was still not within reach and she was going to have to drop and hope it wasn't far. She wriggled forward and closed her eyes as she pushed off. Better to die quickly by falling and breaking her back than being savaged by those dogs.

When she landed at the bottom of the drain all the breath was knocked out of her body. Every bite and cut on her body seemed to protest and scream in rage at her, and her back stung as if a thousand bees had attacked her at once. The fall had only been two or three seconds yet it had felt much longer. Falling through infinite blackness, Charlie had landed at the bottom of the drain and not managed to break her neck or anything else. There was a good four or five inches of water at the bottom of the drain which had softened the landing. As she sat up, Charlie heard the dogs above her scrambling around the top of the drain. If they were brave enough to come down, then they could have her. She knew they were unlikely to, but wasn't sure. They had obviously discovered their fallen comrade and were sending an uninterrupted series of loud barks down the opening to her.

"Yeah, well what are you going to do about it?" Charlie listened to the dogs, but none of them were stupid enough to venture down into the drain. They could probably squeeze through the opening to get her if they wanted, but they also didn't really need to. They had eaten well and were suspicious about the unusual opening in the cage where their waste went to.

"That's what I thought, cowards." Charlie propped herself up and tried to figure out what to do next. The dogs were behind her now, and as long as they stayed up in their kennels she was relatively safe. Still, she didn't want to sit around in a trench full of waste for long. The smell was so powerful and enveloping that she felt overwhelmed by it. What with the loss of blood and shock, she knew that if she stayed where she was, then she was liable to pass out. And if Butcher found out where she had gone, then she was certain he would have no problem in making sure she never got out. It was too risky to sit it out and wait. Nobody was going to come to her rescue. Nobody even knew she was there. It was so hard, though, so hard to fight it. Charlie's head swam and she felt dizzy so she leant back against the wall for a moment. How could Kyler leave her like this? It wasn't fair. Why did he get to go first? He was the fighter the strong one; Charlie missed her mother, and as she waited for the dizzy spell to pass heard a song begin to run through her head.

'*All I feel is the distant wind as you turn your back on me.*'

It was the same song she'd played in her head when Kyler had killed that crow. It used to be her favorite song, and now it was just plain irritating. It reminded her of her old life; of what things used to be like before the corpses took over the world. It reminded her of home, of Kyler, and even her mother. Maybe that was why her head had chosen that song at that time. Maybe that was exactly what she needed to be reminded of.

Sighing, Charlie sat up. She could do nothing, or she could do something. Slowly she began to crawl along the drain. She had no idea where it led or if it would just be a dead end, but she had to do something. She reached an arm up after a few feet and found the roof above her closing in. As she crawled forward another few feet she found the walls getting narrow very quickly, and she banged her throbbing head against the roof. Something with a lot of legs scuttled down across her head and into her hair. She didn't care. The old Charlie would have screamed, but it seemed pretty insignificant if a spider wanted to take refuge in her dirty hair. It was as her head began to pound that she realized she had lost her father's fishing cap somewhere. It had most likely come off when the dogs had attacked, and there was no way of retrieving it now. Bizarrely, she felt guilty for losing it, as if she owed it to her father to get it back, but there was no way she was going back up there.

Charlie pressed on in the darkness and the barking of the killer dogs faded away. She heard the occasional drip of water, but nothing else came to her. She didn't know if she was headed to or away from the house, but it didn't matter. All that was important was that she kept moving. Her body ached and told her to stop, but stopping meant death. She knew that. She knew that Schafer was right about one thing. She had to get away from here.

There was a barrier suddenly in front of her face, and Charlie pushed against it. A rusted metal grill blocked her way, but it moved when she pulled the bottom of it with her right hand. She could pull it up a few inches before the upper nails held it in place. It was enough to get through, although it meant getting right down into the dirty water that surrounded her knees and ran slowly past her.

Pushing herself flat against the bottom of the drain, Charlie forced the grill upward and began to crawl through on her back. It was pure agony. The flesh was still raw and bloody where the dog had ripped her back open right between her shoulder blades, and it felt like her skin was on fire. She could feel the fecal matter seeping into her every pore, binding with her blood, and invading her body with its evil filth. The rusted grate was abrasive against her fingers and cut into her hand as she held it up. Finally, she was through it, and she let go, exhausted. Her face was slick with sweat, and her clothes were heavy with the mix of water and urine. The drain was smaller now and smelt no better than it did before. The darkness was ever present, and she kept telling herself that there would be an end to this. The tunnel couldn't go on forever. Standing up was impossible, and so she got onto her hands and knees and kept going, hoping to find the end soon. The drain appeared endless. There was no light to head for, not a sound other than her own breathing, and as she crawled slowly forward, every agonizing moment brought more excruciating pain to her cuts and wounds. Her right hand was taking all the weight of her body whilst her left arm hung loosely at her side. When she put her hand in a foul lump of excrement, her arm slipped causing her to lose her momentum, and she fell forward once more into the sludge and stinking water that lay six inches deep. Her head smacked against the side of the tunnel, and then her mouth filled with the dirty water. Frantically, Charlie pushed herself up and coughed, retching immediately as some of the warm sludge slid down her throat. Burning bile forced its way up, and Charlie vomited up in the darkness. As she held her trembling body above the waterline, she retched again and again until there was nothing left inside her. Charlie felt overcome by it all. Desperation flooded her, and the exhaustion hit her. They were all dead, and she was halfway there herself. Her left arm was useless, and her legs and back were bitten, probably infected now with God knows what kind of diseases. Butcher had won. By escaping into the kennel and then the drain, Charlie had only succeeded in prolonging her life. What was the point in dying like this, in abject squalor and engulfed in rotten meat and shit?

'*Get away from here. Get Rilla.*'

"I can't. I can't do it," cried Charlie. She sat there sobbing and clutching her left arm. Exactly how long was she supposed to crawl along through this filth? God, how she wished her father were there. He had been right. He had warned her they weren't prepared to go out. He had warned her against going to Attwood's. Her falling tears were for her own plight and pain but also for her father. She missed him. She missed him so much that her heart wanted to burst, and she wanted to crawl back up into the kennel and hold him to her. She missed him because he was her everything. When her mother died they had to rely on each other. It wasn't easy, but nothing was these days. As she recalled her father, she remembered the good things about him; the way he used to laugh and play with her and how happy they were. The fact that they had argued most of the last days and weeks together only made her feel more terrible. There was still love between them, so why had they made it so hard to get along? Why had he made it so hard for her? It had felt at times like he was pushing her away, as if he wanted her to go, as if she really was the greatest disappointment to him. Yet, as she sat in the dark tunnel with blood seeping from her wounds and her clothes soaked in feces, caught between a pack of wild dogs and the zombie-infested streets, something told her that Kyler had meant to say more. He was a fisherman, a man's man, and emotions didn't come out too often. So when he told her something, he meant it to be taken seriously.

Something worm-like crawled over her hand and slithered down onto her thigh. It moved slowly like a worm or a centipede, and she was grateful that it was pitch black in the drain. It tickled her leg as it crawled down and over the knee. Charlie wondered what else was down in the darkness with her. Did bats live in drains or was that caves? The chance of a zombie finding its way in was slim. She was probably surrounded by bugs and cockroaches and all manner of things that scuttled instead of walked and scurried instead of ran.

Charlie didn't really care. She was still sobbing for her lost father to care about trivial things like what insect was clambering over her shoulder. Animals had never been her thing. Her father had taught her to fish once, but she had never really taken to it. Out on the lake in a small boat with her father hadn't been much fun to a teenage girl. She had spent most of her time wishing she was at home with her mother. She would give anything now to have him back and taking her out fishing again. He had taught her how to behave responsibly when out on the water, insisting that she wear a life jacket. She, of course, had argued with him that it made her look unattractive. He had often made her do things that at the time made her feel bad. They argued all too often, especially lately, and yet now when she looked back could see that he was just trying to do the right thing and look after her; more than that, he was trying to get her to look after herself. It was the same when he cut her hair. She hated the way he had roughly chopped it off and made her look like a tomboy, yet was it that bad? It was certainly more practical and coincidentally helped her to live when he had referred to her as his 'son' in front of Butcher. Then there was the time they had argued about the bird, the crow that they had ended up eating. He had told her to take responsibility that day. He had said a lot of things, but that one thing stood out. Putting the bird out of its pain and misery had been the right thing to do. She had to take responsibility for creatures more helpless than herself.

'Get Rilla.'

Kyler had taught her to fight. He had pushed her as far as he could, taught her what to do, but ultimately it came down to her what she should do next. She knew that if she stayed in the tunnel she would surely die. It felt surprisingly easy. Sitting in the dark and letting herself slip away would be probably the easiest option in front of her. But her father never took the easy option; never let her shy away from facing things head on. He had driven her insane over the last few weeks since her mother died, but she finally understood why. He had felt guilt for her mother's passing. The way she had died. Kyler had decided to not let his daughter suffer the same fate. He had tried to make her fight, to see a future, to know that the only way to live now was to fight or die.

Charlie edged herself forward and spat congealed, cloying blood from her mouth. She lowered herself into the filth and stagnant water, and with her right hand extended out in front of her, she began to pull herself along the drain. After only a few feet, she began to hear sounds again, only not voices or barking. She heard splashing sounds and groans. She knew those sounds and drove herself on toward them. The old Charlie would run away from those noises, but now she wanted them. She *needed* them. Using the moans of the dead as a guide, she kept pulling herself forward until she reached the edge of the drain. It emptied out into the ditch or moat that surrounded Attwood's property. It was overgrown with tall reeds, and as she parted them she finally smelt fresh air. The moon was hidden by clouds, yet she could see stars high in the sky, and she pulled herself to the edge of the drain so she could finally sit upright. Her back ached and her right hand throbbed from the exertion of dragging her body along, but that moment by the ditch was glorious. It was as if she had been born again, emerging from that dark tunnel with a fresh outlook. Kyler had been right all along. There were only two options left to people still living in this world. She had been wavering between the two, but she *did* have a choice, and she knew what she had to do next.

'All I feel is the distant wind as you turn your back on me.'

"Not now, brain," said Charlie quietly. Listening to an inane song about things that no longer mattered seemed pointless now. It had served her well once, first as entertainment and then as a distraction, but now she had to retrain her brain. She had to discard her old things that were no longer relevant. She had a job to do.

Charlie spat again and looked out at the moonlit fields in front of her. If she could get up out of the ditch, across the road and home before any of the hundreds of zombies noticed her, she might just make it. Then all she had to do was dress her open wounds and hope she hadn't contracted a fatal disease whilst crawling through half a mile of animal waste and stagnant water contaminated by rotting human bodies.

Charlie lowered herself off the drain and into the water. Her feet sank into the soft dirt, and she unsteadily began to head across the short ditch to the bank. A zombie in the water floated past her, and more on the road above her stumbled by, oblivious to her presence. Charlie smiled. She wasn't going to die today. She was going home.

Only a few feet away lay a zombie trying to climb the bank. As Charlie put her hands on the bank to haul herself up, the corpse looked at her. There was no doubt that its eyes were locked on hers, and the dead body stopped moving. The dead woman let go of the grass, and her putrescent body slipped back into the water. The dead woman groaned and looked at Charlie who returned her look. Both of them stared at each other in silence and then Charlie watched as the dead woman resumed her quest to leave the ditch, grabbing handfuls of wet grass.

She was like *them* now. She was part of them as much as they were a part of her. Charlie pulled herself up the bank and stood still as the zombies filed past her. Maybe it was the smell or the way she looked, or maybe she was so close to death that they couldn't tell the difference between her and themselves. Charlie began to walk slowly through the throng of corpses back to her house. She didn't look back at Attwood's. She didn't need to.

It would still be there when she returned.

To fight.

CHAPTER 12

"Can I just do it now?" asked Tad. "You'll let me drive, won't you?"

Conan shook his head. "Wait."

Tad knew there was no arguing with the big man. They had to wait for his brother, Butcher. As usual, he was taking his time and missing out on the fun. Well, that wasn't entirely true. Butcher was having fun inside the house, but Tad wished he would hurry up.

"Pass me another one, big man." Tad sipped the last dregs of beer from the can and then tossed it behind him into the garden.

Conan reached into the cooler and fished another can out of the melted ice. He passed it to Tad without a word.

"Nice." Tad pressed the cold can briefly against his forehead. The evening was warm and pleasant, and the sun was only just setting now. It was disappearing behind the fence in the west and bathing them all in an orange glow. A few flies buzzed around them all, drawn to the roses and the dead body.

Tad cracked the can open and took a long drink. It had been a long day. He had heard all about their new guests who had arrived in the middle of the night. It had been months since their last arrivals, and Tad was more than excited to learn that they had taken in two girls. Butcher had told him that he had to be patient, that he wasn't to touch them, but it had been almost impossible to resist. The younger girl had spent most of the day locked up with Conan, and Tad couldn't understand why Butcher put up with it. It wasn't natural. Butcher said he needed Conan around, to be 'the muscle', and if that meant letting him have his pleasures in life to keep him happy, then so be it. Tad didn't dislike Conan, but the man was a freak. He was a giant and said little except when prompted. If Tad were in charge, then he would've thrown Conan out. What he liked to do to little girls was disgusting. The thought of Conan with Vicky made Tad's skin crawl, and he turned to thoughts of how he had spent the afternoon. The other girl, the older girl— now *she* was worth thinking about.

Tad burped. "Say, Mom, you think you can get Rilla cleaned up again after Butcher's through? I'm still a little tense and could do with relaxing before tonight. You know what I mean?" Tad raised his can of beer to Conan who said nothing and refused to acknowledge Tad.

"Suit yourself," said Tad. He looked across at the pickup truck and wished Butcher would hurry up.

"Sure, honey," said Verity. She sipped her beer from a glass, preferring not to drink out of a dirty can. "Just as soon as your brother's done. You know how he hates to be rushed into anything. I'll go take a look at the bitch after supper."

"Okay, okay." Tad scratched his nose and fidgeted in his seat. They had brought four chairs out from the dining room, as was their way on a nice warm evening, and planted them in the rose garden. It was a secluded little area to the side of the house and offered a great view from the hill over the town. There was a small gap in the surrounding trees through which they could see Peterborough. The town was quiet now, and Tad wondered if they had seen off the last of the people from that shitty town. At first a lot of people had come to the house looking for help, but over time the numbers had dwindled. Nobody had been able to get over the wall, and Butcher wasn't about to leave the door open. He had told Tad there was a distinct difference between the people out there and them. The outsiders were no good. They just wanted in, to take what Attwood had, to forego the world of the dead, and take refuge in Attwood's property behind its large, strong walls. But by doing so, all they would do is bring death in with them. Butcher had made it quite clear to Tad that on no account should he let any of them in. Now and again they would allow one or two in, just the women, just for some amusement. But they couldn't let any men in. Tad knew that the men would just want to take the place for themselves and had to remain outside the walls. The girls came and went, and the men never got a chance.

Over the last couple of months, they hadn't seen or heard anything, and then last night it was like Christmas. Of course, they had to be careful about who they let in, and most of them didn't pass the grade. Butcher selected who he allowed into the property since Attwood was no longer capable of making those decisions. Tad chuckled and looked up at Attwood. His body still hung on the cross and occasionally he groaned or tried to get free, but the old man was nailed to the cross and not going anywhere.

"Here's to Attwood," said Tad, raising his beer. "May he forever rot in hell, the old bastard." Tad chuckled again but noticed Conan still wasn't responding. "Oh, come on, Conan. Crack a smile, can't you? You'd think after the day you had you might actually be in a good mood for once."

"I'd say he's pretty tired," said Verity, slapping Conan's knee. "He had to clear up the mess from last night *and* got his dick wet. Big day for a big man, huh?"

"Damn straight," said Conan. He belched and picked up another can from the cooler. He crushed the empty can in his hand and dropped it at his feet.

Verity laughed and looked at Tad. "Now stop looking at that truck, you. We've got to wait for your brother. If you go ahead and do anything before he—"

The sound of footsteps on the driveway interrupted Verity, and she looked up to see Rilla approaching them. The girl wore the skimpy green dress that Verity had dressed her in that morning. Why she had to dress the girls up she didn't know as they spent very little time dressed. Verity saw the vacant look in the girl's eyes and the bruises down her bare arms. It was a sight she was familiar with and turned away. "Tad, get a beer for your brother. Looks like he's worked up quite a thirst."

Rilla stumbled toward them and stopped when she reached the chairs. Her lip was cut and a thin trickle of blood ran down her leg, visible below the dress that stopped at the knees.

"Cheers," said Butcher as he took a cold can from Tad. Butcher walked from Tad to Conan to Verity giving them all high fives. "What did I tell you? This place is ours. You want something, and I get it. Right, Conan?"

Conan smiled and nodded.

"Right, Tad?"

"Right on, brother."

Butcher shoved Rilla forward and ordered her to sit in the vacant chair. She sat down slowly and winced when Butcher touched her. "Want a drink?"

Rilla said nothing and stared at the ground.

"I said, you want a drink?" asked Butcher impatiently.

Rilla shook her head slowly.

"I don't think she's thirsty," said Tad. He raised his can and jumped up out of his chair. "I bet you already slipped something down her throat, though, huh?"

Butcher looked at Tad plainly. "Dude, not now. Mom is right there. She is *right* there."

"Oh, yeah, right." Tad lowered his can.

"Nah, I'm just kidding," said Butcher, grinning. He held up his can for Tad to toast. "I'm surprised that girl can even sit down, the day she's had."

Tad laughed nervously and glanced at his mother. Verity was staring out at the sunset, either oblivious to the conversation or willfully ignoring it. She got the girls ready, cleaned them up afterwards, and did as she was told. She seemed content with her lot and never complained.

"So what's going down?" asked Butcher, as he began to tie Rilla to the chair. He bound her ankles together and then brought her arms around the back of the chair. He tied her wrists together and stroked her hair.

"Can I drive?" asked Tad. "You never let me do it. I really want to do this one."

"In a moment, Tad. We'll get to that." Butcher looked at Conan. "I take it we're all cleared up?"

"All dead," replied Conan. "Not much left. One had turned, but I quickly dispatched him. The rest I washed away. Couple of the dogs bought it. Probably that Schafer guy. Looked like he put up a hell of a fight."

"Shame." Butcher knew that meant they were down to two dogs. They would have to start looking for replacements soon. The need to keep them there was getting less and less every day, but he would rather have them than not. If another large group came along he would need them. "Anything useful turn up?"

Conan shook his head. "No. Couple of watches that don't work and a couple of wedding rings. Not much value."

"I did get this sweet hat," said Tad, proudly tipping his new fishing cap to Butcher. "Found it in the kennels. One of the dogs used it as a chew toy after killing the boy. It's pretty comfy."

Butcher ignored his younger brother and turned to Verity. "Dinner nearly ready?"

Verity nodded. "It'll be done shortly."

"Good. After we've eaten I need you to clean our guest up. Maybe find something to pep her up a bit. We've still got some Coke, right? Just enough to give her a quick pick me up. I've got plans."

Verity yawned. "Sure. One of you boys will have to help me clean the dishes though. I'm not doing all the hard graft around here."

"Tad?" Butcher looked at his younger brother who opened his mouth to protest and then thought better of it. "Great."

Conan crushed another beer can in his hands and then tossed it at Attwood's feet.

"Say, where's your gift, Conan? You been busy?" asked Butcher. "Not still got her tied up in the house have you? You should bring her out here. I'll bet she could use a drink."

"I think I broke her," said Conan, bored.

"Can I drive?" asked Tad, excitedly. "Please, Butcher, just let me this one time."

Butcher looked over at the pickup truck. "Shit, Conan, you done with her already?" Victoria was bound up and tied to the back of the truck. A length of rope hung from the bumper and was wrapped around her neck. Her feet and hands were strapped up with cable ties, and yet Butcher could see she was very much alive. She was trying to extricate herself from the ties, but there was no way she was going to get them undone on her own.

"Please?" asked Tad again, as he got up from his chair.

Butcher looked at Conan. "You sure? It's been a while since the last one, and I ain't sure when your next gift is coming along. You understand, big man?"

Conan nodded. "She was fine. Just a little... old."

Butcher slumped down in Tad's vacant seat and looked up at his brother in the waning sunlight. "Okay. Just be careful. You fuck anything up, and you're paying for it."

"*Yes!*" Tad downed his beer and went over to the truck where he disappeared inside the cab and started the engine.

"Right," said Butcher. "I've got one minute. Any advance?"

"Two," said Verity as she watched Victoria twist and turn to free herself from the rope.

"Thirty seconds," said Conan.

"Brave choice," replied Butcher. "Brave choice." He looked over at the pickup truck idling on the driveway, and Tad looked out of the window as he revved the engine. Butcher raised a hand and gave him the thumbs up. "Ladies and gentlemen, start your watches."

The driveway was clear and led down to the annex where it ended. There was room to turn, and usually the truck did a quick turnaround before heading back up to the house. It took no more than a minute to complete the circuit although Tad hadn't driven it before.

"Playtime is over, Conan. You're going to lose," said Butcher, smiling as Tad began to move the pickup down the driveway.

"Stop, what are you doing?" asked Rilla. She only half heard the conversation between them, and was only now realizing that Victoria was tied to the back of the truck. She'd heard them confirm that everyone was dead, including her father, and it was only when they started laying bets that she looked at the truck. As it slowly pulled away she saw Victoria try to get to her feet.

"Quiet," said Butcher as he glanced at his wristwatch. "I've got latrine duty riding on this."

The truck sped up quickly, and the rope behind it extended fully before catching Victoria. She had managed to get to her feet and was trying to jump along. Rilla saw her red eyes and knew that they had hurt her. They had said they would look after her, but it was all a lie. Even the old woman had been in on it. If they had done just half the things to Victoria as they had to Rilla, then she would make sure they paid for it.

"Wait, please, she's only a little girl," pleaded Rilla.

"I said shut up," said Butcher as he saw Tad waving out of the window and grinning like a child in a candy store. "Otherwise, it'll be you strapped to the back of that truck next."

Rilla watched as Victoria was yanked off her feet and her body thrown into the air. As the truck roared down the driveway the rope abruptly went taught and Victoria's body was slammed down onto the driveway. Victoria screamed, unable to put her arms out in front of her to protect herself, and her body began to bounce along the hard tarmac as Tad kept going.

Rilla jumped to her feet. "Stop, right now! Stop it!" she screamed.

"Conan, sort that shit out," said Butcher as he kept half an eye on Victoria and half an eye on his watch.

Conan walked over to Rilla and drew a hand across her face. The slap stung her cheeks, but Rilla knew that Victoria was in far worse pain. And if they didn't stop, she would be dead soon.

"Fuck you," said Rilla, facing Conan. She could feel a bead of blood drip over her bottom lip. "Fuck you, you animals. What the fuck are you—"

Conan squared himself up and then planted a punch right in the center of Rilla's face. The bridge of her nose broke instantly, and her unconscious body was knocked back into the seat behind her.

"Thank you," said Butcher, as Conan calmly returned to his seat.

Tad approached the annex and veered the truck to the left to swing around. Victoria's body was dragged along behind the truck, and as Tad swung around Victoria was slammed into the wall of the annex. Her body left a dent in one of the walls as Tad kept speeding the truck up.

"That has *got* to hurt," said Verity, chuckling.

"Laugh all you like old woman," said Butcher. "Forty seconds. You're out, Conan. It's between you and me now, Mom."

The truck began to come up the driveway to the house, and Butcher could still see Victoria twisting and crying. There were faint cries coming from her body, but if he didn't know who it was, he wouldn't be able to recognize her. Her body was shrouded in blood and her face nothing but a pile of worn away bone and gristle, flesh dangling from it in places, and her nose and eyes just cavities showing her pain.

"Come on, Tad, finish it," whispered Butcher.

Tad suddenly slammed on the brakes and Victoria's body skidded along the drive until it caught up with the truck and bounced into the rear axle. The girl's body was now still, and the crying had stopped.

"Boom!" Butcher stood up and applauded. "She's gone. And that is almost a perfect sixty seconds." He turned to Verity. "Unlucky. You lose again. One week's latrine duty."

Tad got out of the cab and walked around to the back of the truck where he inspected Victoria's remains. Then he went back to the cab, turned the engine off, and ran over to Butcher with a smile across his face.

"Did you see that shit? She is *fucked* up. Her face is just gone, man. She looks worse than those walking corpses out there."

"She dead?" asked Verity.

"Course she is. I don't mess around," replied Tad, defensively.

"Damn. I had two minutes."

"Yeah, like I was gonna let it go that long." Tad fished himself a cold beer from the cooler. "I don't mess around. When I'm going to do something I just do it. I do *everything* fast."

"One day, Tad," said Butcher putting an arm around his brother, "you'll learn that's *not* necessarily a good thing."

Conan let out a snigger.

"Okay, boys, I've had enough. Dinner's ready." Verity got up and began to walk back to the house. "You remember to make sure that dead bitch don't come back. We don't want a fucking zombie walking around the property."

"Shit, I forgot about that," said Tad. "You want me to do it?"

Butcher looked at his younger brother with something approaching pride. "Why not?" Butcher looked at the unconscious Rilla. "You did good, Tad. After dinner, if you clean up that mess you made on the driveway, I'll let you have a go at our other guest before you go out on duty. Burn the remains and then get washed up. You've got a busy night ahead of you."

Tad nodded. "Conan, lend me your gun."

Conan looked at Tad disapprovingly.

"Come on, Conan. You never let me have a go with the Desert Eagle. Just this once? You always say it's impossible to miss with it."

"If you think I'm going to let you get your hands on my baby, you are very *very* mistaken, Tad," said Conan.

"Tad, use your knife," ordered Butcher. "We can't waste the bullets, anyway, so get on with it."

Butcher watched as Tad returned to the truck and the dead girl. "What do you say, Conan, one for the road?"

Conan pulled two more cans of beer out and tossed one to Butcher.

"Amen to that," said Butcher, catching the can mid-air. "Ain't nothing gonna stop us now. What did I tell you? This place is the fucking bomb. You want something, I get it. We got it made here. Those walls are gonna see us through this. We can do *whatever* we want." Butcher watched as Tad rammed a knife through Victoria's head. "Whatever we want, Conan. Ain't nothing or *nobody* gonna stop us."

CHAPTER 13

She tightened the straps around her shoulders and went through a mental checklist of everything to do. Whilst she knew it wouldn't be easy, she had thought through exactly what she needed to do, and now that Attwood's house was directly in front of her, the only thing left was to put the plan into action.

Charlie had traded in her UCLA sweater which had been ripped to shreds like the supple skin on her back for a close-fitting black gym top underneath a black roll-neck jersey she had found in her mother's closet. On top of that she wore a black hooded dressing gown that covered her entire body. Her ripped jeans had been replaced with a fresh pair, and her left arm was wrapped in bandages. For what she was about to do she needed to be quick on her feet and had put on her old grey Converse sneakers. She wasn't going to be winning any fashion awards, but she had dressed appropriately for the occasion and finished her ensemble off with a large Gerber Air Ranger that her father used to take out fishing. There were several knives in her father's garage, but this one was the toughest one she could find. Charlie dry swallowed a couple of tablets and tried to clear her mind. The last twenty-four hours had seen her father killed, and her wounds were still to heal. After getting home before sunrise, she had tried to regain some energy and recuperate, but the knowledge that Victoria and Rilla were still in that house spurred her on. She'd washed out her cuts as best as possible and used her father's whisky as anesthetic when she stitched up the open wounds. Her face has been the hardest and she had had to settle for doing a quick job. The stitches were ragged and crude, and the slashed skin on her cheek was going to leave a scar. Her whole body ached. Her left arm was almost useless, and she had resorted to wrapping the whole thing in bandages. She could still manipulate a couple of fingers slightly, so she lived in hope that it wasn't damaged beyond repair. Her legs, too, throbbed with pain, and she had taken more painkillers in the last few hours put together than she had in the last few years.

Getting to Rilla was her main objective. Butcher had pretended to be Attwood, although she didn't yet know why. Perhaps Attwood was a prisoner in his own home, or perhaps he was just using Butcher to get what he wanted. The fact that they had set those dogs on them told Charlie all she needed to know. Rilla and Victoria were in danger, and she had to get to them. Charlie needed to know what was going on behind those walls.

The black gown hid her well in the dusk that was settling over the Attwood mansion. It also hid her from the zombies. They still meandered around the property, around the fake moat and roads, and slipping through them unnoticed had not been as easy as when she had crawled out of the drain. The bloody knife in her hand was testament to how she had made it this far, and the next part of her plan was by far the most daunting and dangerous. Charlie glanced around her. There were four zombies close by, all men, all strong enough to take her down if they attacked her at once. She felt able to defend herself if they came at her one by one, but if she had learnt one thing from her experiences on the road it was that the dead were unpredictable. Being so close to them was unsettling, but she knew she needed them close by. Too few, and it wouldn't work; too many, and her plan would go out of the window with the most likely result a painful death. Peering up from underneath her hood she saw the camera that they had missed the last time they had come here. It was nestled right in the upper corner of the building, almost hidden by an overhanging branch. She raised a hand and knocked on the door to the annex. Nothing happened, but she didn't expect it to. She knocked again and then slowly lowered her hand and stepped back. The noise had instantly got the attention of the dead, and they began to converge on the doorway. Charlie held her breath and kept her head down, covered by the gown. If she was right, then the door would automatically open. Whoever was watching would see her and let her in. The zombies were out of range of the camera.

As the door clicked open, Charlie smiled. She pushed the door open gently and walked into the room. Just like last time, the door had opened for her. Despite knowing what she was going into, the stench took her breath away, the memories almost making her regret coming back. The floor was still stained with fresh blood, and the scratches on the walls and floor testament to the fight that had taken place only hours ago. As soon as Charlie entered the room she stood to the side and held the door open. One by one the four zombies followed her into the dark room. Once they were in she fished the small black doorstop from her pocket, jammed it into the doorframe, and slipped out of the room allowing the door to close behind her. She kept her back flat against the wall and sidled carefully to the side of the building out of shot of the camera. Now all she had to do was wait. The doorstop was so small as to be practically invisible in the darkness of the evening, and it had stopped the door from closing successfully. Whilst it appeared to be shut, the locking mechanism wouldn't be able to snap into place, leaving her one opportunity before they noticed. Charlie bent down into the tall weeds beside the ditch and relaxed slightly. The zombies were all around her, and people on both sides of the wall were all too eager to kill her, but she had the advantage of knowledge. She knew exactly where they all were and what they wanted. They wouldn't know what hit them.

As she waited and listened, she touched the pendant beneath her jersey. She had cleaned it up as best as she could and gotten most of the blood off. Given even just half a chance then there was no way she would leave it behind. She hadn't been certain that the opportunity to retrieve it would even present itself, and she'd really just been lucky. The swarm of zombies that Schafer had told them about previously had dispersed, and the dead were spread out evenly throughout Peterborough. Getting home was just a vague fuzzy memory now. She had walked through the quiet dark streets on auto-pilot and couldn't recall how she had actually got home. When it had been time to come back to Attwood's, she had navigated her way through town with relative ease, keeping to the shadows and walking slowly through the corpses. Her clothes kept her well-hidden and had let her look for the one particular corpse she had wanted to find. The red dress had been helpful in that respect, and Charlie had finally found her mother outside the florists on Main. She was just staring at the window display as if it was a cinema screen. It wasn't just about retrieving the pendant but also about bringing some closure to her mother's death for both of them. Charlie had swiftly stabbed the Air Ranger blade through Jemma's skull, entering through the ear canal, and killing the brain. Her mother had dropped to the floor and died without even seeing her daughter approach. Charlie felt no remorse for what she did. Her mother was already dead. But as she took the silver heart pendant from her mother's body, she felt guilty. It was like robbing her mother's grave. As Charlie traced its outline now beneath her jersey, she was glad she had taken it. She needed to know that her mother was still with her in some way. If all went well, then she wanted to find something of her father's too. That would not be as easy as getting the pendant, though, and so Charlie sat in the weeds watching and waiting.

After only a couple of minutes she heard voices from inside the annex quickly followed by receding footsteps. A moment later there was the familiar sound of dogs barking. She suspected that Butcher wouldn't risk getting his hands dirty over a few zombies that had inadvertently gotten into the building. He would use the dogs, as usual, to tidy things up. That was her cue, and Charlie shuffled forward slowly across the bridge to ensure that not only did the camera not spot her, but that neither did the zombies in the neighboring fields and roads. She didn't want a crowd of them coming after her. Not yet.

The annex had been left in darkness. Evidently it wasn't worth wasting any power to light it just for a few zombies which made it a little trickier for Charlie. Still, she had been here before and knew the layout of the room. As she slipped into the room, she saw that three of the zombies had already been taken down by the dogs. She removed the doorstop and let the door click shut. The light above it turned red, and she heard the locking mechanism click into place. There was no way back, no way out, no retreat now. Charlie felt pleased. She had no intention of backing out anyway. She let the two dogs finish off the dead men, and they didn't even notice her as she crept to the open panels that led to their kennels. They didn't notice when she crawled down the tunnel and made her way to the drain where she had escaped earlier. The dogs didn't notice when she removed the wire-cutters from the small knapsack beneath her dressing gown and began to snip the wire mesh at the back of the kennel. Though the sun was setting, there was still a faint light which showed Charlie where she was. The last time she was here she had been in pitch black, unable to see anything. Beyond the wire mesh, though, she could now see open ground and further to the house.

As she snipped open the cage that kept the dogs prisoners, she became aware that she wasn't alone. She could hear breathing coming from the tunnel behind her. Hoping it wasn't a zombie, she turned and found a huge Doberman staring at her. Its tongue was hanging from its jaws and saliva dripped to the floor. Its face was covered in blood from the dead, and it snarled as she drew the fish knife out and readied herself.

"Bring it on. I'm ready for you this time, you fucking bitch."

As the dog leapt at her, she quickly pushed herself away and avoided its snapping teeth. Charlie rammed the knife into the top of the dog's skull, and it died instantly, collapsing at her feet.

"One down." Charlie waited for the next dog to appear, but the panel stayed closed, and nothing came. Charlie sighed. "Don't make me come get you," she said, frustrated. The longer she stayed here the longer she risked being discovered, but she had come with set goals and wasn't about to deviate from the plan now. The dogs had to die. It was riskier to leave them alive than to spend a bit of extra time killing them.

Charlie crawled on her knees back to the panel and nudged it open. The four dead men were scattered around the annex in pieces, limbs and hunks of meat discarded like chew toys. In the darkness Charlie didn't even see it coming. The last dog lunged at her as she appeared. It clamped its jaws around her left arm before she had a chance to react and searing pain erupted throughout her body as it sank its teeth into her already savaged arm.

"Not this time," said Charlie through gritted teeth as she pulled the dog closer to her. With her free hand Charlie plunged the knife into the dog's throat. Steaming hot blood poured out from the dog over her, and it let go of her arm instantly. The dog staggered back and then sank to its knees. Charlie looked at her arm. It was pretty much fucked.

"You know, I was going to make this quick," said Charlie to the dog. She crawled over to the whining creature and held the knife above its head. The dog's glassy eyes looked at her and it feebly snapped its jaws at her. "Fuck you. You can just bleed out."

Charlie put her father's old fishing knife between her teeth and crawled back down the tunnel to the cage, leaving the dog to die slowly. After the way her father had died she had no remorse for the dogs. Maybe they were acting the only way they knew, the only way they had been raised to, but that didn't mean they could change or even deserved a chance to. They were dangerous killers, and she had to put them down. In the back of the kennel Charlie finished snipping away at the metal cage and then peeled the wire mesh back. She crawled through onto the dirt, and pulled herself up, free of the kennel. Looking at the house she felt exhilarated. This was what she had come for. This was what they had all come for, yet there was a different reason now. There was more to this than finding sanctuary. Those animals that had killed her father and kidnapped her friends were going to realize that they had chosen the wrong option. They could've opened the door and let them in, but they had decided to keep this place for themselves. Looking at the massive house, she knew they could've all comfortably lived there. It was just greed. Butcher's greed was undoubtedly borne of fear that it would be taken away from him one day. He was nothing more than a kid who refused to share his toys. Well, now he was going to learn the hard way that this new world was all about sharing. The living couldn't afford to be divided anymore. If they didn't, they would die.

A soft rain fell as Charlie quietly walked toward the house. There were two open windows on the second floor and a couple more on the ground floor where light shone out. The trees were thick around the edge of the property, and she could see vehicles on the driveway. There was a bad smell as she approached the vehicles, and she crouched down behind a black sedan as a figure came out of the front door. It was a woman, and Charlie watched as she lit up a cigarette. The old woman sucked at it furiously as if it were the last one on Earth, and within a minute she had thrown the discarded butt to the ground. The woman disappeared back inside the house, closing the front door behind her. Charlie knew she had to get closer to the house and find out exactly who she was dealing with. There didn't seem to be anyone else around, and she slowly made her way around the sedan to get closer to the house. As she passed a pickup truck, she discovered the source of the smell. A body lay at the rear, still tied up. In the dusky gloom Charlie could see the person was dead and had suffered an ignominious fate. The body was too small to be Rilla. Charlie hoped it wasn't Victoria, but something in her heart knew that it was. Had they really killed the girl already? What had an innocent child done to deserve dying like that? Butcher was a sadistic fuck, and Charlie hoped that Rilla was still alive. If Victoria was dead, then Rilla probably didn't have much time left. Charlie felt bad for the little girl although she couldn't have got back to Attwood's any quicker than she had. She began to hurry to the house. There would be no more delays. It was time to end this.

Charlie crept by the wall of the house until she neared one of the windows where light was spilling out into the garden. The window was ajar, allowing her to get close enough to see and hear what was going on inside.

"You've outdone yourself. Cheeseburger and chips. Although I could do without the green stuff on the side of the plate. It's pretty good."

"Okay, enough small talk. I'm worried about those zombies. I still don't see how you let them get in."

Charlie heard two male voices talking and tried to see if she recognized them. As she stuck her head above the window ledge she could just see one of the speakers. It was Butcher. The other man was sat at a table eating, but had his back to her. The room looked like something out of a posh restaurant. Gleaming silver cutlery and candles adorned the huge wooden table. The chairs were lined with velvet and the walls covered in flock wallpaper with a massive chandelier hanging over the center of the table.

"I'm telling you, it looked like one of them knocked on the door. The security camera's probably whacked. What else can I say? I *thought* one of them knocked."

"Zombies don't knock, you idiot."

"Well I know that now, but—"

"All right, enough, Tad. Just don't let it happen again. One of them scraped against the door, and you thought they knocked. It's dark, and you misread the situation. When you've finished dinner you can go back and clean up. I don't want those dead fucks stinking up my annex any longer than they had to. Once the dogs are through, I want you back out there."

"But I thought I could—"

"Just do it, Tad. Don't fight me. I let you do the girl, didn't I? I thought you were getting with the program, and then you do something stupid like letting four zombies in. This is serious shit, Tad. You need to think a bit more about what you're doing."

Charlie watched as Butcher raised a glass of red wine and drank. She moved to the side and saw another man at the table. It was Conan, the huge man who had taken Rilla. As all three men ate, the smoking woman came into the room and Charlie ducked. The woman had looked straight out of the window almost directly at her. The woman walked to the window, and Charlie held her breath as she crouched down in the shadows.

"Can't none of you dumb asses close the window? It's raining out."

Charlie heard the windows being pulled shut, and then the woman walked away. Charlie knew she had been close to being discovered. She could still hear the muffled voices, though, and remained where she was. There were four of them apparently. If that was it, then where was Attwood?

"I'm going upstairs," said Butcher. "Verity, get the bitch cleaned up will you? She ain't good for nothing the state she's in."

"The green dress?" asked the woman.

"Yeah, it needs ironing. And some makeup this time. Rilla's skin is so pale; it's like fucking a ghost."

As she listened to the four people in the room laughing, Charlie didn't know how to feel. There was some relief with confirmation that Rilla was alive. Yet they obviously had her held upstairs and were abusing her. Was it all of them or just Butcher? Who could be so callous as to do that to a young girl?

"I know, I know," said Butcher. "Once we've all had our fair turn with her we'll let Attwood have her. Should be interesting to see that old fuck eat her out."

With more laughter echoing in the room, Charlie crept away from the window and back to the vehicles where she could hide and reformulate her plan. Whatever was going on, they were all in on it. Even the woman had laughed. These people weren't even human anymore. And what about Attwood? Was he just letting them rule the place, letting Butcher tell them what to do? Charlie slid her gown off. It was dirty and wet and would only slow her down now. She had an idea of what and who she would do next, but she had to find a way into the house. She had to make sure Rilla was safe before she went any further. Charlie tried the door handle of the sedan, and it opened easily. She climbed into the front seat and closed the door. The gentle rain tapped on the roof of the car, and she sat watching the house. The four people were sat at a table eating their dinner as if it was a normal day. It was as if they were blocking out the world and what was happening. There were so many people who could be saved, who needed help, and yet they had locked themselves away with no regard for anyone but themselves. They were evil. They had killed to protect what they had when they had more than they could even use. Charlie looked at the mansion. There were probably a dozen bedrooms, not to mention all the other rooms that weren't even being used. Her father would have liked it. Schafer and Magda would've been happy to have found a place like this for Rilla. Jeremy and Lyn would've had a safe place to raise Victoria. That had all been taken away from them by these people. Charlie angrily took off her knapsack and opened it. The few things she had brought with her would be sufficient for what she was going to do next, and she rummaged through the bag until she found what she wanted. She would have to travel light and leave the rest of her supplies in the sedan. The view of the car was obscured from the house by the pickup truck. It was perfect.

Charlie got out of the car and looked at her reflection in a wing mirror. She carefully applied a deep red lipstick she had brought with her and then slipped off the roll-neck jersey, leaving it in the car beside her knapsack. The knife hidden beneath her waist felt good. She remembered when Kyler had given it to her, thinking that she would never need it, at least not on the living. But now she would use it in a heartbeat if she had to. These people didn't deserve a quick death. She jogged back over to the house and found a quiet spot beneath an oak tree to wait. It was only a few feet away, and she could see into the dining room where the four people appeared to be finishing up. The temperature was dropping, but it was still warm, and even the raindrops were pleasant as they fell on Charlie's skin. She waited beneath the tree until she saw the front door of the house open. As expected, a man emerged from it and immediately began walking toward the annex. Charlie watched the man walk. He had a slighter figure than Butcher and was only half the size of Conan. He had light blonde hair sticking out from underneath a cap and looked at the ground as he walked. She wondered if it were he who had killed Victoria. He had 'done the girl.' Either way, he was in with Butcher, and there was no going back now. She tried to remember what Butcher had called him—Todd or Tad something? It didn't really matter. He was already a dead man. As he got closer, Charlie saw that the cap he was wearing was Kyler's fishing cap. That confirmed that he was no better than Butcher. He was a killer. If he was anything like Butcher, then he had probably raped Rilla too. He would be the second to die.

Charlie waited until Tad was out of sight and then ran to the front door. Unlocked, she said a prayer and opened it, wondering if she was going to come face to face with Butcher or one of the others. Instead, she found the hallway empty. The quietness of the room was unnerving. There was a stairway to her left with plush red carpet and another huge chandelier hanging above her. As she stepped into the room she closed the front door behind her. They obviously felt no need to lock it anymore. There were three doors she could choose to go through and an open doorway to the right which appeared to lead toward the dining room. The only light in the hallway was coming from that corridor to the dining room. A couple of candles at the top of the staircase told her that they were either conserving power or more likely being cautious. Perhaps they didn't have enough energy to sustain running the entire place. It would be unnecessary to light up all the rooms. Equally, if they lit up the whole house it would be seen from the top of the hill across Peterborough and beyond. Did they really want the place to be a beacon for the dead? Or perhaps they were more concerned about attracting the living.

Charlie slipped off her shoes and hid them underneath a hat stand alongside several other pairs. Her bare feet would make her footsteps quieter, and she hoped that every room was carpeted. The carpet in the hallway was thick and would hide her movements. She listened, hearing clattering noises from somewhere deeper within the house. Somebody was clearing away the dishes which meant at least one of them was occupied in the kitchen. With one outside that meant there were only two left, plus Attwood. The odds of getting to Rilla first were increasing by the second, and Charlie marched over to the staircase. She ascended slowly, watching out for any creaking floorboards. She found none. Reaching the top of the staircase had been easy, and the flickering candles showed her two options. To the left was a long corridor with what appeared to be several doors and to the right the same. There was no immediate clue as to what direction she should go to search for Rilla. The options were too numerous and Charlie stepped to the left into the thick shadows so she had time to think. The stairs were dark, but the candles gave off enough light for her to be seen if anyone came by. Charlie closed her eyes and listened. There had to be something. She didn't have time to search the whole mansion. Rilla didn't have time. The house was gloomy, but Charlie had become used to the darkness. After the kennel and the tunnel, after the night in Peterborough's streets and the company of zombies, she found the darkness almost soothing now. She could hide in the dark and found light uncomfortable. She liked it now, the protection the darkness gave her. It was no longer an enemy but a compatriot, complicit in her plans. In the darkness she could be anyone she wanted to be.

A faint hissing sound caught Charlie's ear. It disappeared and then came back again. It was coming from behind one of the doors to the right. Charlie looked down the stairs at the front door. It was still quiet, so she darted across to the other corridor from where the noise was coming from. As she made her way slowly down the dark corridor, heading further into blackness, she heard the hissing sound again and then it stopped abruptly. There was a faint rattling sound and then a smacking sound, as if two wet pieces of leather had been slapped together. Charlie edged further down the corridor and noticed that a sliver of light was coming out from beneath one of the doors. She made her way to it and stopped when she was a couple of feet away. She heard another smacking sound and a muffled voice. She had found someone, though she couldn't hear who. Charlie drew the Air Ranger out and put one hand on the door handle. The golden knob was cold and slipping in quietly unnoticed was impossible. She was going to have to go for it.

"Fight or die, Dad," Charlie said, and she flung open the door.

"Who the hell are you?"

Charlie tried to gather her thoughts quickly as she barged into the room, the sharp blade out in front of her. Rilla lay on top of a bed wearing a freshly laundered green dress that stopped above the knee. Her lip was bleeding, and her hands were bound. As Charlie entered the large room Rilla looked at her with growing surprise on her face. Beside the bed was the old woman holding a mirror and hairbrush, and next to her was an ironing board, the iron still steaming, and a small bedside table full of make-up.

"What are you doing in—?"

Before the old woman could finish her question Charlie rushed forward and lunged for her. The old woman was surprised, but not enough to wait to be stabbed, and she threw the mirror at Charlie as she attacked. The mirror glanced off Charlie's head and she ignored it. It had given the old woman enough time to prepare for the attack, though, and she raised her arms in defense. Charlie sliced the knife through the woman's outstretched palm, and they fell onto the bed together in a heap. Charlie grabbed the woman but the bed was soft, and it was impossible to pin her down. Charlie tried to ram the knife through her again, but the old woman moved quickly, bringing a knee up into Charlie's stomach.

As Charlie rolled away in pain she saw Rilla sit up and throw her bound arms around the woman. Charlie looked for her knife, but it was lost in the folds of the bedclothes, and she was desperately trying to suck in air as she looked for a weapon. Rilla had a hold of the woman, but Charlie could see Rilla was weak. The old woman leant forward slightly, and then smashed her head backward, causing the base of her skull to smack into Rilla's face. Rilla screamed out in pain and let go of the woman who crawled across the bed to Charlie with murderous intent in her eyes.

"Wait," said Charlie, but it was too late for talking.

The old woman planted a fist in Charlie's face and sent her flying off the bed. The old woman followed her and kicked Charlie in the gut again as she crawled across the floor around the foot of the bed.

"You come into *my* house and attack me?" Verity kicked Charlie again. "Who the fuck are you?"

Charlie felt another foot in her gut, and she put a hand on a leg of the ironing board for support as the breath was knocked out of her once again.

"Holy shit, you her girlfriend or something?" asked Verity, as she stared at Charlie. "You really think you can come in here and do as you please? Butcher is going to fuck you up."

Charlie used the legs of the ironing board to get to her feet. The old woman was staring at her, and Charlie knew that she was as bad as Butcher. Rilla was on the bed dazed and bleeding, and Charlie knew she had to stop the old woman from alerting the others.

"Why?" asked Charlie clutching her stomach. "Why are you doing this?"

"Look at you," replied Verity. "Pathetic. You come to us with your hands out, and when we bring one of you in this is how you repay us. With violence. That's why we can't let you all in. We select only the *prime cuts*, don't you see that? The annoying little girl was good for Conan, but it's you two who I'm most curious about. My boys have had their fun with this bitch, but you offer something new. They haven't had a blonde in a while."

Charlie's eyes were drawn to the knife on the bed. Rilla was crawling up against the headboard, and her movement had exposed the knife. Verity saw it too and was nearer to it than Charlie.

"Let me take Rilla out of here, and I'll let you live," said Charlie. She was beginning to regain her breath now, but her stomach hurt, and the cut on her face was bleeding again. "I'll give you that much. One chance. Take it."

Verity laughed until it descended into a cackle. Thirty years of smoking meant she had little energy for fighting. "I don't think so, darling. We're going to feed you to the fucking wolves."

As Verity lunged for the knife on the bed Charlie turned to the ironing board next to her. She had been inching ever closer to the hot iron the whole time they had been talking, and as Verity turned her back, Charlie seized her chance. She grabbed the iron and brought it down on Verity's back, the clothes sizzling beneath it. Verity screamed in pain and whirled around.

"You fucking bitch." Verity had grabbed the knife and intended to use it. "You fucking—"

Charlie smashed the iron across Verity's face, and the woman went down, stunned. Verity still held the knife in her hand, but a large red bruise was blossoming on the left side of her face. The skin was red raw, and Verity was shaking.

"Wait—" said Verity, but Charlie had no intention of waiting or giving her that one chance anymore.

Charlie got to her knees and bent over the old woman. There was still malevolence in her eyes, and Charlie saw the woman bring her hand up with the intention of using the knife. Charlie easily knocked the knife from her grasp and smashed the iron across the old woman's face again. She couldn't afford the woman to get away, and Charlie straddled her, pinning the woman's arm beneath her knees.

"You know how my father died? You know how Rilla's parents died?"

Verity shook her head feebly, her energy sapped and her nose broken. "Please, I don't know anything about that. It wasn't me."

Charlie put her face close to Verity's. "Fucking liar," she spat. "You know *exactly* what's going on here. You killed them. They died in agony, just like you."

"What?"

Charlie plunged the hot iron down onto Verity's face and held it there. The skin immediately began to burn, and though Verity tried to turn away she couldn't free herself from underneath Charlie. The burning flesh began to sizzle and steam reached Charlie's nostrils. She lifted the iron up, bringing with it large chunks of flesh from Verity's face. Much of the searing skin had stuck to the plate of the iron including Verity's lips.

Beneath her knees, Charlie could feel the old woman's body trembling. One of her eyes had exploded, and the other looked up at Charlie with something approaching fear. The old woman's mouth tried to form words, but blood spilled over her raw lips as she tried to speak.

"P-p-please. My son—"

"Pathetic." Charlie plunged the iron down again, thrusting it down onto Verity's face and holding it there with both hands. The smell of cooking flesh reminded Charlie of summer BBQ's in the back yard and Kyler sizzling steaks for them all.

'I want to kiss your mouth, hold your hand, and all I feel is the distant wind as you turn your back on me.'

No, I can't block this out, thought Charlie. The old woman's screams were muffled beneath the iron, and the song that erupted into Charlie's head was not required anymore. It had been a defense mechanism once, something she did when she wanted to lose herself in the old world when there were no zombies. Those days were gone, and so was the old Charlie. She dismissed the song and pressed down harder. The old woman was still wriggling even though Charlie had all her weight on the iron. The iron slipped slightly as Charlie felt the woman's jaw collapse. Several teeth spilled out amongst the blood pouring from the woman's face, and Charlie smelt piss as the old woman's bowels loosened just before she stopped moving.

Finally, Charlie let go of the iron and sat back. Her arms ached from the effort of holding it in place but it was over now. The woman was dead. She didn't feel particularly happy or relieved, but it was something that had to be done. Just like snapping a bird's neck, sometimes things just had to end.

"Charlie?"

Charlie looked up and saw Rilla at the end of the bed. She was staring at the old woman through red eyes.

"Is she dead?"

Charlie nodded.

"Good." Rilla looked at Charlie and smiled. She leant forward and brushed Charlie's cheek. "Is it really you? What happened? I thought you were dead."

"Me too." Charlie left the iron sizzling on Verity's corpse and got to her feet. She found the knife on the bed and cut Rilla's hands free before sinking down onto the bed, grateful for the rest. She just needed a moment to gather her thoughts. If the others had heard the shouting and screaming, then she wouldn't have long.

Rilla put her arms around Charlie's neck and began sobbing, unable to stem the flow.

"It's okay," whispered Charlie. "It's all right now."

CHAPTER 14

Scared to let go, Rilla kept her arms around Charlie but brought her face around so she could look into Charlie's eyes. "They killed her. Vicky was only ten. They killed her for no good reason just so they could have a laugh. It was just a game to them."

Charlie suspected as much. The burnt remains had looked small, and she figured Victoria wouldn't have as much use as Rilla.

"I'm guessing they didn't treat you too good." Charlie pushed a lock of hair out of Rilla's eyes. "Look, Vicky was just a plaything to them. If they'd kept her here, they would be doing to her exactly what they've done to you. No one should go through that. Vicky seemed like a sweet girl, and I wish I could have got to know her a bit better. But maybe she's better off out of this."

Rilla shrugged. "It's not fair, Charlie. Why did they have to do this? Why couldn't they just..."

As Rilla broke down again, Charlie felt a lump in her throat. She didn't have time to get sentimental now. There was a fight to be won. Seeing what they had done to Rilla and guessing what they had done to Victoria was more horrible than she had imagined. What kind of men were they? And this woman had helped them. Somehow that was even worse.

"How did you find me?" asked Rilla. "How did you make it? I thought you were dead. They said everyone was dead. When we came in... Did my parents...?"

Charlie kissed Rilla's forehead. "I'm sorry, but nobody else made it. They set a pack of dogs on us. It was nasty, dead nasty. Your father got me out. He fought back and killed one of the dogs. It bought me enough time to get out of there. Getting out of the property wasn't easy, but I guess I realized that giving up wasn't an option. When your father helped me, when he saved me from being ripped apart by those dogs, he asked me to get you. He wanted me to get you out of here, Rilla, and that's what I'm going to do. They're not going to touch you again."

Rilla sighed deeply. She traced her index finger gently across Charlie's cut cheek, making the skin tingle. There were some basic stitches holding her skin together that looked painful and raw. "What did they do to you? How did you survive?" Rilla looked at Charlie's hands. There were several cuts on her right hand, and her left hand was bandaged up completely. Dark blood had soaked through the bandage.

"It doesn't matter," said Charlie. "I can't go back and undo it. I wish I could've done more for the others, for my father, for yours... I'm sorry I couldn't get here any quicker. This time yesterday I was walking through the streets just trying to get back home."

"You walked?" Rilla wiped her eyes. "Past the corpses?"

Charlie nodded and took Rilla's hand. "I just walked. I think they thought I was like them. My face was cut, and I was covered in blood. One of the dogs ripped me open like a box of tissues. Anyway, when I got home I just crawled into bed. I found some painkillers and took a shit-load of them. I managed to sleep a while, and when I woke up it was day. I knew I had to come back. I wasn't going to leave you here no matter what happened to me. If it wasn't for Schafer, I'd be dead. So I found a first aid kit and set to work cleaning myself up. I'm not much of a nurse and stitching my face back together was even harder than it looks. I've got more painkillers flowing around my body than blood, but I'm not complaining. I brought some things with me to help us. Most importantly, I've got something I didn't have before, something that my father was trying to instill in me over the last few weeks that I couldn't see before. He taught me how to survive. He taught me to have belief in myself, and that's something they can't defeat. They can cut me, kick me, and throw me to the dogs. But I'm *alive*, Rilla. I'm alive, and I'm not going to waste what life I've got left. I'm shattered, but that's not going to stop me. I'll sleep when I'm dead."

"So what now?" Rilla brought Charlie's hand up to her face and held it against her cheek. The touch of someone other than Butcher and Tad was reassuring. Charlie's skin was soft and warm, and

Rilla wanted to feel safe again. She hadn't felt safe in a long time and was certain she would die that night. Now that Charlie was here it felt different. She felt protected. Charlie was only a few years older than her, yet she had felt a bond with her from the moment they had met. Even back at Kyler's house Charlie had looked out for her.

"Rilla, we don't have much time," said Charlie, getting off the bed. "I have to do more work. I need you to stay safe. I need you to stay in the house and hide, and let me take care of this."

"No," said Rilla quickly, jumping up off the bed too. "I want to stay with you. I don't want to be here anymore."

"Tough. You're staying put. You're in no condition to help me do what I have to do." Charlie looked at the skimpy green dress that Rilla wore and her bare feet. There was no way she was letting her come along. "No, you're staying here. I need you to trust me, Rilla. I've got this far, and I need you to trust me just a little bit longer. I promise you, this will end tonight."

"Here." Rilla held out the knife to Charlie. "I guess you'd better take this then."

Charlie refused it. "Keep it. I don't need it. Follow me back downstairs and get to the sedan parked out front. Stay there until I come get you. Come on, we don't have much time."

Leaving the room behind, the two girls hurried back into the dark corridor. Charlie listened carefully in case the men had been alerted to her presence by the dying screams of the old woman, yet nobody came rushing up the stairs to meet her. As they got back to the front door, Charlie heard noises still coming from deeper in the house somewhere. The house was so large that it had hidden the woman's cries. So much the better for them. Charlie carefully opened the front door and checked the area was clear. There was no sign of anyone.

"Let's go."

Leading Rilla by the hand back to the sedan, Charlie knew she had to get to the annex next and quickly. As Rilla climbed into the back of the sedan, Charlie took a length of cord from her knapsack and instructed Rilla to keep her head down and stay out of sight.

"You're coming back, right?" asked Rilla as she lay on the back seat of the car. "You're coming back?"

Charlie nodded and patted Rilla's bare foot as she closed the door. The girl looked half scared to death. It was the safest place for her right now. Charlie couldn't worry about looking after her when she had to concentrate on finding the others.

With Rilla safely hidden, Charlie jogged quietly through the dark evening to the annex. It was quiet, but as the large building loomed up out of the darkness, she saw a faint light on inside. She had hoped to beat the man to it, wanting to be able to surprise him, but she was going to have to change tack. She looked back at Attwood's house. To all intents and purposes it was deserted. There was Butcher and Conan to deal with, probably still within the bowels of the house, but right now she had one to take care of right here: the one who had been told to clean up the zombies, Todd or Tad. Charlie stealthily made her way to the annex and the open door. She cautiously peered inside.

Tad lifted the fishing cap from his head, wiped the sweat away from his brow, and sighed. He straightened up to stretch his back and threw the long-handled broom down in disgust. Why did Butcher think he could order him around like this? It wasn't his fault the zombies had got in. It was just an accident. He had managed to sweep up most of the remains, but it was the death of the dogs that sickened him. The zombies had managed to kill one, and there was something particularly sad about it. It was just an animal doing what it had to do. It was protecting its master. That would mean they were going to have to get more dogs, and Butcher wouldn't be happy about it. Tad hadn't even heard any noise coming from the kennels and knew that if the last dog had been injured he was going to have to check on it.

"Fuck this." Tad wanted to get back to the house and enjoy some time with Rilla. Butcher always bossed him about and talked to him like an idiot. It really had looked like someone had knocked on the door. How was he to know he was only letting in a few corpses? Anyone could have made the same mistake in the darkness. Tad turned back to the doorway, determined to leave and go back to Rilla. If Butcher didn't like it he could clean this shit up himself. There was nothing here that wouldn't wait until morning.

In the open doorway Tad saw a figure. They were standing outside in the dark, and Tad raised a hand to his eyes. "Butcher, that you?"

"I'm not Butcher."

The voice was female, but all Tad saw was a shadowy figure. He pulled out a gun and pointed it at the doorway. "Get in here. Verity?"

"I'm not Verity."

Tad was sweating, but it wasn't just from the exertion of cleaning up the dead zombies. Whoever this was, they were calm and just standing there watching him as if this were an everyday occurrence. Suddenly it dawned on Tad that it must be Rilla. There was no one else it could possibly be. He hoped there wasn't going to be any trouble as the gun he had was useless. It was just for show. The only weapon he had on him was the knife tucked into his boots.

"Rilla? What the fuck are you doing out here? How did you get out?" Tad knew that there was no way Butcher would just let her go.

"I slipped past him when he wasn't looking. I couldn't wait anymore. It's you I want. It's always been you."

Tad couldn't quite believe what he was hearing. "You got past Butcher to come and find *me*? Far out." Tad could see the outline of the mansion behind the girl, and wondered if this wasn't some sort of test or trick the others were playing. "Bullshit. I bet Butcher put you up to this."

"Well, if you don't want me." Charlie turned and began walking away from the annex. She kept to the shadows and headed for the protective canopy of an old oak tree.

"Wait, hold on," said Tad. If he did what Butcher had told him to do, then he would spend the next hour wiping up blood and bits of dead bodies. Rilla had come to him. To *him*. She was cute, and Butcher would never know. Tad could just say he found her out here and take her back to the house when he was through with her. Tad rushed outside and saw the girl standing beneath the tree. "Just hold on a moment."

Tad raced to the upper floor and control panel from where he turned out the lights and locked the doors. Then he quickly jogged back down and headed straight for his prize. It was dark under the tree, far too dark to see properly, and he kept his gun in his hand just in case this was a trick. Park of him couldn't believe it yet he wanted to. There was no sign of the others, and he didn't know how long he would have before they came looking for her. The girl held nothing in her hands and was offering herself to him. Perhaps this wouldn't be such a bad evening after all.

"Rilla?"

The girl was facing the tree, her back to him. He put a hand on her shoulder and slid it down to her hip.

Charlie shuddered inwardly. She had half expected to be dragged in to face Butcher, but it looked as if this man was either drunk or stupid. It was almost too easy. When she felt his hand on her hip she knew she didn't have long. She could try to grab the gun off him but it was too risky, plus she didn't want to make too much noise, not just yet. She flexed her neck.

"Take me. Now."

The gun in her back disappeared, and then she felt his warm breath on her neck. Both his hands cupped her breasts and his mouth kissed her bare shoulder. Charlie smiled as she let the cord unravel from her left hand. It had been coiled up, hidden from view, and as the man began to squeeze her breasts she gasped.

"Wait."

Charlie stepped out of Tad's embrace and turned around. She stepped forward, and a tiny sliver of faint light from the house hit her face.

Tad saw the red lips and blue eyes, but it didn't register in his brain that it wasn't Rilla until he caught a glimpse of the short blonde hair. "Wait, you're—"

Knowing that he was off guard and the gun was tucked into his pants, Charlie swiftly wrapped the cord around Tad's neck and jumped around to stand behind him. Both ends of the cord were wrapped around her wrists so there was no chance she might lose her grip, and she pulled it together tightly.

Tad tried to slip his fingers underneath the cord around his neck, but he was too slow, and couldn't even get a single finger underneath. He gurgled and stumbled forward. Charlie went with him, all the while pulling the cord tighter and tighter. Tad fell to his knees and continued to try to get the cord away from his neck, but it was strangling him, taking away all of his breath. He tried to get more air into his lungs but it was impossible.

Charlie leant over Tad, her warm breath on the back of his neck. "The only thing that's going to be *fucked* around here is you." Charlie gritted her teeth and pulled the cord so it was completely tense. She could feel Tad's body trembling as he fought her, and even though her arms ached she was not about to let go. The length of cord that she had brought with her from Kyler's garage was strong and wouldn't break. It was like an anaconda wrapped around the man's neck, and there was no way out for him. He had killed for the last time. He was fighting, and Charlie struggled to stay on her feet, but the more he fought her, the harder she pulled the cord. In the darkness, she could do whatever she wanted to.

Tad's eyes bulged out, and as his body went limp, Charlie kept hold of the cord. She could feel spit and blood dripping from his mouth over her fingers, but she wanted to make sure he was dead. She wanted to know he wasn't going to get up again, and so she let the cord begin to cut into his skin until it felt like she was going to pull his head off. The man's legs kicked feebly and then there was nothing. When she finally let go, Tad's body slumped forward against the oak tree. Charlie stood there panting, staring at him. She dropped the cord and bent over the body. There was no breath coming from his mouth, and she retrieved the gun from his belt. It was still too early to use it. Soon the man would be back up and walking around, but she would deal with that later. The living were far more dangerous. She plucked the hat from his head and put it on her own.

"That's *mine*." Why did people think they could just take what they wanted? She had given up on understanding this new world. Her father had warned her of people like this. He had thought the answer might be to build a wall between the living and the dead; between those who had life and those who wanted it. But separating them was never going to work. Death was as much a part of life as anything, and no wall was going to stop it.

Charlie nestled her back against the oak tree and looked at the house as she regained her breath. Two left. Butcher and Conan. If

Attwood was still around, then he was keeping a low profile. He would keep. Who was next was really just who came out first looking for this one. She didn't care who she killed next. It was just a means to an end. Kyler would be pleased with her. She had thought he was insane spending all that time readying for a fight. All along he had been right. The world was a different place now. When it came to them and us, it wasn't the walking corpses he was talking about.

Charlie headed back to the sedan, intending to check on Rilla, when she saw movement from the house. A figure came out, and Charlie darted behind the pickup truck. She needed whoever it was to get much closer to her. She wasn't sure if they were armed, either, and couldn't afford to take any chances. Holding the gun down at her side, she waited to see what direction they headed for. The figure seemed to pause and think before heading for the cars. She had hoped they would go for the annex. That way they would get ahead of her, and she could take them out from behind. A clean shot in the back of the head would do it. But if they came to the parked vehicles, they might find Rilla. That would complicate things.

The footsteps got closer, and Charlie peered around the edge of the truck. It was Conan. The size of him seemed even bigger than she remembered. He looked like a sumo wrestler except his bulk was all muscle and no fat.

"Yo, Tad, you fucking around out here? What're you doing? We've cleaned up inside, so if you're done out here we'll get to work on the girl."

Confrontation used to scare her. Charlie would shy away from arguments, and even when Jackson had dumped her she had let him off easy. Kyler had told her as much. She had lost her head when it had fallen apart. So much had happened since then that she had to stop herself from bursting out laughing. Remembering how she used to be felt like a dream. She had gone from nothing, from an ordinary girl, to standing outside a millionaire's mansion holding a gun having just killed two people. Charlie smiled and stepped out from behind the truck and pointed Tad's gun at Conan.

"Hold it."

Conan had been about to discover Rilla in the sedan, and it seemed like now was as good a time as any. It wouldn't make any difference now if she made some noise. She needed to anyway, and shooting Conan dead in cold blood just as he had Jeremy would be fitting.

"Who the fuck are you?" Conan pulled at his white goatee with curiosity. There was no sense of fear in his voice. He stared at Charlie. "How did you... what did you do with Tad?"

Charlie smiled sweetly. "Tad? He's a little short of breath right now. Don't worry. He'll be up on his feet soon. He's just another of those walking zombies now, just like you."

Charlie pulled the trigger and the gun clicked. Nothing happened. She pulled it again and still nothing happened.

Conan grinned. "Empty, bitch."

He charged at her, and Charlie had only a split second to decide what to do. Tad's gun was a dud, for show only. Just like the man himself; all style and no substance. Charlie knew she could stay and fight, but the man was like a giant, and overpowering him would be virtually impossible. The other option was to run, but she hated that option. She really hated running now; hated turning away from a fight. She had to take a long-term view, though, and knew if she could lose him in the darkness she could regain the advantage. Charlie turned on her heels and ran into the darkness away from the house.

Conan ran after her, his lumbering bulk sending tremors through the ground. "You're dead, you know that?" he shouted, but the girl kept running. She was a stranger, and yet there was something about her blue eyes that was familiar. He felt like he had looked into those eyes before, but he couldn't place them. It was irrelevant. He was going to beat her to a pulp and worry about it later. Nobody took a shot at him. He knew he was lucky the gun wasn't loaded. The girl obviously didn't know that either which made him wonder what she was doing here. If she had come to kill him, then why not bring a loaded gun?

Tad.

As Conan chased after her he realized she had gotten the gun off Tad. She had killed him and taken his gun except she hadn't checked to see if it was actually loaded. It was just like that stupid fool to not carry a loaded weapon. The idiot fuck deserved what he got.

They were in the gardens of the house now, and Charlie had no idea where she was going. She was leading him away from Rilla which was one of her aims, but she didn't seem to be making much ground. She glanced around as she ran and could still see and hear the big man following her. He was surprisingly quick on his feet, and Charlie knew she was going to do well to give him the slip. The ground beneath her bare feet was soft, and her only advantage now was that she was dressed in black. Conan was still behind her, and she turned back to look for some place to hide when she suddenly hit something and went flying.

The cooler spilled out warm water over the ground and Charlie screamed as she hit the dirt. With her face literally planted in the rose garden, Charlie grabbed the rose bush and ignored the sharp thorns that dug into her skin. Her shin was throbbing from where she had run straight into the cooler. Maybe running around in the dark hadn't been such a good idea. As she got to her feet, she heard a moaning sound coming from above her.

"What the hell?" Charlie couldn't understand what she was looking at. The windows of the house didn't give off enough light for her to see clearly out in the garden, but it looked like a huge cross. There appeared to be a man strung up on it, yet the sounds emitted from above her were not the sounds of a living man or even someone in pain. They were the sounds of the dead.

"I see you met Attwood," said Conan, as he planted a fist into Charlie's face.

Once more Charlie found herself falling and collapsing into a thorny rose bush. Her face felt like a freight train had slammed into it, and blood gushed from her nose. A rough hand grabbed her left arm, and she squealed in pain. In the darkness she heard laughter.

"That hurt?" asked Conan, laughing and holding Charlie in front of him. There was no doubt she would drop like a stone if he didn't support her.

She looked at him through glazed eyes. The sucker punch to the side of the head had knocked her for six. The whole world was fuzzy. She knew enough. Conan had caught her. She also knew that Attwood had been caught in their web just like her. He was as dead as everyone else they came across.

"What do you think, Attwood? Think I should let this bitch go?"

Charlie heard the zombie moan, and then Conan punched her again. He caught her full in the face, and she went down clutching her head. Everything was spinning, and she was sure her nose was broken. The bone felt like it was shattered, and she wanted to close her eyes as the pain spread around her body. She couldn't fight him. She couldn't do it. She touched the silver pendant around her neck and let the blood spill from her mouth. He was going to kill her, and she couldn't stop it. She felt Conan's huge arms lift her to her feet again, and through swollen eyes, she looked at him.

"Still standing, huh?" asked Conan. "Impressive."

Charlie spat and felt one of her teeth come loose with her tongue. She sucked and spat it out along with a mouthful of warm blood. "I'll never give up," she said quietly.

"Is that so? You hear that Attwood? We got ourselves a fighter. Well, I don't quit either. I've never shied away from a fight, and I'm not starting now. I could just shoot you but why spoil a good thing? I think a good old fashioned fist fight is what we both want, right?"

Conan let go of Charlie and aimed his fist. The punch landed on her jaw, and yet again Charlie fell to the ground. Conan laughed and stood over her. "Come on. Get up. Get to your feet, and show me you're a fighter."

Charlie's head was full of concrete, her thoughts like cold soup. The gun was useless. Attwood was dead. She wanted to go home. She had taken too much for granted. She had taken her life for granted and thought she could defeat them all on her own, but she was wrong. She wanted to get vengeance for her father, but as she cradled her aching body on the soft wet ground she knew she had failed. The rain had petered out to nothing, and she was going to die alone.

"I'm sorry, Dad," Charlie whimpered. Her body felt light and she waited for Conan to lift her to her feet just so that he could strike her again. He wouldn't stop. He enjoyed it. He would keep going until he had beaten her senseless, and then he would keep going until she was just mulch for the roses. Charlie rolled onto her back and looked up at Conan. The crucified body of Attwood loomed over them both, and as Charlie looked up at Conan she began to laugh.

Conan clenched his hands into fists. "What? You think dying is funny?"

"No." Charlie coughed and winced, wishing she had more painkillers on her. Kyler hadn't told her how painful fighting could be. "I'm just looking forward to seeing the shock on your face when I kill you."

"I don't think so." Conan bent over Charlie. "I was going to save you for Butcher, but I think I'll just kill you now."

CHAPTER 15

When Rilla plunged the knife into Conan's neck it took a moment for the realization he's been struck to sink it. His expression turned from anger to curiosity, and as he was about to hit Charlie he faltered. He put a hand to his neck and touched Kyler's fishing knife. The three-inch blade had penetrated his throat and only the very hilt remained exposed. Conan stumbled back, copious blood pouring from his open wound like an exposed oil well.

"What the fuck?"

Rilla picked up the discarded cooler and swung it round to smash Conan in the face. He finally went down in a heap at the base of the crucifix, and Rilla dropped the cooler to turn to Charlie.

"Are you gonna be okay?" she asked, helping Charlie to her feet.

Charlie swayed as she stood and put her weight on Rilla who slipped an arm around her waist. "I will be." It hurt to think let alone speak. She didn't know what a broken jaw felt like, but Conan had done his best to give her one. Her left eye had swollen shut, and her mouth kept filling with blood from where Conan had knocked her teeth out. "You should be in the car. I told you to wait."

"I might not be where you are, but I'm getting there. My parents made me strong, much stronger than what you've seen from me so far. I wasn't about to let you do this on your own."

"Thanks," whispered Charlie. She looked at Conan. He was injured, but he was far from dead. She had nothing left to kill him with except her bare hands. She could try to snap his neck, but she was shattered. The beating he had given her on top of the dog attack had left her weak, and she wasn't sure she had it in her.

"We can't leave him like this," said Rilla, as if reading Charlie's mind.

"No, we can't." Charlie took a whistle out from her pocket, one she hadn't used since her high-school netball days. "I've got a plan."

Charlie blew loudly on the whistle sending a shrieking noise through the quiet air. When she stopped, Rilla looked at her with amazement.

"What the hell are you doing?"

"Trust me," said Charlie. She spotted her fishing cap on the ground and picked it up. There was blood on it, but she didn't care and placed it on her head. "Get me back to the sedan and just trust me. I've got an idea."

"What about the gun?" asked Rilla. She looked at Conan. "Shouldn't we—"

"Leave it. We don't need it."

It only took a minute for them to reach the sedan, and Rilla helped Charlie into the front seat. As they sat in the comfort of the luxury car, Rilla turned to Charlie. "So what are we waiting for?"

Charlie peered through the windshield. It should be any moment now. Her breath was starting to fog up the glass and she wiped her hand through the mist. In the gloom outside she saw movement, a lone figure stumbling through the garden in the direction of the crucifix. Charlie smiled. "That," said Charlie, pointing out Tad to Rilla.

They watched as the resurrected body of Tad stumbled past them oblivious to their presence. Rilla could see the mottled bruised skin around his neck and the distended tongue that hung from his open mouth. His eyes were pure white, and as he walked into the rose garden, Rilla turned to Charlie.

"I took care of him." Charlie answered, without waiting for the question. "And now he's going to take care of Conan."

A few seconds later, with Tad out of sight, they heard the screams begin. They came from the darkness and echoed off the moon and stars. There was no mistake. Tad had found the weakened Conan. Charlie didn't need to see him rip out the big man's throat. She didn't need to see Tad tear chunks of his flesh out, or to see Conan beg for his life as Tad tore him open. She knew he was dead. There was a certain poetry and satisfaction in knowing that Conan had been killed by one of *them*. The huge walls they lived behind hadn't protected them as they thought, and now they would both become zombies. Even the old woman, if her brain hadn't been destroyed, would probably return. They would all turn into the things they most hated. Eventually they would be the ones on the other side of the wall, forced to try to navigate a dangerous world and find others. They would join them on the other side of the wall, and this place would become a safe shelter once more. The only potential problem now was Butcher.

"Rilla, that whistle and all the noise we made will have brought a lot more of the dead to this place," said Charlie. Her head was pounding. "You know, I bet they're piled up outside just begging to get in."

"I know. How are we going to get rid of them? What do we do now?" asked Rilla. "I just want this over, Charlie. I just want this to be all over. How do we get out of here with those corpses at the door?"

"We're not leaving," replied Charlie. "I want the zombies to come. I *want* them here."

"Are you insane? What about Butcher? What about this place? You saw what they did to Attwood. We can't stay here now."

Charlie tensed up as pain racked her body. She sucked in a breath and let it go slowly. For a moment she thought she might pass out, but she couldn't stop now. Kyler had taught her that once you started something you finished it. She wanted to sleep, but there was still something she had to do. "Look in that knapsack will you, please? There are some painkillers."

Rilla found a bottle of white tablets and poured some into her hand. She took three and handed them to Charlie.

After she had swallowed the pills, Charlie took Rilla's hand. "When this is done I'm probably going to crash. I need to know you can handle this, Rilla. When Butcher is gone I'll try to help you clean this place up. Those two in the rose garden and maybe that woman in the house will need dealing with. You need to put them down, you understand? The ones outside these walls won't get in. If we can make it through tonight, then we can do it, Rilla. We can turn this place into the sanctuary that it's supposed to be."

Rilla leant over to Charlie and pulled her close. Hiding in the sedan earlier she had been scared. She had been scared for herself and for Charlie, but now that they were together again she felt stronger. There was something about being with Charlie that made her feel confident. Charlie had been through the wars, and Rilla could see the tiredness etched all over her young face. Her short blonde hair was covered in blood and dirt, and the stitched holding her cheek together had come loose. There didn't seem to be much choice but to follow through with whatever plan Charlie had and finish this. After what Butcher had done to her, Rilla wanted to do it. If Charlie believed in it, then so did she. Rilla tucked a lock of blonde hair behind Charlie's ear and smiled. Later, when all this was over, she would have to tend to Charlie's wounds. She was bruised and bleeding all over, and it would be a long time before she was ready to fight again. If what she said was true, then maybe they wouldn't have to fight again. Maybe they could turn this place around. Attwood certainly had no claims on it anymore. Rilla saw no reason why they couldn't work together and make a go of it.

"Okay. What do I do? And *don't* tell me to wait here."

Charlie smiled back, proud of Rilla and pleased she had come back. There was something growing between them that she hadn't felt for anyone for a long time. Since her mother had died, Charlie had felt very alone in the world, but since Rilla had burst into her life she had found something to fight for. This wasn't just about vengeance anymore. Their own futures were on the line, and they were inexplicably bound together now no matter what happened.

"Follow me."

* * *

Butcher stared at the video screen blankly. The road outside Attwood's was quiet. A few zombies occasionally passed by, but from the viewpoint of the camera above the annex door, there was little to arouse his interest. He would ask Conan to keep watch for a while and go see if Rilla was ready. After eating he had been watching the monitor on his own, but the security room was far from the action and he was bored. He tapped the tip of a large knife on the wooden desk and then frowned. Was that a burning smell?

"Verity, you cooking again?"

Butcher left the security room and its black and white TV screens, and made his way through the house to the stairway. The burning smell grew stronger as he got closer to the front door, and as he reached the bottom of the stairs he realized the smell wasn't coming from the kitchen but upstairs.

"Conan? That you? What are you doing?"

Butcher shook his head and sighed as he ascended the stairs. "Do I have to do everything myself? Jesus, they'd burn the place down if they didn't have me to keep a watch on them."

Up on the second floor the smell of burning was stronger, and Butcher knew the only people up here were Rilla and his mother.

"Christ, what are you doing in there?" Butcher angrily marched down to the bedroom. There were no fireplaces up here which only meant someone had been lazy or stupid or both. Verity liked to smoke, but she was supposed to go outside. Butcher hated the smell of it.

"Mom, if you're going to burn the house down with one of your fucking cigarettes, then you can—"

As Butcher threw back the door, he was surprised to find the room empty. The bed was a mess, and there was blood on the white sheets. Grey smoke drifted lazily through the air, and Butcher noticed the ironing board at the foot of the bed had collapsed. A pair of feet stuck out by the end of the bed, motionless.

"Shit." Butcher dropped the knife and approached the body carefully. He knew from the sloppy clothes that it wasn't Rilla, and while the face had been burned beyond recognition, he knew who it was. There was an iron embedded in his mother's face, and Butcher howled. He lifted the iron off his mother's dead body and pulled clumps of singed hair and skin with it. There would be no open casket for what was left of Verity.

"I'm going to kill that fucking bitch." Butcher wouldn't cry for his mother yet. He wanted revenge. He wanted to know how Rilla had managed to get away and do this. Where were the others? Why had nobody else come?

As Butcher ran back down the smoking corridor, he began to shout. "Conan. Tad? Get your fucking asses out here, now!"

Back at the front door Butcher waited, but neither Tad nor Conan appeared. There was a long whistling sound as if someone was about to kick off a soccer game in the rose garden. "What the fuck is going on?"

Butcher raced to the kitchen but found only a neatly piled stack of dishes and no Conan. "Guess it's up to me then." Pulling a meat cleaver out from one of the kitchen drawers, Butcher ran to the dining room. "Conan, you in here?"

The house was silent. For the first time since taking over Attwood's, Butcher felt unnerved. There was something off. He was angry and knew that Rilla had done something. Perhaps Conan had already found her and was teaching her a lesson. But there was something more going on that he couldn't see or understand yet. Butcher returned to the front door and opened it slowly. When he looked outside he saw nothing unusual. It was dark, and the rain had brought the fresh smell of the garden to his nose. He heard the faint groans from Attwood. The vehicles were parked up where they had been left, so he knew that Rilla hadn't tried to smash her way out.

Stepping out of the house, Butcher didn't know where to turn next. Rilla could be hiding anywhere. Conan was probably out looking for her which only left Tad. Was he still cleaning up the zombies in the annex? He could use an extra pair of eyes in his search for Rilla, and Butcher headed toward the entrance of the property.

A groaning sound came from behind the pickup truck, and Butcher looked over his shoulder. A bulky shape emerged from the darkness.

"Conan? Where the fuck have you been? Rilla's killed Verity and taken off. I'm just going to get Tad now. You need to get your shit together and—"

Butcher stopped. There was something about the way Conan moved unsteadily and the way his eyes appeared to be glazed over that made Butcher aware something had gone horribly wrong.

"Conan?"

The man bumped against the truck and then headed for Butcher. His stiff limbs made him walk awkwardly, and Butcher could tell he was dead. Another figure emerged from behind Conan, and Butcher saw his dead brother.

"No." It came out as a whisper, a denial of what he was seeing. "No," said Butcher again, as shivers ran up and down his spine. "She can't have done all of this."

Butcher retreated away from the advancing zombies, unable to look anymore at the corpses of Tad and Conan as they walked toward him with their arms outstretched. His head was spinning. How had Rilla done this? Had he underestimated her? Had she been fooling him all along? He had made a mistake in letting her in He should've kept the door locked.

As Butcher wheeled around he saw light coming from the annex. Somebody was in there. It had to be Rilla. There was nobody else left to operate the controls. She was trying to escape, but if she opened that front door then she would let *them* in. Butcher began to run toward the annex and saw that the door was open. A figure stood in the middle of the room, the single light bulb illuminating her.

"Rilla!" Butcher saw a flash of green as she darted out of sight. It *was* her. As soon as he caught up with her he would gut her and let Tad eat her alive. He was going to enjoy watching her die. "Rilla, wait there. You can't run from me."

Butcher charged into the annex and flung the door shut behind him. He didn't want her slipping past him and getting away. This was going to be the end for her. There was still a crude mess of body parts in the room left over from when Tad had accidentally let the zombies in earlier. There was no sign of Rilla though. No green dress, no sight or sound that she was anywhere.

"Rilla? Time's up. Come out, come out, and we'll play a game. I think it's time you joined your parents."

The door clicked shut behind Butcher, and he saw the light above it turn red. Then the green lights above the panels turned red, and he heard the locking mechanism to the dogs' kennel turn.

"What are you playing at, Rilla? You can't hide from me." Butcher tried to open the panels but they were fastened shut. Had she gone into the kennel? How had she got past the dogs? And if she had, then who was operating the controls?

A deafening whistle obliterated Butcher's thoughts as it echoed sharply around the room. Butcher put his hands over his ears and returned to the center of the room. He looked up at the gantry where he had stood a day earlier and condemned five people to a grisly death. The dark figure removed the whistle from their mouth and stared at him.

"Rilla? How did you get up there so fast? Open this fucking door right now."

Charlie stepped forward in order to let Butcher see her clearly. Slowly she removed the blue and green fishing cap from her head to expose her short blonde hair. "Remember me?"

Butcher frowned. "You look like someone I killed. That asshole's son? But you look... different."

"Close. I'm that asshole's *daughter*. You saw what you wanted to see and made an assumption based on what I looked like. You made a mistake, Butcher. All you had to do was open the door and let us in. Instead you turned your back on me, on us. You could have changed the world, but instead you stuck to your stereotypes and out of date views. We weren't a threat to you. You just assumed that everyone on the other side of the wall was a danger to you; that they couldn't possibly help or contribute. You judged us all the same, and now it's come back to bite you in the ass. Now you're going to pay for your selfish, callous attitude."

"But... but how did you get out? How did you get over the walls? There's no way through them, I made sure. I made sure that they were big and strong, that nothing could get through." Butcher looked at the door to the road that led to Peterborough. The red light was on indicating it was still locked. "You can't have gone through that way. No way."

The door behind Charlie opened, and then Rilla appeared. She smiled at Charlie and then looked down at Butcher.

"There's more than one way to skin a cat, dickhead."

"No trouble?" Charlie asked Rilla. She had told her how to get out of the annex through the kennel and the wire she had cut a hole through earlier. Butcher had walked right into their trap and now he was stuck like a pig.

Rilla shook her head. "Just Tad and Conan wandering around like a pair of hillbillies who sniffed too much glue. They're heading our way, but we can take care of them. We killed them once; we can do it again."

Charlie smiled weakly. The game was nearly over. She wanted to rest but she had to see it through to the end. "Cover your ears a second."

Rilla did as Charlie instructed and then blew on the whistle long and hard. When she was through, the two of them looked down at Butcher.

"Jesus, what is with that? You are off the planet. You're going to deafen us all with that shit." Butcher rubbed his temples. The shrill blast from the whistle set his teeth on edge, and he kept picturing Verity with her face burnt away. He imagined Conan lumbering around in the darkness and Tad behind him. He couldn't understand how it had all gone so wrong. He was angry with Rilla and himself for letting it get this far. He should've just killed them all when he had the chance. He waved the meat cleaver in the air. "I'm going to chop the both of you up into little pieces and feed you to my dogs."

"I don't think so," said Rilla. She despised Butcher and everything he stood for. He belonged in the darkness. She was with Charlie now and everything he had done to her could be erased. She didn't want to dwell on it or remember the horrible things he had done. She just wanted him dead.

Butcher pointed angrily up at the gantry. "You two cunts had better let me out of here right now, or I am going to kill you *both* very slowly, very painfully. You hear me?"

Neither Rilla nor Charlie responded.

"Do you fucking here me?" shouted Butcher, apoplectic with rage. His face had turned red, and the single light bulb above him only heightened how alone he felt. He suddenly realized how vulnerable he was and how he had left the others in the same position. He remembered what he had done to them and what fate awaited him. The dogs were on the other side of the panel, and he wasn't sure he would be able to control them. They were used to seeing him through a wire cage, and he hadn't exactly treated them well. He had trained them to kill, and if they came face to face with him, then he suspected that was exactly what they would do. "Let me out of here!"

"The problem is, Butcher, you just ain't good for nothing. I don't think we want to let you go," said Charlie, her hands hovering above the control panel. "I'm going to feed you to the wolves."

Butcher looked around the room and recalled how he had told her the same thing. He shook his head. "You're not doing shit. You can't do nothing to me. I'll kill the dogs with my bare hands, and then I'm coming to get you."

"Oh yeah?" Charlie raised her hand above the control panel. "You think?"

"Woah, hold on, hold on," said Butcher. It couldn't end like this, not here, not now. He had the cleaver, but the dogs were fast, and he was all alone. "Look, I made this place what it is. You need me. We can run this place together if that's what you want." Butcher decided he had to try acting contrite. It didn't sit well with him, but if he had to beg for his life then he would. He just had to play the part right and could seek his revenge later. "The wall around this place keeps *them* out, you know. You don't have to do this. All we have to do is keep *them* on the outside, and we stay on this side. There's no need for all of this." Butcher attempted a smile, hoping it would appeal to her compassionate side. "You're safe now. You, too, Rilla. I was just angry before. I was out of my head, you know. It was Conan. He kept pushing me, and I guess I fell for it. Look, we can start over. Okay? Let's just go back to the house together. What do you say?"

"I say that you're delusional," said Rilla.

"No wall can keep you safe forever." Charlie took Rilla's hand in hers. It was partly for support and partly because what they were about to do she wanted to do together. She kept talking to Butcher as she moved their hands over the control panel. "Build it as high as you fucking want, but eventually someone will find a way through. I'm proof of that. Walls can fall, you know. They divide us and provide you with a false illusion of safety that means you get complacent. You think you can hide behind these walls forever? You think you can keep *them* out forever? The corpses will get in one day. I got in, didn't I? And I'm willing to bet there are more like me out there who need help, who need to find a better life; you're not a part of that world, Butcher. People like you just want more and more to squirrel away what you've got just for yourself. Well, that world is over. You're not the future, Butcher. You're part of history now."

Charlie and Rilla fingers depressed a button, and Butcher heard the door unlock. The lights above the panels to the kennels remained red, as did the light above the door to the house. He turned around and saw the green light above the exit.

"Fuck me. So you're letting me go?" Butcher looked up at Charlie and Rilla. "After all this, you're just letting me go?"

"Not exactly. I said I was going to feed you to the wolves and that's exactly what we're doing." Charlie looked at Rilla proudly. "We're giving you every opportunity that you gave us."

Butcher watched as the exit door opened and a large, dead corpse stepped through. Butcher finally realized then what all the whistling had been about. It had been a siren for the dead. Another corpse came through the open doorway and another one behind that. Butcher saw a zombie wearing a turban, the man's black beard covered in blood. Another zombie wore a sari that had been ripped apart to expose the hideous rotting flesh beneath. More and more came into the room, women and children, all different shapes and sizes and yet all the same; they were all dead. Butcher looked horrified as the zombies ambled toward him, pressing him back.

"What are you doing? What is this?" Butcher shouted.

Charlie smiled. She stepped back from the controls. "You think we'd let you go? You're zombiekill."

Butcher looked around the room, but there was no way out. Everything was locked down tight, and there was no way past the corpses. They kept filing into the room and were almost on him. Butcher ran for the door and began frantically pulling at it, trying to get his fingers around the frame and get the door open. A fingernail broke off but he kept going, desperate to get out. The door to Attwood's house was locked shut, and no amount of violence would open it.

"You fuckers, open this fucking door. Open it now, you evil fucking witches!"

Charlie leant over the control panel and smiled as Butcher scrambled to get the door open. "Fight or die, Butcher. That's your only choice now."

As the first zombie reached him, Butcher swung his cleaver at it, and it lodged itself firmly in the man's head. The zombie reeled backward and fell down dead but was replaced quickly by another. Butcher tried to throw punches at them, but he was too slow. The dead woman in the sari grabbed his right arm and sank her teeth into his wrist. Blood spurted out vociferously, and Butcher felt one of the dead children grab his crotch. Small teeth began to nip at his upper thigh, and fingers clawed at his legs. A black man with half of his face missing pushed his way forward and began to rip at Butcher's clothes. Another man, his arms eaten away to just bloody stumps, nestled his head in the crook of Butcher's neck and began to bite the soft skin. A slim white woman with bright red hair and two pits of maggots where her eyes used to be sank her teeth into his face and pulled off a hunk of meat from his forehead. She swallowed the supple skin quickly and then sank her teeth back into him. Her jaw clamped around his eye socket, and he could feel her teeth ripping out his eyeball. His arms were held in a vice by the others, and there was literally nothing he could do to fight them off.

Butcher screamed as the zombies overwhelmed him. He sank to his knees with teeth and fingers ripping open his skin, tasting his delicate flesh and drinking his warm blood. He wanted to push them back but their numbers were too great. The annex was full of them. They had succeeded in getting in at last, and the faint light was enough for him to see that he couldn't fight them off. The pain was like nothing he had ever experienced, and he defecated as he realized he was dying. He was slowly being eaten alive, and as an arm was wrenched from its socket, he let out one last bloodcurdling scream.

Smiling, Charlie opened the door that led down to the grounds of Attwood's property. Rilla joined her in the doorway, the sounds of the dead and dying beneath them. The single bulb gave them a little light and showed them that the corpses of Tad and Conan were still down there, drawn by the whistling.

"Let's take care of those two," said Charlie. She touched the pendant hanging around her neck, and the faint echoes of an old song trickled through her mind.

'*I want to kiss your mouth, hold your hand, and all I feel is the distant wind as you turn your back on me.*'

Rilla nodded. "Then what?"

"I don't know," said Charlie honestly. "We could stay here and try to help others? There must be more people out there like us."

"Or we could run. We could get as far away from this fucking place as possible," suggested Rilla.

"I'm not going to turn away and forget."

Rilla looked at Charlie, puzzled.

"It's something my Mom said once just before she died. She never ran away from anything or anyone. There *are* others out there, Rilla; others who haven't been given a second chance like you and me. Truth is I hadn't thought much past getting back here, finding you, and dealing with Butcher. I guess we've got time to figure it out. I just know that I need to rest," said Charlie.

Get Rilla.

The darkness enveloping Charlie had served her well. It was done. It was finally over. She wiggled a loose tooth at the back of her jaw and pulled her father's cap down on her aching head. "I need some more painkillers. Then I think I'm going to sleep for at least a week. There's only one thing I know for sure, Rilla. As long as we're together, we'll be okay. From now on it's you and me."

"You and me," said Rilla, grasping Charlie's hand. "*Forever.*"

"As for the future?" Charlie leant her weary head on Rilla's shoulder. "I guess we'll see."

THE END

Acknowledgements

I hope you find 'Zombiekill' entertaining and yet perhaps more than just another zombie novel. With what is going on in the world there are some serious questions we need to ask ourselves about what direction man is headed for: division or unity?

Please check out the numerous quality novels Severed Press have also have produced at www.severedpress.com.

Also consider leaving a review and pay a visit to my website www.russwatts.co or look at my other titles:

The Afflicted
The Grave
The Ocean King
Devouring the Dead
Devouring the Dead 2: Nemesis
Goliath
Hamsikker
Hamsikker 2
Hamsikker 3

CHECK OUT OTHER GREAT ZOMBIE NOVELS

DEAD ASCENT
by Jason McPhearson

The dead have risen and they are hungry...

Grizzled war veteran turned game warden, Brayden James and a small group of survivors, fight their way through the rugged wilderness of southern Appalachia to an isolated cabin in the hope of finding sanctuary. Every terrifying step they make they are stalked by a growing mass of staggering corpses, and a raging forest fire, set by the government in hopes of containing the virus.

As all logical routes off the mountain are cut off from them, they seek the higher ground, but they soon realize there is little hope of escape when the dead walk and the world burns.

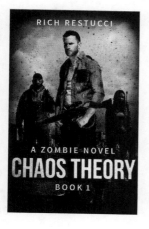

CHAOS THEORY
by Rich Restucci

The world has fallen to a relentless enemy beyond reason or mercy. With no remorse they rend the planet with tooth and nail.

One man stands against the scourge of death that consumes all.

Teamed with a genius survivalist and a teenage girl, he must flee the teeming dead, the evils of humans left unchecked, and those that would seek to use him. His best weapon to stave off the horrors of this new world? His wit.

CHECK OUT OTHER GREAT ZOMBIE NOVELS

DEAD PULSE RISING
by K. Michael Gibson

Slavering hordes of the walking dead rule the streets of Baltimore, their decaying forms shambling across the ruined city, voracious and unstoppable. The remaining survivors hide desperately, for all hope seems lost... until an armored fortress on wheels plows through the ghouls, crushing bones and decayed flesh. The vehicle stops and two men emerge from its doors, armed to the teeth and ready to cancel the apocalypse.

TOWER OF THE DEAD
by J.V. Roberts

Markus is a hardworking man that just wants a better life for his family. But when a virus sweeps through the halls of his high-rise apartment complex, those plans are put on hold. Trapped on the sixteenth floor with no hope of rescue, Markus must fight his way down to safety with his wife and young daughter in tow.

Floor by bloody floor they must battle through hordes of the hungry dead on a terrifying mission to survive the TOWER OF THE DEAD.

CHECK OUT OTHER GREAT ZOMBIE NOVELS

RUN
by Rich Restucci

The dead have risen, and they are hungry.

Slow and plodding, they are Legion. The undead hunt the living. Stop and they will catch you. Hide and they will find you. If you have a heartbeat you do the only thing you can: You run.

Survivors escape to an island stronghold: A cop and his daughter, a computer nerd, a garbage man with a piece of rebar, and an escapee from a mental hospital with a life-saving secret. After reaching Alcatraz, the ever expanding group of survivors realize that the infected are not the only threat.

Caught between the viciousness of the undead, and the heartlessness of the living, what choice is there? Run.

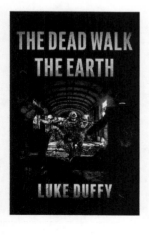

THE DEAD WALK THE EARTH
by Luke Duffy

As the flames of war threaten to engulf the globe, a new threat emerges.

A 'deadly flu', the like of which no one has ever seen or imagined, relentlessly spreads, gripping the world by the throat and slowly squeezing the life from humanity.

Eight soldiers, accustomed to operating below the radar, carrying out the dirty work of a modern democracy, become trapped within the carnage of a new and terrifying world.

Deniable and completely expendable. That is how their government considers them, and as the dead begin to walk, Stan and his men must fight to survive.

CHECK OUT OTHER GREAT ZOMBIE NOVELS

Z BURBIA
by Jake Bible

Whispering Pines is a classic, quiet, private American subdivision on the edge of Asheville, NC, set in the pristine Blue Ridge Mountains. Which is good since the zombie apocalypse has come to Western North Carolina and really put suburban living to the test!

Surrounded by a sea of the undead, the residents of Whispering Pines have adapted their bucolic life of block parties to scavenging parties, common area groundskeeping to immediate area warfare, neighborhood beautification to neighborhood fortification.

But, even in the best of times, suburban living has its ups and downs what with nosy neighbors, a strict Home Owners' Association, and a property management company that believes the words "strict interpretation" are holy words when applied to the HOA covenants. Now with the zombie apocalypse upon them even those innocuous, daily irritations quickly become dramatic struggles for personal identity, family security, and straight up survival.

ZOMBIE RULES
by David Achord

Zach Gunderson's life sucked and then the zombie apocalypse began.

Rick, an aging Vietnam veteran, alcoholic, and prepper, convinces Zach that the apocalypse is on the horizon. The two of them take refuge at a remote farm. As the zombie plague rages, they face a terrifying fight for survival.

They soon learn however that the walking dead are not the only monsters.

CHECK OUT OTHER GREAT ZOMBIE NOVELS

900 MILES
by S. Johnathan Davis

John is a killer, but that wasn't his day job before the Apocalypse.

In a harrowing 900 mile race against time to get to his wife just as the dead begin to rise, John, a business man trapped in New York, soon learns that the zombies are the least of his worries, as he sees first-hand the horror of what man is capable of with no rules, no consequences and death at every turn.

Teaming up with an ex-army pilot named Kyle, they escape New York only to stumble across a man who says that he has the key to a rumored underground stronghold called Avalon..... Will they find safety? Will they make it to Johns wife before it's too late?

Get ready to follow John and Kyle in this fast paced thriller that mixes zombie horror with gladiator style arena action!

WHITE FLAG OF THE DEAD
by Joseph Talluto

Millions died when the Enillo Virus swept the earth. Millions more were lost when the victims of the plague refused to stay dead, instead rising to slaughter and feed on those left alive. For survivors like John Talon and his son Jake, they are faced with a choice: Do they submit to the dead, raising the white flag of surrender? Or do they find the will to fight, to try and hang on to the last shreds or humanity?

CHECK OUT OTHER GREAT ZOMBIE NOVELS

VACCINATION
by Phillip Tomasso

What if the H7N9 vaccination wasn't just a preventative measure against swine flu?

It seemed like the flu came out of nowhere and yet, in no time at all the government manufactured a vaccination. Were lab workers diligent, or could the virus itself have been man-made? Chase McKinney works as a dispatcher at 9-1-1. Taking emergency calls, it becomes immediately obvious that the entire city is infected with the walking dead. His first goal is to reach and save his two children.

Could the walls built by the U.S.A. to keep out illegal aliens, and the fact the Mexican government could not afford to vaccinate their citizens against the flu, make the southern border the only plausible destination for safety?

ZOMBIE, INC
by Chris Dougherty

"WELCOME! To Zombie, Inc. The United Five State Republic's leading manufacturer of zombie defense systems! In business since 2027, Zombie, Inc. puts YOU first. YOUR safety is our MAIN GOAL! Our many home defense options - from Ze Fence® to Ze Popper® to Ze Shed® - fit every need and every budget. Use Scan Code "TELL ME MORE!" for your FREE, in-home*, no obligation consultation! *Schedule your appointment with the confidence that you will NEVER HAVE TO LEAVE YOUR HOME! It isn't safe out there and we know it better than most! Our sales staff is FULLY TRAINED to handle any and all adversarial encounters with the living and the undead". Twenty-five years after the deadly plague, the United Five State Republic's most successful company, Zombie, Inc., is in trouble. Will a simple case of dwindling supply and lessening demand be the end of them or will Zombie, Inc. find a way, however unpalatable, to survive?

Printed in Great Britain
by Amazon